TRIDENT FORCE

MICHAEL HOWE

BERKLEY BOOKS, NEW YORK

THE BERKLEY PUBLISHING GROUP
Published by the Penguin Group
Penguin Group (USA) Inc.
375 Hudson Street, New York, New York 10014, USA
Penguin Group (Canada), 90 Eglinton Avenue East, Suite 700, Toronto, Ontario M4P 2Y3, Canada
(a division of Pearson Penguin Canada Inc.)
Penguin Books Ltd., 80 Strand, London WC2R 0RL, England
Penguin Group Ireland, 25 St. Stephen's Green, Dublin 2, Ireland (a division of Penguin Books Ltd.)
Penguin Group (Australia), 250 Camberwell Road, Camberwell, Victoria 3124, Australia
(a division of Pearson Australia Group Pty. Ltd.)
Penguin Books India Pvt. Ltd., 11 Community Centre, Panchsheel Park, New Delhi—110 017, India
Penguin Group (NZ), 67 Apollo Drive, Rosedale, North Shore 0632, New Zealand
(a division of Pearson New Zealand Ltd.)
Penguin Books (South Africa) (Pty.) Ltd., 24 Sturdee Avenue, Rosebank, Johannesburg 2196,
South Africa

Penguin Books Ltd., Registered Offices: 80 Strand, London WC2R 0RL, England

TRIDENT FORCE

A Berkley Book /published by arrangement with the author

PRINTING HISTORY
Berkley edition / December 2008

Cover illustration by Edwin Herder.
Cover design by Judith Lagerman.
Interior text design by Laura K. Corless.

For information, address: The Berkley Publishing Group,
a division of Penguin Group (USA) Inc.,
375 Hudson Street, New York, New York 10014.

ISBN: 978-0-425-22488-5

BERKLEY®
Berkley Books are published by The Berkley Publishing Group,
a division of Penguin Group (USA) Inc.,
375 Hudson Street, New York, New York 10014.
BERKLEY® is a registered trademark of Penguin Group (USA) Inc.
The "B" design is a trademark of Penguin Group (USA) Inc.

PRINTED IN THE UNITED STATES OF AMERICA

10 9 8 7 6 5 4 3 2 1

TRIDENT FORCE

1

Rio de Janeiro

Carlos Coccoli inhaled his cigarette in long, slow drags as he leaned over the safety railing and looked twelve stories down into Graving Dock Number Three. Behind him, half a mile and two security fences away, lay the industrial north-east of Rio de Janeiro. In front lay the wide, dark waters of the Baia de Guanabara.

Despite the late hour, the blue-white glare of the Xenon floods lighted the hole with the intensity of the tropical noon sun. He studied the dock's gray-black concrete sides; the various cave-like mezzanines and work platforms built into those gray-black sides; the puddles of black water that glistened on the dock floor and the row of keel blacks lined up along the bottom about a hundred feet from the far wall. The dock was over twelve hundred feet long and over five hundred wide. Built to accept all but the most insanely large ships. It was so big, thought Carlos, that it had made *Aurora Australis*, the ship that had occupied it up till a few hours before, look like a toy. They could easily have fit three *Aurora*s in there.

"Umberto," called Carlos over his shoulder, "I now see

why you like working here so. This dock reminds you of that quarry you used to work in."

"I'd be better off back there," replied Umberto, who was standing on the concrete apron a few yards back from the edge of the dock, in the dense shadow created by a work shed and the framework of one of the many surrounding cranes.

Carlos didn't want to hear that sort of thing but said nothing as he joined his taller companion in the shadows. They stood there, dressed in light gray coveralls with Tecmar badges sewn to them, and smoked in silence. Even after dark the yard was still very busy, but the area around Graving Dock Number Three was also almost unsettlingly quiet. There were no air compressors roaring. There was no banging and crashing of steel on steel. No shrieking of hull and deck plates being cut to precise shapes. No screeching of railroad wheels on tracks. There were no truck horns and backing alarms. Even the sounds of the city, very much alive on the far side of the security fences surrounding the yard, were all but lost in the thick night air.

Where, the day before, the cruise ship *Aurora Australis* had rested now only a row of keel blocks, surrounded by black puddles of water, remained on the dock's floor. Once the overhaul had been completed, the dock had been flooded and the steel doors opened. Tugs had worked the cruise ship out into the channel; the doors had been closed again and the dock pumped dry, leaving the lingering smell of petroleum and burnt steel, which permeates all shipyards. Tomorrow the blocks would be repositioned in preparation for the dock's next guest, but tonight it slept.

"It's hotter than hell," snarled Umberto as he swatted what sounded to him like a mosquito.

"No hotter than usual," replied Carlos, speaking and moving with the abrupt self-confidence of a young man who knows he's headed up in a world filled with fools. "You worried all of a sudden?" As he spoke, he looked out over the dark waters of the Baia de Guanabara, the tear-shaped body of water that separates Rio from Niterói to the east. He watched the car lights moving across the distant Rio-Niterói bridge. The great span had been there all his life, and now was probably the last time he would see it. He wondered briefly if he would miss it. Of course not! The tourists might find Rio enchanting, but for millions of *cariocas*, including Carlos, it was nothing more than a suffocating prison filled with poverty and frustration. A prison that was becoming more and more crowded as the rural poor flooded in, thinking life was better in the big city.

Thanks to Omar he now had the chance to escape. Within a few minutes he would be very rich; able to visit practically any bridge in the world. Able to do practically anything, for that matter.

"Hell, no! Why should I be?"

"Having second thoughts?"

"Shit, no. Have I ever?" The expression on Umberto's face seemed to belie his words.

"Good. With what they're paying us, we'll never have to have second thoughts again about anything."

"Where the hell is he? Who the hell is he? Really?"

Carlos glanced at him, snorted, then looked away again. While Graving Dock Number Three might be sleeping, the rest of the shipyard was not. A quarter of a mile away, a Venezuelan ULLC, a supertanker, was parked in Graving Dock Number Two, bathed in its own banks of brilliant floods while its bottom was cleaned, repaired and painted. Another half mile beyond that a deep-drilling rig was under construction for Petrobras, the Brazilian national oil company. Up and down the coast of South America, the shipbuilding business was booming. From where Carlos and Umberto stood, however, the noise of the rest of the yard was barely a muted mumble, almost as if it were coming from another planet.

"You do understand that we have to disappear forever . . . tonight. We can't be in Rio or anywhere nearby tomorrow morning."

"Those new IDs he's supposed to bring us . . ."

"He showed me mine. They're good."

"What about Anna?"

"I told you, I'm not bringing her. She's stupid. I can't trust her. With the money we're getting I can do much better. You and me are both going to be rich and free as birds."

"How does Omar know we did it right? That we didn't cheat him?"

"He has some way of checking. Omar's no fool. Probably somebody in the crew. Somebody's got to detonate the damn things."

"You think a lot of them will get killed?"

"Their asses are going to be blown to hell. I'm going to love it. They've been raping us and everybody else for centuries. They don't mind a few of us dying if they can make some money on the deal, so why should we let a few of them stand between us and millions of dollars? U.S dollars. Even the sheiks who own this place don't like them."

"You think Omar is working for him? The sultan?"

"Seems likely. He's some sort of Arab, I think, though he talks almost like a *carioca*."

"Is the sultan an Arab?"

"Is there some other kind?"

Umberto was silent and Carlos cursed to himself. The fool was having second thoughts, he concluded as he looked out over the harbor, at the lights sparkling along the Niterói shore and at the full moon, huge and yellow, hanging above it. Umberto was far too nervous—it was hard to believe he had worked for years as a blaster in a quarry.

Whatever he may have done in the past, he was now having second thoughts about their recent and future activities. Losing his nerve. In this condition he was dangerous. Dangerous to Carlos. And Carlos started to have second thoughts about him.

As Carlos considered what to do about his tall, thin co-conspirator, the light of a pair of headlights swept across the concrete apron. As they moved side to side, the beams dodged some air compressors and welding machines, only to fully illuminate others. Periodically they dipped down and reflected on the railroad tracks set into the apron.

"This must be him," said Umberto, a note of relief in his voice.

"Yes," agreed Carlos, watching as a beat-up van with "Estaleiro Tecmar" written on its side pulled up to the crane and stopped.

"Isn't this a surprise," commented the van's driver, a thin, darkish man, dressed in a blue coveralls identical to those worn by his victims. The driver could have been either Arab or Latin and would have fit into practically any crowd anywhere. "Carlos and Umberto taking the night air under a crane."

"Don't be funny," snapped Carlos, irritated at their employer's tone. "Our work was satisfactory, wasn't it?"

"Very much so. The oppressed of the world are very much in your debt."

Before either victim could react, the driver raised a small-caliber pistol and shot each in the forehead. The pistol made a breathy pop when it was fired, one easily mistaken for the sound of a pneumatic tool being disconnected from the air hose that had provided its power. The two ship fitters each grunted and collapsed to the grimy concrete, where they twitched slightly. The driver opened the door and stepped down onto the apron.

Pop. Pop. To be certain, he fired a second shot into each head, from a different angle than the first. He then loaded the two cadavers onto a plastic tarpaulin in the back of the van, washed away the small, obvious pools of blood with a five-gallon jug of water he had brought with him, and drove off.

To the south, over the city, there was a distant flash of lightning. Then another.

* * *

The air was humid, hazy and heavy as the sun first peeked over the horizon. Anna Olivieros lay in bed, watching the pink wall of her bedroom brighten, and wished she were dead.

Carlos had not come home that night. True, he had stayed out other nights, but she knew that this time was different. The past few days he'd been so distant. It was as if she weren't even there. She'd tried to convince herself that he had another girlfriend. That would have hurt but it would have been bearable. But it wasn't true. Carlos had been busy with some project, some clever, unsavory project. He often was. But this time was different, she knew in her heart. He'd moved on to something bigger. This time he had left her and she was certain she'd never see him again.

The last thing in the world she wanted to do was get up, but she did. She dragged herself out of her bed and headed for the bathroom. Life does go on, she told herself, knowing that was true but not totally relevant. More to the point, she had to work to eat, and that, she knew, was something she would want to do. As for the apartment, she suspected that without money from Carlos it was history.

Realizing she was running late and struck with a sudden terror that she might lose her job in addition to losing Carlos, Anna picked up the pace, her actions reflecting habit more than conscious thought. She showered, dressed in something, made up her face, combed her hair and was out the door, her heels clacking, in less than half an hour.

If Anna's apartment and neighborhood were far from grand, they were also far from *favela.* No tin and cardboard shacks with muddy dirt floors. The building was of concrete and had electricity, running hot and cold water and an elevator. The interior walls and floors were worn but reasonably clean. Despite the almost overwhelming pain at losing Carlos, she was able to feel how much she would miss living in the building, which she wouldn't be able to afford on her own income. Unless some miracle occurred, her next stop would be both lonely and wretched.

Muggy though the morning was, it was still early. In another hour it would be much worse. When Anna stepped out the front door of the apartment building, she stepped into the vibrant flow of life that is Brazil. The crowds flowing both directions along the sidewalk weren't exactly dancing the rumba, but they were moving rapidly and purposefully. Out in the road, the solid mass of cars, trucks and buses executed their own incomprehensible ballet—jerking and twisting and weaving around and between one another. As they danced, they filled the already super-saturated air with the blasts of their horns.

Anna turned toward the bus stop, only to see the bus pulling away, leaving a dense tail of diesel smoke. She cursed quietly, then debated with herself whether to try to catch the bus at the next stop or wait for the next one at her normal stop.

Did it really matter? she wondered numbly. Her mother hadn't liked Carlos. Neither had her brother. They didn't trust him, and neither, really, did she. He was handsome, flashy, vibrant, and she knew that she was plain. Worst of all, she was in love with him. Now all she could do was hope against hope that she was wrong. With a sigh, she decided she couldn't run with her heels on, so she turned toward the stop she used every day.

Distracted as she was, Anna didn't at first notice the white SUV with heavily tinted windows parked between her and the bus stop. Out of the corner of her eye she did, however, notice Oswaldo, the handsome young street thug standing beside the car. Impossible as it seemed to her, she found him even more attractive than Carlos. The fact was that everybody who'd ever laid eyes on him would have agreed that he was a very presentable and attractive young man. Except when he was beating your face to a pulp with a two-by-four or shoving a knife into your navel.

"Anna, my love!" shouted Oswaldo as he reached out and grabbed her passing arm. Using her momentum, he then swung her around in one smooth motion and ushered her into the SUV before she understood what was happening. He jumped in behind her, slammed the door behind him, and the van sped off, weaving through the heavy, but not impossible, traffic. Without pausing, Oswaldo wrapped a thin line around Anna's neck and quickly twisted it tight. He wanted to silence and strangle her, not to cut her head off. He watched with pleasure as her startled look turned to one of fear, her hands clutched frantically at her throat and her mouth opened wide, screaming silently. He slammed her in the side of the head when her body tried to struggle. He looked again at her face. Her eyes looked as if they were about to pop out. He considered relaxing the garrote slightly, deceiving her into believing that she might yet draw another breath, but he resisted the temptation. The job had to be done quickly and thoroughly.

If any of the passersby had even noticed the incident, they would have undoubtedly assumed that the handsome lad was giving a friend a ride. Unable to see through the windows, they would have had no way of knowing that Anna Olivieros was dead four minutes after the SUV pulled away from the curb.

* * *

Moored next to the finishing dock at the Estaleiro Tecmar yard, the white hull and upper works of the expedition cruise ship *Aurora Australis* glowed in the morning sun. Highlighting this great expanse of white, the ship's Day-Glo orange covered lifeboats/survival capsules hung like beads along the sides of her superstructure.

Roughly five hundred feet in length, with a net register tonnage of slightly under twenty-five thousand and powered by two huge, German diesels, *Aurora* was as small as cruise ships go. She was nothing in comparison with the immense floating hotels, over a thousand feet long, that made their long-established circuits around the Caribbean, but then she wasn't a standard cruise ship. Rather, she was one of the smallish group of ships designed to take—in her case five hundred—affluent adventurers on expeditions to out-of-the-way places and, along the way, provide a level of luxury almost equal to that offered by their larger cousins.

Aurora was built tough—ice-reinforced hull, numerous redundant systems, an unusually high level of stability—to enable her to overcome the dangers of nature. But it is next to impossible to design and build a ship strong enough to resist the dangers posed by determined and resourceful men of ill will.

* * *

Mamoud al Hussein, the executive who provided on-scene representation for the foreign owner of the Estaleiro Tecmar, stood in the living room of his house. The house, of which he had for short periods of time been quite proud, was a large, modern concrete-and-glass structure set in Rio's high southern hills. All surrounded by a high wall and equally high-tech security system. The view was magnificent—the Atlantic to the south, the center of the city to the east and the Baia de Guanabara beyond. As he watched the sun continue its journey from Africa, Mamoud listened to the sultan's prime minister on the phone and thought just how fortunate he was to have the view he did. And how regrettable it was that he could no longer enjoy it emotionally as much as he appreciated it intellectually.

"From what you report, Mamoud, it all appears to be going well. Operating profits are up and the operation is beginning to develop an international reputation for quality and innovation."

"Thank you, Your Exellency."

As he spoke, Mamoud smiled slightly. Everything *was* going very well. The charges were in place, and Omar assured him that the heart of the man on the ship burned with a fury equal to Mamoud's. Although neither the prime minister nor the sultan realized it, His Highness was doing much to make the world a better place, much more than simply operating a cutting-edge shipyard. He was facilitating a cosmically good deed, a most virtuous act, without even knowing it.

In fact, the sultan might not even consider it a virtuous act at all.

While His Highness ranted endlessly to the masses of his subjects about his devotion to his faith, his true love was cash. Business. When it came to cash, His Highness was just as ruthless as the most vicious terrorist.

"We are so pleased, Mamoud, that we are considering moving you on to a totally new project, one which will be exceptionally challenging. Assuming you are ready to move on."

"I'm confident that the local management at Tecmar is well able to follow through on the program, Your Excellency."

"Good. You are familiar with our plan to build a new solar panel factory, are you not?"

"Yes, Your Excellency. The last I heard no decision had been made on where to build it."

"For various reasons, both economic and political, it has been decided to build it in North Africa. We would like you to take charge of it and ensure that, despite the obvious challenges, it is a success."

"I'm honored, Your Excellency. It sounds like a very interesting project. When should I plan to leave here?"

"Plan on another month in Brasil, then a couple weeks of vacation if you wish, then come to the capital to assemble your team."

"I look forward to it, Your Exellency."

Mamoud the engineer couldn't help but be pleased with the news. Mamoud the terrorist was also perfectly satisfied with it. There was nothing further for him to do in Rio.

Mamoud al Hussein was very much a man of science. He had a Ph.D. in engineering. He'd taught at both MIT and Caltech, owned a dozen major patents and gloried in the scientific method.

Mamoud al Hussein was also very much a man of faith. He had concluded, at an early age, that there existed concepts—good and evil, dignity, justice were examples he might use—that are utterly meaningless to science. The applications made by humans of these concepts were totally explicable to him, but the existence of the concepts, by themselves, was not. Thus, he concluded there was some sort of entity from which these concepts originated, and he was willing to call that corpus God.

For Mamoud al Hussein, there was no conflict between faith and science. Science constituted the revelation of God's wonders. The scientific method was one route to God. The great Arab scientists and philosophers of the First Millennium had no problem with the juxtaposition, so why should he? And whenever he thought of the millions of Christians and Moslems who had devoted, and still did devote, so much time and hate to fighting science, he felt ill.

Mamoud believed deeply that science and faith must coexist, yet everywhere he looked he saw faith under attack. More now than ever before, in his view. By the ignorant, foolish masses of the world, who were increasingly beguiled by their growing material prosperity. By the cynical, hateful institutions of politics and the media. For them, faith was a joke, something to be hugged when necessary and laughed at contemptuously when it threatened to cramp their style.

This abuse of faith—and the abuse of reason that was part of the process—infuriated Mamoud well beyond any state that might be called reasonable. It created within him a white-hot rage that burned in his guts day and night, even though no sign of it ever slipped through his façade of calm, measured reason. So powerful was the flame that it instantly vaporized the deep, emotional pleasure he had once felt from the company of a woman or from a view such as the one he was now observing or even from the thrill of an engineering triumph. He remained fully capable of appreciating but utterly unable to enjoy.

For years Mamoud had kept his silence, but the current situation was now intolerable. It was a situation that a man of his intellect, his abilities, his ego simply could not allow to continue. He had to speak out, to act. To make an unforgettable statement, a grim one if necessary, that would be seen by all. If, in time, this manifestation of faith—or another—led to his destruction, so be it.

South Florida

"God damn it!" growled Chief Boatswain's Mate (DV) Jerry Andrews as he squatted, squirming, in the rank, black mud, imprisoned on all sides by the head-high salt grass.

Mike Chambers, CO of the Trident Force, agreed silently as he squatted beside Andrews in the awful mud. The black gunk. The blowtorch sun. The sharp, tough grasses that made the dry squeaking sound of centuries-old dead bones as they rubbed against each other. The vicious horseflies that jabbed, sliced or bit every cxposed part of their bodies—not to mention the yellowish-brown clouds of chiggers that hissed around their heads—all of which continued to attack despite the fact that Chambers and his people were totally soaked in DEET and undoubtedly developing some totally new type of cancer. It was sheer torture. And it was intended to be sheer torture.

Twenty years ago he might have considered the drill something close to sport. A test of physical skill and determination. A chance to prove himself to himself, if to nobody else. Not anymore. Now it was, at best, a vile necessity—an exercise to maintain certain skills that were but only a part of his current mission.

Captain Michael Chambers, USN, commanded a top-secret, super-low-profile antiterrorism intelligence and intervention/strike group that reported directly to the secretary of defense. The Force had been created to deal with nautical incidents and other threats to U.S. ports, shipping and other maritime interests, especially those involving sticky questions concerning sovereignty and intervention authority.

Mike himself had joined the SEALs upon graduation from the Naval Academy. After several years of special operations, he decided that maybe the navy really was about boats and ships. He transferred back to the fleet and, over the years, rose to command an LPH, one of the helicopter amphibious assault ships that had developed into the backbone of the navy's force projection mission. When SECDEF himself first offered the Trident job to Mike, he had demurred, but then agreed when assured that once he finished setting up the Force and running it for a year or two, he would get his flag.

The "firing range" on which Chambers and his team were suffering was just one of a number established to help the nation's many special operations units keep their skills honed. There was a jungle firing range and a desert firing range, as well as arctic, alpine, urban, coastal and deep ocean firing ranges. And they weren't just a place where you stood with ear protectors hung over your head and fired at a target or two. They were nightmare stages on which you waged near-total, personal war. All simulated, of course.

"Watch it, Chief!" growled Chambers as he waved his arms, hoping the other side would note the moving grass. Jerry was getting a little old for this too, he thought. Jerry and Lynn were grandparents, for that matter, although they'd gotten an early start.

Their souls weren't over the hill, thought Chambers, a

little resentfully, but their bodies weren't as well tuned as they once were.

Each firing range had at least one objective, which was defended by one force and attacked by another. Neither side knew the true identity or precise size of the other. Thus, Mike and his Trident Force might be competing with one of the CIA special groups. Or maybe a normal SEAL detachment. Or Army Rangers or a contingent of the Delta Force. Or the president's security force. Or even some obscure group of DEA agents. Or any of the special mercenary forces now employed by the government. Or anybody else the secretary of defense and his minions thought might contribute something to the felony. Not only did Mike now not know, but he was supposed to never know the other side's identity. And the same for the other side. The only thing of which either could be reasonably sure was that the other's armament was as basic as their own. The drill was supposed to be a test of wits and stamina, not who had the biggest weapons budget.

The marsh firing range on which Mike and his fellows were pinned down was located in the middle of the Big Cypress National Preserve in the southern tip of Florida, not far from the Miccosukee Reservation. The objective was a ratty little long-abandoned village of crumbling mud and daub huts.

The morning had started out cool as Mike and his Force team commenced their eight-mile slog toward the objective. So cool was it that it took almost fifteen minutes for the big blobs of sweat to begin appearing on their jungle greens. They forced their way through three or four miles of sharp-edged, head-high grass. Then the sun and the deep, glue-like muck—"God's own crap" as Jerry called it—began to wear them down. They maintained their alertness, however, and were rewarded. Around mid-morning they spotted a contingent of the other force emplaced on a small, brush-covered hummock that stood between them and the objective. As far as Mike could tell, the defenders hadn't spotted them.

Chambers's initial thought was to detour around the hummock and move on directly to the objective, but it seemed clear that was not practical. They would be spotted unless they detoured so far that they would not make it to the objective before the end of the exercise.

Among the many iron-hard rules of warfare, two stand out: Never attack an entrenched, very possibly superior enemy head-on, and never divide your forces. If you violate one of these rules—or both—and win, nobody says a word. If you violate one—even to execute the other—and things don't work out, you will be hanged. By the journalists and other armchair generals and by the court-martial.

On the assumption they hadn't been spotted, Mike decided to surprise the defenders. He sent Ted Anderson and Jack Kudloe—both twenty-something SEAL petty officers who were still fast and nimble—off to the left to circle around behind the defenders. He, Jerry and Alex Mahan the older members of the team, would provide the diversion.

The first part of the plan seemed to have worked well enough. After Ted and Jack had gotten well clear of them, Mike and his companions continued along their original track, making just enough muted ruckus to attract attention. In due course they'd been spotted and brought under fire, which they returned. Each side was firing M-16s with blanks and lasers, which triggered the sensors attached to every participant's clothing. Now it was just a matter of avoiding the lasers and waiting for evidence of Ted and Jack's attack from the rear. Unless, of course, the defenders spotted the two SEALs prematurely or decided to send out a party to track down Mike's group.

"They've got us well pinned down, Boss," observed Jerry. "You have a backup plan?"

"Try to sprint past them."

"Umm," replied Andrews noncommittally, as he wiped away some of the sweat pouring into his already-red eyes.

"I think we may be okay," said Alex quietly. "Ted and Jack have been circling around for more than half an hour and don't seem to have been spotted."

Mike nodded in agreement He'd asked her to talk quietly, while he and Jerry did the opposite, to avoid giving away her gender. While he wasn't sure how he could make use of it, every little bit of information the other side didn't have was to his advantage.

Unlike the other members of the Force, Alex had never been in the navy. She had, however, been both a crack CIA analyst and field operative. She possessed a reputation for having a steel-trap mind, a high level of accurate intuition and a ferocious attention to detail. Alex was also fluent in four languages and had an advanced degree in engineering, but her greatest qualification was her network of contacts. She had, over the years, managed to develop and maintain dependable contacts not only in the CIA, but also at the DIA, the NSA, the DEA and most of the countless Homeland Security agencies. In a word, graceful Alex knew everybody. While the politicians in power loved to babble about the seamless cooperation they were building among the various intelligence agencies, the reality was that the cooperation was still far from seamless. No matter what the press releases said, people still had friends and enemies, self-interests, ambitions and agendas.

Suddenly all hell broke loose on the hummock. The volume and rate of gunfire exploded, its *crack, crack, crack* mixed with loud shouting. Then Mike could hear the *pop* of dye grenades.

"That's it," he shouted, standing as he did. "It's now or never, so let's hit it!"

Without waiting for a reply Mike charged forward, as best he could, keeping his graying crew-cut hair below the top of the grass except when he popped up to fire. To his right, Jerry—big, tough but far from young—was doing the same, beginning to pant as his feet sank deep into the mud every few steps. To his left, tall, willowy Alex was gliding over the mud, her long, dark hair made up into a tight bun, as she tried to dance and weave between the stands of stiff, thick grass that Jerry was attempting to bulldoze.

Shortly before they reached the hummock, Mike realized the defenders seemed to have stopped firing. Fifty squishy, slippery paces later he and his team broke into the open and then charged up onto the slightly raised hummock. They came upon the sort of scene that Mike truly hated.

One of the defenders, a big, red-haired guy, was lying on his back. Leaning over him, forcing the barrel of his rifle into the redhead's neck was Jack Kudloe. The SEAL was screaming, "I killed you, you son of a bitch. I killed you," over and over again, his face red with uncontrolled fury. The redhead kept trying to protest that he had only been hit in the leg. Ted and two of the defenders, both of whose mud-caked greens were highlighted by dye from the grenades, were trying to pull Kudloe off his victim. So far with little success.

Fury flashed through Mike's icy blue eyes only to immediately morph into cold calculation. He'd seen it too many times before. Wind a man up too tight, suggest that he was allowed to play by special rules, and you were asking for trouble. No matter how intense their training, many men—under the proper circumstances—lost sight of the objective and, in the process, lost all self-control. And any man who lost control was of no more use to an organization like the Trident Force than would be a mad dog.

The missions assigned to Chambers's group went far beyond the straightforward sabotage and assassination that characterized so many black ops. They tended to be delicate, complex and infinitely frustrating. Chambers was as interested in self-control, flexibility, brains and a minimum of couth as he was in killing skills. A little sea time was also a big plus.

What irritated him the most at the moment was that he'd personally selected Kudloe not two weeks before to replace a man who'd been badly injured and put on the retired list. Now he discovered that his handpicked replacement suffered from uncontrollable bloodlust. Well, damn it, he'd made a mistake.

"Get the hell off that man, Kudloe," bellowed Chambers.

The enraged SEAL paid no attention whatsoever.

Chambers walked around to Kudloe's head, stooped down and jammed the barrel of his M-16 under the SEAL's armpit. He then lifted and pushed on the stock, using the weapon as a lever to pry the attacker off his victim. Kudloe grunted and turned toward him, rage still in his eyes.

"Get off that man immediately!" repeated Chambers.

Kudloe leaned back, taking the pressure off the rifle. "Oh, shit!" he mumbled. Fortunately for him, he didn't add "fuck you." Even more fortunately, real knives were not permitted on the firing ranges.

His eyes still pale with anger, Mike glanced to his side at Alex, who was standing with her rifle under her arm. She was shaking her head to herself and looking at Kudloe with an expression of distaste. She understood how things had to be done if the Trident Force was to achieve anything.

A voice squawked out of the radio clipped to Mike's belt. The same voice emerged at the same time from the radio clipped to the fourth defender, who was thereby marked as the opposition's leader. Mike and the other leader exchanged glances then both looked up in the sky to where the monitor drone was now slow-flying directly overhead. "The attacking force is scored with having overrun the defending force and suffering no casualties," announced the stereophonic voice of the exercise mediator, who had been spying on the whole drill from above. "The attacking force is reminded that it has less than two hours remaining to reach and take the objective."

"Damn!" mumbled the defense leader. He then shrugged his shoulders.

"Good work," said Mike to his team. "Even you, Kudloe. Up to a point. Now let's hit the road. We don't have much time. And Kudloe, your performance for the rest of the day will determine whether I transfer you back to a regular SEAL unit or to storekeepers school or to the brig."

He looked up at the blazing sun, took a deep breath of the rich, hot, organic air—it tasted of salt and long-dead seafood and sun-baked salt hay—and gritted his teeth. How many more defenders lay ahead? he wondered. Were they all concentrated in the objective or had they established other little outposts on other hummocks? How many roving patrols did they have out?

They never told you how big the other side was. That was supposed to be part of the fun.

* * *

Ramon Fuentes, Captain, United States Marine Corps, tried hard to convince himself that he felt left out; that he'd rather be on the firing line with the rest of the Force than where he was, stuck inside the Force's drab, windowless, concrete block facility, staring at a computer, surrounded by the smell of the wax on the floor tiles and waiting for something to happen. He tried, but he couldn't do it.

He could crawl through mud, fire an M-16—or anything else—and suffer the god damned horseflies as well as any man—or woman. Better, in fact. But the pleasures of the field—whether it be Paris Island, Quantico or Little Creek—couldn't possibly compare with the pleasure of having a leisurely family lunch with your wife and daughter. Each of whom had taken time out of her busy day to join him for an hour or two in the admittedly under-decorated, but well air-conditioned and bug-free conference room.

Sandy and little Jamie had left, but the glow continued as he stared at the snippets of news rolling down the computer monitor. They were much like newspaper headlines, except they were directed at a very select, need-to-know audience.

The phone rang. "SecResGruTwo, Captain Fuentes speaking, sir."

"Ray, this is Alan. Give me Mike," said the deputy secretary of defense who served as liaison between SECDEF, himself and the Force.

"He's out at the firing range with the rest of the team."

"I have to talk to him."

"Is this an emergency? I can alert him, have him break off the exercise."

"No. Not yet. Maybe not at all. Will he be coming back to the office today?"

"Yes."

"Have him call me then."

"Aye, aye."

Ray Fuentes didn't really trust Alan Parker. He'd seen the bureaucrat change his story one too many times in order to protect his own ample ass. To be on the safe side, the marine officer relayed the message verbatim to the firing range, for delivery to Chambers as soon as possible. Half an hour later the firing range reported back that the message had been delivered and that Captain Chambers was going to take it at face value and return the call when he got back to his office.

* * *

Fuentes was struggling halfheartedly with some paperwork when the security lock clicked and the outside door opened. In, out of the dark, marched Mike Chambers—mud-covered, sweat-soaked and looking slightly cranky.

"How'd it go, sir?"

"In the end it was a draw. They—whoever the hell they were—must have had at least twenty people at the objective . . . Ray, we missed you. Please open the garage door."

Ray pressed the garage door opener while Chambers

stepped out in front of the building. "I want all the gear cleaned and restowed to Jerry's satisfaction. Then you can shower.

"And, Kudloe, most of what you did today was outstanding, but I can't tolerate any team member losing control, so you turn in all your gear to Chief Andrews after you've helped stow the other gear. Tomorrow you report to SpecOpsGroup Four. Your orders will be there." Normally he wouldn't have delivered the rebuke so publicly, but the entire Force had seen the incident and knew what the result would be.

"Aye, sir," replied Kudloe. At least, he thought, he wasn't going to storekeepers school.

"Boss," said Alex, who had walked over to Chambers and was even muddier, "am I going to be able to come up with some paperwork for Kudloe? I assume you want it done tonight."

"After you get a shower. For the authority, just cite the SECDEF directive that set us up. And while you're at it, ask SpecOpsGroup Four to have Vincent, that SEAL who was second on our want list, report here tomorrow morning. Same authority."

While Alex showered and immediately got to work on her computer and the rest of the Force continued to clean and stow its gear, Mike collapsed into the chair behind his desk. My God, he thought, the air-conditioning is heavenly. After wiping his clean hand across his still muddy face, he picked up the phone and called Alan Parker.

"How was the exercise?"

"Satisfactory. Whoever we were going against had five times as many people as we did. What's up?"

"What do you know about *Aurora Australis*?"

"She's a cruise ship, isn't she? Goes to the Arctic, or the Antarctic."

"The Antarctic. And at the moment she's headed there with five hundred passengers to watch the ice melt. Many of those passengers are very important people, including a United States senator and a United States congressman."

"I can see she might be a target but . . ."

"But there're a thousand more just as tempting at any given time. I know. In this case, however, there are a few other odds and ends. The ship just completed a major overhaul at the Estaleira Tecmar shipyard in Rio. Tecmar belongs to a very wealthy sultan, a Moslem. And our sources report that two ship fitters seem to have disappeared in Rio along with the girlfriend of one. The men had worked at the Estaleira Tecmar. And then to complicate matters, the ship's owners are Canadian and she flies the Ecuadorian flag."

Mike spent a moment digesting Alan's words. None of the facts were in any way unusual in the twenty-first century world, but they made him a little uneasy. When you've spent a lot of time at sea, you tend to become very sensitive to little things—a vibration that shouldn't be there, a line flapping when it should be secured, a ship rolling in a manner that isn't "quite right," a nagging squishing sound.

"You have anything really solid?"

"Not exactly. At this point it might be a political problem as much as anything else. The president's going to be all over SECDEF if something happens—especially with the senator and the congressman and countless politically active environmentalists aboard."

"Why don't you just suggest the ship return to port or even evacuate the politicians?"

"Because SECDEF doesn't think we know enough to justify it. Some of our allies, even our closest ones, are starting to make rude remarks about our trigger fingers and 'boots in their faces' policies."

"And . . . ?"

"There are three media teams aboard broadcasting live."

"Three!"

"Yes."

"Damn."

"You're being tasked to do something about the situation. Make sure nothing bad happens. And make sure we don't piss anybody off unless absolutely necessary."

"Thanks."

"What are you going to do?"

"Haven't the faintest idea at the moment. I will by tomorrow morning."

"Get back to me."

"Roger."

Mike hung up, walked into Alex's office and described the conversation to her. "I want everybody here tomorrow. Zero six hundred. Including Vincent."

"Aye, aye, Boss," replied Alex with a fixed look. She's tired, he thought. They're all tired, except Ray. He didn't like having to tell them to come in early, but it wouldn't hurt them. And they'd all volunteered to join the Force.

"And would you dig around in you magical way and see if you can come up with anything useful on *Aurora* or the shipyard or the ship fitters or anything else relevant."

"You've got it, Boss. I've already canceled the one date I've been invited on this year."

Mike looked at her again and knew she was just zapping him. Alex had no trouble finding men, although she was something of a loner and tended to keep her own counsel.

* * *

"I can only find eighty-six of these concussion grenades," growled Jerry Andrews, his head and shoulders jammed down into a box of grenades. Jerry, the oldest member of the Trident Force, was a navy chief boatswain's mate and master diver. In addition to being in charge of all things nautical and of ensuring the rest of the team didn't kill themselves diving, Jerry was also in charge of all the group's gear and weapons.

"Sorry, Jerry," replied Alex, who was sitting on a box of

half-pound TNT charges, "but your inventory says there should be ninety-one . . ."

Jerry grumbled something then stood up. "Okay, I found 'em in a small box on top of the flash-bangs. What's next?"

"Morning, guys," said Mike Chambers cheerfully as he stood in the door between the "playroom"—where boats and other non-explosive toys were stored—and the Force's small magazine. "You certainly got an early start." It was a few minutes after six A.M.

"Morning, Boss," they replied almost in unison.

"Jerry smelled something in the air and wanted to get this done before he was unable to do it because you had him doing something else," added Alex. "And I was already here anyway."

Mike nodded, realizing she was telling him she'd spent the night researching for him. "Thanks, Alex," he said, thinking she really did look like she could use a little sleep. "Is Vincent here yet?"

"Yes, sir," came the voice of the unit's newest member, Rick Vincent.

"Can you relieve Alex here or are you all wrapped up in something really important?"

"I'm on my way, sir."

"Alex, after you get Rick up to speed on that inventory, will you please come over to my office?"

"Five minutes."

Alex stepped into Chambers's Spartan office and found the captain seated behind his desk chewing on a cup of black coffee. He motioned her to one of the two not-very-comfortable guest chairs.

"I've been thinking all night about that cruise ship. Alan's right, it's an uncommonly tempting target."

Alex smiled. "So what do you want to do?"

She's back in the groove, he decided as he scanned the walls of the office, his eyes settling briefly on photos of various ships and friends—more than a few of whom were now dead. Unless she was busy circulating her résumé. "Initially I want to do a little very quiet research. I want to send Ray and . . . Ted down to Brazil for a day or two to look around."

"Ted doesn't speak Portuguese."

"But he does know a little Spanish and that will have to do. Anyway, we both know Ray will want to do most of the talking."

"You have a cover in mind?"

"I spent a little time on the Web and noticed there was a fire in that yard two months ago, while *Aurora* was still there. Nobody was injured but there was a certain amount of property damage."

"Was it anywhere near the ship?"

"About half a mile away, as far as I can tell, but Ray and Ted should make sure. What's important at the moment is that it's just the sort of thing one of their insurance underwriters might want to know a little more about."

"Between primary and extended coverage and reinsurance, an operation like that, especially a maritime one, is bound to have half a dozen underwriters."

"Exactly! And you're bound to have a contact at one of them who can provide us with some credentials. I want you to find out who all the underwriters are while I call Alan and get him to okay the plan."

After Alex had headed off to her office, Mike picked up the secure phone and called Alan Parker.

"Yes, Mike?" asked Alan, a career bureaucrat who had the amazing ability to remind you, by the tone of his very first word, that he was your superior.

"I've come up with a plan, at least a start, on this *Aurora Australis* business and a little direction, a little focus, would help."

"Okay?"

"Is there anybody, any group, who your people believe might be especially tempted by *Aurora* and her passenger list?"

"Aside from the Business Round Table we haven't been able to identify any specific group that especially dislikes environmentalists . . ."

Alan paused as Mike laughed dutifully at the joke.

"If anybody really is targeting that ship, they probably don't care who the victims are as long as there are a lot of bloody bodies lying around and a few survivors screaming into a sea of TV cameras."

"Especially with the media already on hand to provide instant exposure. You have nothing else?"

"No."

"Very well. I'm going to send two of my men to Rio to snoop around for a day or two."

"You going to use any cover?"

"Insurance investigators. There was a small fire there a month or two ago."

"If they find something?"

"We'll go from there."

"And if they don't?"

"We'll go from there."

"No incidents!"

"No incidents."

"Will they be armed?"

"Since they'll be flying commercial, I'll have to arrange for one of Alex's friends to deliver sidearms to them after they arrive."

"If there aren't going to be any incidents, why are they to be armed?"

"Because half the country is armed."

"Okay, I'll take it to SECDEF."

"Roger."

Mike hung up and walked into Alex's office. "Find anything?"

"Yup. Eight underwriters in all, two of which I can get to. I've already arranged for Ray and Ted to represent Anglo-Swiss Re."

"Where are they?"

"Ted's here. Ray called to say he'll be a few minutes late. He has to pick up some medicine for his kid and I told him a few minutes would be okay."

"Anything serious?"

"No. He seemed to think it was just one of those kid things."

"Very well. As soon as Ray gets here, I want the four of us to go over all of this."

"Roger, Boss."

Six hours later, Ramon Fuentes, captain of marines and very talented linguist, boarded a flight from Tampa to Miami. Along with him was Ted Anderson, the wiry, fast-moving black SEAL petty officer. Once in Miami, the two boarded a direct overnight flight to Rio de Janeiro.

3

The South Atlantic

Captain Arthur Covington, sparkling in his immaculate white uniform—short-sleeved shirt, knee-length shorts with kneesocks, and black shoulder boards with four gold stripes—stood on the bridge of *Aurora Australis*. Below him, the white and Day-Glo cruise ship sliced through the choppy waters of the immense estuary at the mouth of the Rio de la Plata. Astern, to port and over the horizon, lay Montevideo, Uruguay. Even farther behind, and to starboard, lay Buenos Aires, Argentina, where they'd loaded their passengers. Although they'd yet to pass Cape San Antonio, they were, for all intents and purposes, out in the South Atlantic.

"It's a beautiful day, Captain."

Covington turned and smiled at his chief mate. "Yes it is, Mr. Winters."

The two officers stood in silence a few moments, savoring the salt air, the glint of the afternoon sun on the foam-speckled blue sea and the very gentle rise and fall as the ship's bow met that sea. "The overhaul seems to have gone extremely well, unless there've been problems you or the chief engineer have neglected to tell me about."

"As far as I know, there haven't been any. It appears to me the Brazilians did very good work for us. The ship's far from new, but she's acting pretty frisky at the moment."

And neither of us is particularly new either, thought Covington as his sense of well-being began to drift away. But we both know our business. "This is what? Our thirty-somethingth Antarctic voyage . . ."

"Thirty-second, I figure, Captain."

"So we should have it all down pretty damn well by now. And we do. Ice in all its forms, storms such as are rarely seen anywhere else in the world, passengers on ego trips—we both know how to handle them. But still, I'm not comfortable about this particular expedition."

Arthur Covington's mind was far from inflexible. He couldn't have survived thirty years of highly varied service at sea if it weren't. Still, he found the current expedition both unusual and a little unsettling. He'd never before commanded a politically driven expedition, especially one on which the sponsor—Greenpeace—had selected and even subsidized so many of the passengers and had demanded so much control over the itinerary. And he was expected to provide an experience that would serve a highly specific objective: to convince the passengers that Antarctica was melting and, therefore, by extension, that we the people were causing the melting.

As for the basic premise, Covington had no doubt the globe was warming at the moment. His mind remained open, however, about the precise mix of causes.

"It's too damn political, Mister," continued the captain. "We—you, I and *Aurora*—are being set up in the middle of a culture war."

"You're not the only person who thinks we're a target, Captain. They keep sending us those special warnings."

"Useless warnings, Mr. Winters. 'Your ship might well be an attractive target for terrorists. Special care should be exercised at all times.' They keep saying it over and over, but I haven't the slightest idea what we can do that we're not already doing—except return to BA and forget about the whole damn thing."

"I couldn't agree with you more, Captain. We've searched the ship twice as it is, just in case they're talking about bombs, rather than guided missiles or six guys wearing ski masks."

"What more do we do to ensure nothing happens? Strip-search everybody—starting with Senator Bergstrom—twice a day?"

Winters closed his eyes slightly and shook his head.

"And all this media, Mister," continued the captain. "Crews from three different networks. Some of the passengers have even brought their own media advisors to deal with the media persons, and they're all getting under my skin before we've even gotten out of the Plate Estuary."

"I've already had two run-ins."

"I'm convinced some of these people are more interested in being seen than in seeing. Especially the senator and that congressman. Either could have jumped on a government flight anytime he wanted to visit the icy south. But they knew the media coverage might be a little scanty if they did it that way."

Covington lapsed into silence and the two continued to stand, looking forward at the passengers milling around the bow. Most were talking as they watched the gulls and the white-capped waves glide by. Even from where he was, Covington could recognize the famous writer with his equally famous, carefully tinted, snow-white hair. And the emaciated actress with whom the writer was talking. She had once been even more famous than the writer. And there was Rod Johnson, the Greenpeace coordinator, or commissar if you didn't particularly like him. He was impossible to miss in his checked wool woodsman's shirt, especially when half the passengers were sweating in their T-shirts.

"I'm pleased they're able to enjoy the weather," remarked Winters. "If we'd sailed from Ushuaia, they'd probably not see the sun for a week or two."

"Ah!" sighed Covington. "I suppose we might as well get it over with now. Before it cuts into the Welcome Aboard Party."

"I suppose so, Captain."

Covington walked over to the bulkhead and raised the public-address system to his mouth. "Ladies and gentlemen, this is Captain Covington. As you were informed when you first boarded *Aurora*, we are required by both government and company regulations to conduct a lifeboat drill shortly after getting under way. We will conduct this drill in a few minutes, as soon as I review it with you. When you boarded, you were informed of the number of the boat to which you have been assigned. That number is also found on the door inside your cabin. Please remember that odd number boats are on the starboard, or right, side of the ship, and even numbered boats are on the port, or left, side of the ship. Numbers one and two are the farthest forward and the numbers go up as you walk aft. Please also remember that personal flotation devices—what used to be called life jackets—are stored in your cabin in a locker marked PFDs. In a real emergency the word would be passed over this public-address system for you to report to your lifeboat stations, and you would do this as rapidly as possible, after picking up and putting on your PFD. In this drill you will do the same, so now please walk—walk, this is not a race—to your cabin, get and put on your PFD and report to your assigned boat. When you are told the drill is completed, we ask that you return your PFDs to the locker from which they came so you can find them again. At all times, whether in this drill or in a real emergency, you are required to obey the orders of the ship's officers and other personnel and you are also encouraged to ask for their assistance.

"Now commence the drill!"

The two officers watched the reactions of the passengers they could see, the ones on the forward weather decks, many of whom had been looking up at the bridge, their sunglasses glinting in the sun, during the announcement. At first, very little happened. Then they all seemed to find something terribly important to say to one another. Then they started moving hesitantly toward the doors into the ship.

"As usual, they didn't really believe you'd do this to them," remarked Winters wryly.

Covington just smiled.

* * *

Fifteen minutes into the boat drill Arthur Covington turned to his chief mate. "It's time, Mister, for you and me to take a tour of the boat deck. See how this is really going."

"I'm with you, Captain."

After nodding at the mate of the watch to carry on, Covington led the way down two ladders to the starboard boat deck, where they encountered the predictable level of confusion. With no true emergency in sight, it wasn't a matter of panic but one of confusion and growing irritation. Many of those who had found their boats were already getting bored standing next to them, while those who couldn't find their stations were becoming both frustrated and embarrassed. And then there were those who couldn't—or wouldn't—put their PFDs on properly.

Covington and Winters crossed through the superstructure to the port side and found the same situation. As they walked slowly aft, with the ship rising and falling gently beneath them, the captain became aware of a tall, balding man walking with them. Their unknown companion was dressed in expensive-looking slacks and a polo shirt embroidered with the crest of a very prestigious golf club, and his hands were clasped behind his back.

Covington stopped and turned to him.

"James Ives, Captain," said the new arrival as he offered his hand. "I'm the CEO of Universal Systems and Solutions. Do you always have this much confusion when you run this drill?"

"Are you on your way to your lifeboat station, Mr. Ives?" asked Covington.

"I never participate in this sort of exercise anymore. Once you've reached my level . . ."

Covington paused a second. "I totally understand your position, Jim, and I hope you understand mine. Yes, these drills are always confused, but this isn't the navy, so they're not expected to be perfect. They're designed to make sure everybody knows where his PFD and lifeboat are located. It's also been my experience that men at your level are in an excellent position to set a stellar example for your less-accomplished fellow passengers."

Ives looked coldly at him a moment and then walked off. Covington neither knew nor cared where the CEO of Universal Systems and Solutions was headed.

A few moments later Winters spotted a video camera operator recording the drill. "Have you reported to your lifeboat?" asked the chief mate.

"No," replied the operator, waving for him to stand aside.

"You're required to do so," said Winters, standing directly in front of the camera's lens.

"I'm a videojournalist!" snapped the young woman. "You just don't want the world to see this confused mess. If there's a real accident, all these people will be killed."

"You're a passenger, and I will take that camera from you in fifteen seconds if you do not go where you are required to go."

The girl gave the chief mate the sort of look she undoubtedly reserved for New York cops who told her to get behind the barricade along with everybody else. She then turned and walked off.

"I have to go change into trousers and brush my teeth

for the Welcome Aboard Party," remarked Covington half an hour later, after he'd secured from the drill. "It's too bad *Aurora* isn't bigger—then she might have a staff captain to handle the social stuff while I concentrate on dodging icebergs."

* * *

Senator Alvin Bergstrom leaned on the rail and looked out to starboard as the golden sun lowered itself into the white-speckled blue sea. To his left, his PR coordinator, Babs Martin, had her glasses firmly in place and her back to the rail while she looked over the passengers, young and old but most affluent, chatting, nibbling and drinking at the Welcome Aboard Party. To his right—and almost shoulder to shoulder with him—Linda, young, desirable Linda in her shirt and jeans, was also leaning over the varnished rail cap, admiring the sun or the sea or perhaps just her own thoughts.

The senator took a deep breath. He couldn't decide which he found more refreshing—the fine wind that massaged his tired, sixty-five-year-old face and scalp as if it were the most delicate of lovers or the very attractive young lobbyist whose attention and smiles seemed to promise the same loving treatment. "Yes, Linda," he replied to the young woman as he turned toward her, "all reasonable people agree something decisive must be done . . ."

"I totally agree with you, Senator," said Linda, looking intently into the senator's strikingly blue eyes, "and that's why we've to first stabilize the climate and then get it back to where it belongs. We simply have got to get the temperature down!"

"Yes . . . ," replied Bergstrom, glancing up at the video cameraman who was shooting down at them from the boat deck.

"The problem, Senator, is greed. Too many people are making too much money by trashing the environment, and they've got to be stopped."

"I couldn't agree more, Linda. Deb, my wife, reminded me of that just a few days ago. It's too bad she couldn't come on this expedition—she's a very solid environmentalist, my whole family is—but she's not been feeling well recently. Now, in the way of a little background, tell me something about yourself. What kind of music do you like? Sports? What do you think about when you're with your boyfriend?"

Babs frowned when she heard the question. In the past four years she'd had to make half a dozen of Bergstrom's indiscretions disappear. In some cases, she'd been unable to bury them as deeply as she would have liked, so she'd had to confuse the facts so thoroughly that Solomon would have found it impossible to guess what had really happened. It had cost a great deal of money—and in several cases destroyed the reputations of an innocent or two—but the objective had always been attained. Alvin Bergstrom, in public, was folksy and convincing. With his twinkling eyes and open face, he was able to look anybody straight-on while he rumbled the most utter nonsense. His polls remained almost 90 percent positive, and that's all that mattered to the people to whom Babs really reported.

"Senator Bergstrom, it's good to see you."

Babs watched as the senator turned. "Why, it's Jim Ives. How are you, Jim?"

"Looking forward to the voyage, Senator, although I'm a little bit nervous about the ship's governance."

"You mean the way it's run?"

"Yes, that lifeboat drill was a disaster."

"I suspect it went as well as they ever do."

"We should have a drink this evening, Senator. As you may know, we've set up a new consulting arm that may well be able to help the government with all this warming business."

"Not this evening, I'm afraid, but in the next day or two. Babs will set it up."

"I look forward to it."

"Okay, Babs?" said the senator as Ives walked away.

"I'll take care of it."

* * *

Arthur Covington paused partway down the ladder from the boat deck to the main deck aft, as a rogue cloud of acrid stack gas, unwilling for some reason to blow promptly downwind, wrapped itself around his head just as he was inhaling, then dissolved in the clear air. His sinuses screamed briefly and then the incident was over.

He examined his ship critically. The paint work was clean and bright and the varnished rails gleamed, although here and there deep discolorations hinted at the ship's age. Some of the other expedition ships preferred the rough and ready look, but Covington liked to maintain certain standards. And the catering staff, he was also delighted to note, had done their usual fine job. What had once been a small pool—the Brazilians had done an excellent job of decking it over—was now surrounded by dozens of small round tables and countless chairs, all bordered by rows of long tables serving drinks and hors d'oeuvres. The fact that *Aurora* was an expedition cruise ship did not mean that her passengers were willing to settle for anything less than the best.

Covington took a moment to scan the crowd from his vantage point. Many—most—were in shorts or blue jeans. A few—generally the older ones—were slightly more formal. All were standing around chatting as they somehow managed to drink, nibble on hors d'oeuvres and wave their hands, all at the same time. Welcome Aboard Parties were the same on all ships, he decided. Whatever their mission.

Covington's eyes settled briefly on Senator Bergstrom. Although the plump little man was his most "senior" passenger, he decided not to rush over, since the senator was clearly busy with the gorgeous young thing whose eyes were so green he could feel their attraction from where he was. Next he spotted the movie actor, Lloyd what's-his-name. Once again, no action on his part was required immediately, since Lloyd . . . Llewellyn, that was his last name . . . was surrounded by and very busy with a flock of twenty-something ecologists. And the writer with the beautiful white hair. He was alone, looking desperately for somebody to approach him and chat. The captain could feel the man's unease and even disappointment, but he simply didn't feel literary enough at the moment to do anything about it.

The good news from Covington's point of view was that he didn't have to make a welcome aboard speech. The bad news was that he had to wander through the crowd and shake every hand that wanted to be shaken. Just like a politician. Taking a deep breath, he stepped down the ladder. As he did, something slammed into both his shins, knocking him back and down until he found himself sitting on the step.

"Oh my gosh, I'm so terribly sorry!"

Covington looked down and saw a little girl of about eight. Katie something or other, he thought. He'd noticed her name because she was the youngest person aboard the ship. "Are you all right?"

"Oh yes," said the girl-dervish. "Are you hurt?"

"No, I'm fine."

"Oh, I'm so sorry," continued Katie. "Somebody told me that if I ran up these stairs I could get a better look at . . ." As she paused, a look of horror crossed her face. "You're not the captain, are you?"

Covington couldn't help but burst into laughter. "Yes, Katie, I'm the captain."

"Ohhhhhh!"

"And you're Katie Sanders. I'm very glad to meet you and I'm also very glad you could come along on this trip."

"Thank you. They—Mom and Dad—told me we're going to see hundreds and hundreds of penguins. I love penguins."

"I will show you hundreds of penguins but you have to do me a favor . . ."

"Yes?"

"Please don't run around without looking where you are going. It's all too easy to fall over the side of a ship and very, very hard to pick you up again if you do." As he spoke, Covington's eyes scanned the rails to ensure that the netting had been installed along them precisely to prevent people like Katie Sanders from rocketing over the side.

"Yes. Of course."

"Good. Now, part of my job," continued Covington as he pulled himself up, "is to go around and meet as many of those people as want to meet me. If you will excuse me, I'm sure we will get a chance to talk more later."

"Will you come meet my mom and dad? I know they want to meet you."

"Sounds to me like the very best place to start. You lead the way."

As the tall officer in white followed the little girl in shorts and a T-shirt, he noticed a hint of perfume mixed with the strong smells of food that surrounded him. The band then finished its break and broke into a mellow version of a popular rock tune. Covington found himself smiling again, not at the band but at the thought that one of the video cameras had caught his collision with Katie. What, he wondered, would the home office make of it?

"Captain," said Katie, "this is my dad, Tim, and my mom, Dana. Mom and Dad, this is the captain of the ship."

"Arthur Covington," said the captain quickly, offering his hand first to Dana.

Katie's parents, who had been startled to see Katie leading what was obviously the captain toward them, struggled to recover their composure as they shook Covington's hand.

"I congratulate you," continued Covington, thinking as he did that Tim and Dana both looked so young they could have been Katie's older siblings. "I wish more people had the wisdom and confidence to bring kids with them on these expeditions of ours."

"We were a little worried about the rides ashore in the rubber boats," said Dana. "They say the water's bitterly cold and sometimes rough. But we decided this was probably the opportunity of a lifetime for all of us. Katie *will* be able to go ashore, won't she?"

"Absolutely. I know for a fact that Katie's as nimble as she is tough. If I were to worry about anybody, it would be some of our older passengers." As he spoke, Covington watched out the corner of his eye as Katie ambled over to a table of hors d'oeuvres and scooped up a cracker with caviar. After touching it carefully with the tip of her tongue, the girl made a face and, believing nobody was watching, threw it over the rail.

The band finished the tune, and after a pause, the bandleader asked for silence. "Welcome to *Aurora Australis*," she intoned over the microphone. "We're so glad you could join us. Although I'm sure you will all agree that the expedition itself is a grand treat, I'm thrilled to announce that we have another one for you. Among our many illustrious expedition members, one is named Chrissie Clark. Yes, *the* Chrissie Clark! Our own Chrissie Clark. And as her special contribution to ending global warming and saving the environment, Chrissie has volunteered to sing for us from time to time. Starting right now!"

As the crowd burst into shrieks of delight, Covington studied the singer a moment. She was a nice-looking girl. Not just because she was slender, well built and had an open, friendly face, but because she seemed to radiate a natural warmth. It's something that all entertainers try to do, he thought, but only the most successful really manage to pull off. He turned back to the Sanders. "I can't tell you how much I've enjoyed meeting you three. And," he added quietly, "I want you to bring Katie up to the bridge sometime."

"Is that permitted?"

"It is if the captain says it is."

"She'll love it," said Tim.

"And so will Tim," remarked Dana dryly.

"Good. Send word to me when you're ready. Now, I'm paid to circulate, so I must do so. Again, welcome aboard."

While Chrissie Clark belted out several of her latest hits, and the under-forty set swayed and bumped to her words and tunes, Covington worked his way more or less at random through the crowd, greeting and chatting as he went.

Despite his current social duties, Arthur Covington could never forget he was *Aurora*'s master. By law he was almost totally responsible for the ship and all those aboard, and no matter what limits the law might put on his liability, what wiggle room it might allow him in the case of error, he held himself to be absolutely and totally responsible. Even while chatting with several highly influential businessmen, he couldn't prevent his eyes from wandering almost continuously around his ship, checking that all was in order. He glanced up and forward and was most gratified to notice one of the enginemen standing beside the winch of the aft-most lifeboat on the port side. The man was, at the moment, staring aft at the party, but Covington was certain he was there checking the winch and performing preventive maintenance. He held his chief engineer in high regard and was pleased to have his confidence reaffirmed. Within less than a heartbeat, however, his sense of well-being blew away with the warm breeze when he caught sight of Congressman Peter Evans, his second most important politician-passenger, and realized the man was staring almost angrily at him.

Evans had a reputation for being intensely ambitious, not to mention proud, and would expect Covington to approach him rather than the other way around. Pasting his smile back on, the captain turned and headed toward the congressman, who, he noted, had his wife, Penny, at his side. Penny, he understood, was from old money, and most seemed to feel that much of her husband's success had grown out of that very same weedy old green.

"Congressman Evans," said Covington as he wormed his way through the small crowd surrounding Evans and offered his hand. "Welcome aboard *Aurora*."

"Thank you, Captain," replied Evans, now beaming. Unlike Chrissie Clark's, however, Peter Evans's good cheer was totally forced. He simply did not seem comfortable, which seemed strange since most politicians are addicted to crowds. It was only then that Covington realized Evans had arranged for a news crew to be on hand to tape the great moment. Cameraman, soundgirl and reporter—all undoubtedly primed by Evans to ask just the right questions.

A media show, thought the captain. A scripted media show. That was what the whole expedition was supposed to be.

* * *

Marcello Cagayan paused in his labors—he was lubricating the winch on one of the lifeboat davits—and looked aft at the party as he unthinkingly wiped the bluish grease off his hands with a rag. His most basic, and dominant, impulses were hatred and contempt, although a very slight twinge of jealousy was also present. He hated all those people milling around on the deck beneath him. For their smugness; their greed; their stupidity. He hated them because up until now they had not only believed they were powerful, but were, in fact, powerful. He hated them because whenever they noticed him—assuming they ever did—they would see nothing more than a powerless little brown monkey. Unworthy of comment.

But the world was changing fast. The world had already changed. Omar was right. They thought they had the power. They thought they were in control. But they weren't. On this ship, Marcello Cagayan, the puny little brown monkey, had the power. He was the one who would control who would live and when all would die.

"Hey, man." Marcello turned. It was Vido, one of the Ecuadorian deckhands. "Looks like a damn good party."

"Yeah," stuttered Cagayan as Vido passed by, carrying a large roll of white nylon line. Vido was okay, thought Cagayan. He never called him a *mono*, never treated him like a fool. If anybody survived, Cagayan hoped it might be Vido, although he certainly wouldn't change anything to guarantee it.

Marcello had been born into parasite-ridden poverty on one of the southern islands in the Philippines. His father, a subsistence farmer, had died when he was young. Killed by government troops who claimed that he was a rebel. Even though they knew better. His mother had died when he was even younger. Of poverty.

Marcello could well remember the day his father died. He'd stood there with the rest of the village in terrified silence when the officer told his father to kneel before him and beg. He saw the expression on the officer's face when he pulled the trigger and blew a big hole in his father's head.

At the time he'd felt great sadness and great fear. His father, the central authority of his young life, had been destroyed by an even greater authority. Only later had he come to understand strength and weakness and power. Only later had he understood that the officer's expression was not one of simple pleasure, but the near-divine pleasure of forcing one's will on others. Of exercising power.

After his father's death there was little to keep Marcello in the hot, fever-infested, frequently muddy village of his birth. At the age of eight he wandered off in the general direction of the ocean, a course that was not difficult to determine since he was on an island.

4

Houston

"What do you think of this bottle, Mamoud?" asked Bob Gilchrest, chairman of Oceanic Petrotransporters, LLC, as he partially filled Mamoud al Hussein's glass with red wine. The two men were sitting, with half a dozen others, in one of the private dining rooms in one of Houston's more exclusive clubs. The room was done in a heavy, traditional Spanish style. Dark wood paneling, heavy oak furniture. It was a style that still reflected, especially in some of its details, the tastes of the Arabs who had dominated Spain for so many centuries.

Mamoud tasted it. "Very fine, Bob. Much better than that product you served me earlier . . . Did you say that was from West Texas?"

"And I admit they're better at making oil there than wine," continued the ship owner in a deep, slow drawl.

"Still, I salute their effort."

"And I salute your efforts the past six years. You've turned Tecmar into one of the world's cutting-edge yards."

"Most of the credit goes to Lorenzo and his Brazilians." As he spoke, Mamoud nodded toward Lorenzo Almeida, the president of Tecmar. "They're the ones who put together the proposal you accepted a few hours ago to overhaul six liquid natural gas carriers and they're the ones who will execute it. All I did was a little cheerleading."

"You sound as if you're about to retire."

"No, but I understand His Highness has another project for me."

"Really! Can you talk about it?"

"I don't see why not. We've been planning to build a new solar panel factory. It's a business His Highness wants to be in, and I have been asked to build it and get it started."

"Where?"

"North Africa. But please don't worry, Lorenzo and his team are totally capable of handling this project and any others you may ask him to undertake."

"I know that, Mamoud. We'd have never given you this contract if we weren't confident that Lorenzo could handle it himself, just in case something happened to you."

Mamoud smiled and looked around the table. He hadn't allowed himself the liberty of relaxing much recently, but tonight a sense of comfortable satisfaction was almost forcing itself on him. He and Lorenzo *had* landed a huge contract and Lorenzo *had* proven to be a very apt pupil. The men at the dinner table with him were all skilled engineers or other technicians, and he always enjoyed the company of such men. But then, as the topic of conversation changed to topics more mundane and, to him, childish, his perpetual unease returned. Their utter conviction that their successes were totally the result of their own personal perfection, their total inability to think of science as merely one portion of something far greater, grated on his nerves and soul. To them, engineering was a means to enhancing one's paycheck rather than a means of approaching and glorifying God. Some of these men, he reflected, might even believe that they were men of faith but he suspected they were just deceiving themselves.

It was through logic of just this sort that Mamoud al Hussein had managed to alienate himself from a major portion of the human race.

"Bob," Mamoud finally said after looking at his watch about half an hour later, "today has been one of the truly great days of my life, but I must get back to Rio. There are also a number of odds and ends I want to complete so Lorenzo doesn't find himself tripping over them six months from now."

"I hate to see you go, old friend . . ."

"Any questions or problems, give me a call. Or ask Lorenzo—he'll be in Houston for another week or so."

After good-byes all around and a quick drive to the airport, Mamoud was airborne in the Tecmar jet an hour and a half later. As the plane had taxied across the apron, the thought of *Aurora Australis* passed briefly through his mind. What he was doing was distasteful, he admitted to himself for the millionth time, but necessary. There was nothing more to think about, since he had done all he could and now the matter would play itself out, one way or another. He closed his eyes and was almost immediately asleep.

5

Rio de Janeiro

The big jet floated slowly down toward the white-capped waters of the Baia de Guanabara, its four huge engines purring at the newly born sun.

Ted, who had won the window seat in a game of scissors, paper, rocks, watched as the heavily industrialized Ilha do Governador came into view. And then the runways of Jobim International Airport at the western end of the island.

"You get enough sleep?" asked Ray.

"I've slept in worse places . . ."

"Good. I like working with a guy who's alert. On his toes. Can sleep anywhere."

"Having a clean conscience helps."

"You finish that overview Alex made up for us?"

"Fascinating stuff. Alex has a way of making the weirdest crap seem reasonable."

Both were careful not to mention that the overview was an explanation of basic insurance practices and terms—subrogation, common average and the like. It was highly unlikely that anybody was eavesdropping, but the possibility always existed. And any informed listener would find it odd for two insurance investigators to be boning up on the basic vocabulary of the industry.

Half an hour later the plane had landed with only a modest bump and the two were walking down the Jetway, briefcases in their hands.

"Ray," said Ted in a low voice, "you really think we're going to come up with anything on this trip? I mean, I know the Old Man seems to think we might, but I have my doubts."

"It's a long shot, but let's see what happens."

"I'm with you."

The two continued in silence to the baggage carousel, where, under the watchful eyes of two combat-equipped paratroopers, they snatched up their duffels and flowed with the crowd to the Immigration desks.

"This place reminds me of L.A.," remarked Ted. "From what I read, I thought everybody would look like you or me, but half the people here look Japanese, Chinese or Arab."

"You missed the Indians—from India. Everybody seems to want something the Brazilians have—gold, airplanes, computer chips, sugarcane for ethanol, ears and mouths for cell phones—the place is a free-for-all."

"Our kind of place?"

Ray just shook his head. When he reached the head of the line, he launched into a fluid Brazilian Portuguese. The Immigration officer lifted his left eyebrow briefly then returned to a bland, bureaucratic scowl.

"Reason for your visit, *Senhor*?"

"Business, *Senhor*."

"What business are you in?"

"Insurance, *Senhor*. We will be consulting with one of our accounts, a shipyard a few kilometers from here."

"How long do you plan to stay?"

"A week or less."

When it was Ted's turn, he considered trying his halting Spanish but decided discretion was the better part of valor and stuck to English, which the official spoke perfectly.

The officer typed each of their names into the computer in front of him and pushed enter. While the official glanced back and forth between them and the monitor, Ted glanced around at the video cameras and wondered if he'd ever get used to being under surveillance for essentially the rest of his life.

"Very well," said the officer finally, his face breaking into a totally unexpected smile. "Welcome to Brazil."

While the Customs inspector palpated their bags, Ray noticed a young man waving a sign reading "Mr. Fuentes—Mr. Anderson." "That's one good sign," said Ray to Ted. "Our driver's here."

When Ray waved at the driver, the inspector frowned but said nothing.

"Welcome to Rio," said the sign-bearer in perfect English as Ray and Ted stepped out into the main concourse. "I'm Salvador. I've been sent by Tecmar to pick you up. Your firm alerted us you were on your way."

"That's most gracious of them," replied Ray.

"I've been instructed to take you anywhere you wish. Mr. Palmeira, our chief operating officer, is hoping to meet with you at two in the afternoon, but in the meantime you may wish to go to your hotel and freshen up, or we can go directly to the shipyard if you wish to begin your inspection immediately."

"What about Mr. Almeida, your CEO?"

"He's in Houston at the moment with Mr. al Hussein. They are completing the details of a very major contract—to overhaul and modernize six liquefied gas tankers for a company there. He won't be back until next week. If you wish, we can set up a videoconference."

Ray glanced at the time bug on a departure display. It wasn't even eight local time. "Salvador, I think the best plan is for you to take us to the hotel so we can clean up and catch some sleep. Then pick us up in time to meet with Mr. Palmeira."

"Of course, sir."

Much to Ted's disappointment, the hotel Alex had booked them into was not in the south of the city—along the Copacabana or Ipanema beaches. Rather, it was a commercial establishment located in the northeast, not far from the Rio-Niterói Bridge and the Tecmar shipyard. It was a district badly abused by history, economics and demographics, one filled with once-elegant houses, now serving as tenements, and a wide selection of dreary, dirty factories and warehouses. The hotel itself was old and faded, its plaster moldings and worn, but once-elegant rugs spoke of a more prosperous past. On one side was a small park that might once have been a wonderland. Now it was a land neither Ted nor Ray would care to be in after dark. What the hell! thought the SEAL. This is a working trip and the boss must want us in the middle of the action. At least it seems clean and the air-conditioning seems solid.

Or they were there because Alex had decided to save the taxpayers a little money.

"This was delivered for you about an hour ago, *Senhor*," said the desk clerk to Ray as they were checking in. "The messenger said it is important that you review these documents right away."

"*Obrigado*," said Ray, accepting the package, which he then handed to Ted.

"We hope you will enjoy your stay in Rio."

"We hope so too," replied the marine as they turned and walked to the self-service elevator.

"Bugs?" asked Ted. Once the door had closed, the car smelled faintly of hot lubricating oil and some sort of fried food.

"Always possible but let's assume not. Nobody at Tecmar knew where we're staying until we told Salvador."

Ted shrugged his shoulders.

Without a bellboy to guide them, it took several minutes to find the room. Once they were in the room and the door was closed, Ted dove into the parcel from Alex's friends and pulled out two small-caliber Berettas, two shoulder holsters and twenty rounds of ammunition. "Kinda small," he remarked, holding one of the automatics up for Ray to see.

"We're undercover, remember?" As he said it, Ray took a deep breath and thought how stale the air tasted, despite the air-conditioning.

While Ray started to unpack, Ted disassembled the weapons, just to make sure they were in good working order. He then carefully examined the ammunition. It wasn't that he didn't trust Alex's friends, but he was very much aware that different people have different objectives in this life. Even when the same government was cutting checks for all of them.

"I guess we have to wear these," he remarked, holding up the wrinkled jacket he had just pulled from his duffel. "Damn hot, though."

"You think we'd be any better off sticking them under our shirts? Or in our pockets?"

"In this heat these jackets are kind of a giveaway that we're armed."

"I know. We'll deal with it," said Ray as he punched a number into the telephone. He immediately launched into a torrent of fluid Portuguese. After stopping to listen a few moments, he said "*bom*" and then hung up only to immediately place another call.

"You ready?" asked Ray after completing the second call.

"Everything all set?"

"Yup. The rental car's on its way. The concierge will call us when it arrives."

"And the sidearms?"

"We'll keep them in our briefcases for now. Remember, whether or not people really believe we're insurance investigators, we will continue to act as if we are. We have to assume that somebody is keeping an eye on us, even if they *do* believe we're really from Anglo-Swiss Re. Insurance inspectors make people just as nervous as the DEA does."

"Roger."

The phone rang. The car had arrived. "That's it, Pal. We're off for a little sightseeing."

For the next three hours, with Ray driving the worn-out Honda Alex had rented them and Ted reading the detailed map she had somehow come up with, the two scouted the area around Estaleiro Tecmar. The area—jammed with old factories interspersed among tumbledown, makeshift dwellings, many of which didn't qualify for the term "house"—proved to be even more severely run down than their hotel's surroundings. The streets, with three or four exceptions, were narrow, twisted and dirty. Spotted here and there were small commercial nodes containing a few stores and several bars and restaurants, none of which looked very appetizing. And the air was filled on one block with the smells of solvents and smoke, while on the next it reeked of sizzling cooking oil and whatever was being cooked in it.

"Think you can find your way around here at night?" asked Ray as he stopped beside a vacant lot, figuring the rubbish-strewn open land would give them a better chance of spotting any lurking muggers.

"Hell no! This is a tangled mess."

"Reminds me of some parts of San Juan I'd rather forget. Maybe they've been cleaned up by now. Okay, back to the hotel. Let's hope we've learned enough."

"Something is always better than nothing."

* * *

Roberto Palmeira, chief operating officer of the Tecmar shipyard, sat at the head of the table in the yard's primary conference room. Behind him, a large window looked out over Graving Dock One and beyond, across the Baia de Guanabara to the city of Niterói. Running under the window was a long, oak table, the center of which was dominated by a gorgeous, but flashy, potted plant with huge orange-and-black flowers. Around the table were Ted and Ray, along with the yard's security and fire chiefs.

"I'm still at a little bit of a loss about your visit, gentlemen," said Palmeira after Salvador had made the introductions and then discreetly left. "The fire that interests you was far from large and we made no claim for it. And, quite honestly, shipyards tend to have fires from time to time and our record is, I believe, quite good. Still, I can understand that our underwriters might wish to send safety engineers to consult with us. But you are not safety engineers, are you?"

"No, sir, we are not," replied Ray. "Anglo-Swiss Re is more than satisfied with the technical details of your safety systems. We're more interested in the human element. Would you mind reviewing what is known about the incident?"

"As we stated in the report, the fire was caused by a careless welder working too close to combustible materials. Both the welder and his supervisor were discharged."

"According to your report, drugs were involved . . ."

"Yes, they were. Shipyards are very dangerous places—I'm sure I don't have to tell you that—so we've had a random drug testing program for many years. Unfortunately, we also have six thousand workers and, shamefully, drugs are very common in Rio—as they are in a number of North American cities. We work closely with the federal police. We do what we can but . . ."

"We understand the problem is very difficult to control . . . Now, our preliminary investigations indicate that two of your shipfitters—a Carlos Coccoli and an Umberto Rojas—appear to have disappeared without formally quitting a week or so after the fire. And the girlfriend of Coccoli was also reported as missing."

An expression of serious confusion spread across Palmeira's face. "Gentlemen, we have thousands of workers and Brazil is a very big nation. People come and go all the time. Some leave—for the Amazonian gold fields, for New York, for God knows where—without even collecting the wages we owe them. When opportunity presents itself, people seem quick to chase it. Especially with Christmas approaching. Why are these two men of such interest to you?"

"We've received indications that they may be—or have been—important members of the drug regime in your yard."

"Have the federal police been informed?"

"Not yet. As soon as we have something solid, we will ask you to inform them."

Palmeira turned to the security chief. "Is anything known about this Rojas and Coccoli?"

"I'll check, sir," replied the security chief, an expression of intense irritation on his face. He then pulled out his cell phone and dialed.

"He should have that information for you in no time," remarked the yard's COO as they waited. "We have a very complete computerized personnel system—and an equally up-to-date security and access program."

"The last record we have is their leaving through the south gate at 10:02 on the night of November 27," reported the security chief. His relief that he had something solid to report was all too obvious. "Coccoli was born in Rio, although he listed no relatives, just his girlfriend," he continued, listening to his phone and pausing from time to time. He came to us when he was eighteen. He was started on menial work and did so well that we put him in our shipfitters training program. Again he did well, and has been well respected by his supervisors. As for Rojas, he is originally from Para State to the north. He did welding for a gold mining company there, so we put him to the same task. No family listed, but that is not uncommon."

"Is that a normal time to leave? The end of a shift?"

"No," replied Palmeira, his perplexity still evident. "What project were they working on?"

Again, the security chief consulted his cell phone. "They had just completed the *Aurora Austalis* overhaul."

Ted and Ray both struggled not to look at the other.

"Ah!" said Palmeira, clearly relieved. "She is an older ship and that overhaul was a very complex and challenging project. It's very likely they would hang around the yard for a while, have a beer with some of their coworkers and celebrate the completion of the project."

The executive paused a moment, a frown on his face, then continued: "We allow no alcohol in the yard except for one canteen where the workers can have a beer or two *after* they have finished their shifts."

"Can you give us a list of the other shipfitters with whom they worked and where we can find them?"

"It might be best to leave this to the federal police. Drugs is a very violent business."

"We're primarily interested in determining if there's any connection between these two and the fire—and the possibility of further fires. Sabotage, perhaps."

"Of course!" Palmeira smiled, not believing a word of it.

Five minutes later—proving that the Tecmar shipyard really was totally up-to-date—the computer printer resting on a small table along one wall burst into life. Roberto Palmeira picked up the printout and scanned it. "Here are ten men who worked with Coccoli and Rojas on *Aurora*. All are in the yard now, so you can go talk to them. I will be pleased to provide you with a vehicle that you can drive yourselves, but I urge you to let Salvador drive for you. Some of these job sites are difficult to find, and Salvador will in no way interfere with your inquiries. He will stay in the vehicle if you wish."

"If we're going to find ten men in one afternoon, we're going to need Salvador's help," said Ted, speaking for the first time.

* * *

With Salvador driving, Ray and Ted crisscrossed the Tecmar shipyard—visiting graving docks that baked in the tropical afternoon sun; fabrication and assembly shops filled with the screeching, pounding roar of steel being forced into useful shapes and forms and the ever-present smells of cut metal and petroleum in all its many forms and flavors—tracking down and interviewing the men on the list of shipfitters who had worked with Coccoli and Rojas. All seemed to agree that Carlos Coccoli was exceptionally brash and ambitious, although that was not so strange for a young man. Umberto Rojas had struck most as somewhat withdrawn. Everybody agreed they were good workers. Nobody knew anything about their personal lives, although one or two—after taking great care to describe themselves as solid family men who had only been passing by on the way to the bus—thought they'd seen the two patronizing some of the seedier bars and other establishments that lined the grimy streets surrounding the yard.

"Those guys weren't willing to admit anything," said Ted as he walked through the door into the hotel room, stretched out on the bed's worn spread and soaked up the air-conditioning, stale air and all. "They obviously knew more but didn't want to admit it."

"Yeah, this is one of those places where it's dangerous to know or say too much. But I think we found what the boss sent us here for this morning."

"You mean that the two guys worked on *Aurora Australis*?"

"Right."

"But nothing's happened to the ship. Nothing's been found. There's no intelligence . . ."

"I know, but the boss seems to think there might be something, and I must admit that their having worked on the cruise ship just adds another dot to the picture."

"It's still pretty thin. Don't you think we're getting a little carried away with the 'connecting the dots' business?"

"What about the yard itself?" asked Ray, knowing that

Ted had been a third-class shipfitter before transferring to the SEALs.

"The yard impressed me. Cleaner, better organized than the two we had overhauls in before I joined the 'chosen.' "

"You didn't notice anything odd, out of place? Something the boss might want to know about?"

"No. That's one squared-away yard—as yards go."

"I'm going to check in with the boss," said Ray as he rigged a scrambler onto his cell phone.

Ted lay there, listening to Ray explain the situation to Mike Chambers. And he listened to the silence when Ray was listening to their boss. "Aye, aye, sir," said the marine finally as he flipped the phone closed. "We're in luck, Ted. We're going partying tonight and SECDEF's picking up the tab."

"You mean those dumps opposite the shipyard?"

"How did you guess? It seems the Agency has a stringer in the area who thinks she may know them. A B-girl at a place called the 'Bar Tiffany.' We're going to listen and try not to attract too much attention to ourselves. Remember, no incidents. If this girl knows something, fine. If not, that's fine too."

"The 'Bar Tiffany'?"

"Yes, the girl's named Dani."

"What's the address?" asked Ted, opening Alex's map as he did.

Ray gave it to him.

"Hell, we must have passed this place at least twice today but I don't remember it. I don't remember seeing anyplace I really wanted to go into."

"All right, damn it, if we have to go we have to go. Let's hit it!" he concluded, sitting up.

"Not so fast. Nightlife around here doesn't start until late. This Dani's expecting us between midnight and one, so get a little shut-eye because you're going to need it."

"Why?"

"Because unless we find something truly astounding, the boss plans to redeploy us tomorrow."

"To where?"

"He didn't say."

* * *

Mamoud al Hussein picked up the quietly ringing phone. "Yes, Roberto," he said, looking at the caller ID.

"I'm very sorry to bother you now, Mamoud, when you're trying to rest up from your trip, but there's something very strange about these insurance inspectors who met with me today."

"Yes?"

"They said they are here to look into the 'personnel situation' in the yard. Specifically the drug situation. And that makes sense. And they are very interested in two particular shipfitters who left our employ several weeks ago. They suggested these two men were involved with drugs, and of course they may well have been, but why are they interested in these two? I'm very sorry, but I have a gut feeling that they are interested in something else. Unfortunately, I don't know what it is. I know this isn't much, but I thought you should know."

"Have you checked again with the insurance company?"

"Yes. They say they are their people."

"Very well, Roberto. Thank you. Would you arrange for a meeting with them tomorrow? Perhaps I can figure out what they are up to."

"Consider it done."

Mamoud hung up and looked out the window at the late afternoon sun just disappearing behind the mountains to the west. Should he act or would any action be an overreaction? He had no idea who these two really were. They might well be insurance people interested in the narcotics problems in the yard. That made perfect sense. They might be practically anybody else.

In theory, the mechanism had been set in motion along its destined course and there was nothing more for him to do. Indeed, he reminded himself, by interfering he might very well destroy his own well-thought-out construct. On the other hand, midcourse corrections were common in even the greatest of engineering endeavors. Think of NASA.

Action was called for, he decided. Especially since it entailed very little risk to either him personally or to the operation. He took a cell phone out of his desk drawer. It belonged to a young girl who never existed.

"There were two men at the yard today who are supposed to be insurance inspectors . . . Yes, you know of them? I want you to arrange for them to die tonight, victims of the city's ceaseless, random violence . . . Yes, I think it is reasonable to assume they will go out. They are young men. Young men who seem very curious about Tecmar and a great many other things. Watch their hotel. At the very least they will go out for dinner."

6

The South Atlantic

The sun rose to find *Aurora Australis* at latitude 42 degrees, 33 minutes south, roughly two hundred miles east of Argentina. The ship was now within the fabled Roaring Forties, a geographic band known for its boisterous winds. By dawn the sea had made up into a serious chop and the temperature had dropped significantly, but the sky remained almost cloudless. It was, in fact, the last fine day *Aurora*, her passengers or crew would see for quite some time.

"Good morning, Congressman," said Wendell Gardner as he stepped on the treadmill beside that being used by Peter Evans. Wendell was one of the team leaders who would supervise the expeditions ashore.

"Morning, Wendell," replied Evans, looking out the side of his eye at the shaggy young man about whom he had such mixed feelings. On the one hand, the fellow—who had made it a point to approach him repeatedly—was an utter fanatic. His theories and proposals were far beyond anything Evans could allow himself to be seen embracing, even in the existing, overheated media environment.

Several of his important backers would never stand for it. On the other hand, he couldn't just tell him to buzz off. The media would interpret that as an outright rejection of all that is good and pure on Earth. And they were everywhere!

But he might still be of use, thought the congressman as he twisted the speed control up one notch. Just about everybody can be useful in some way.

"The approach I suggested to you last night, sir, that you propose a law forcing foreign governments to comply with our environmental laws . . . What do you think of it?"

"A lot's already being done in that direction. We prohibit the import of certain products into the United States, for example, that haven't been manufactured in accord with our laws."

"Yes, but those rogue countries trade with each other! We have to find some way of controlling their behavior before it's too late."

"I promise you," replied Evans as he looked ahead and puffed slightly, "that I'll look further into it. I agree we have to take control. We need some new legislation with real teeth in it.

"Wendell," continued Evans quietly, hoping that none of the other toilers in the ship's fitness center could hear him, "just how dangerous is the process of our transferring ashore by those rubber boats?"

"It isn't, sir. If the weather's too rough, we don't go ashore. Otherwise, we've got it all worked out."

"It's not possible to fall over, or be swept over the side of the boat?" Evans said as his feet continued to glide over the simulated track.

"No, sir. We're prepared to prevent that."

"And ashore . . . what are the dangers there? Have you ever had anybody slip into the water and drown? Are there crevasses that split open without warning? What about storms that suddenly hit?"

"This isn't our first expedition, Congressman. We've got it all worked out. Everybody's closely supervised. You will be safer ashore than when you are aboard this ship."

"I'm sorry for being so insistent," continued Evans, "but I'm a little worried about my wife. And I tell you this in full confidence. She's always been very solid on the environment—all you have to do is look at our contributions to see that—and up until recently she's always loved the outdoors, but something has happened to her the past six months. She seems to go through bouts of depression and almost suicidal clumsiness—or carelessness. The doctors don't really seem to know what's brought this all on, but it's very worrisome to me. I'm hoping this trip will pull her out of it, but at the same time I worry that she might injure herself, either through carelessness or possibly even intentionally."

"Everything will be fine, Congressman. I'll keep an eye on her."

I damn well hope so, thought Evans. I want as much media coverage as I can get, but I don't want any of Penny flapping and floundering in icy water, screeching and screaming.

Without ever having stopped jogging, Evans turned back to his machine and set the pace a little higher for himself. He then looked around the fitness facility, at the row upon row of treadmills and weight machines of various sorts, the majority in use. There was a lot of sweat being spilled, he thought. For many of *Aurora*'s passengers, personal fitness was just as much of a moral issue as was environmental concern.

Despite the brochures, he'd assumed, until he got aboard the ship, that *Aurora* would be a little on the Spartan side. He'd been wrong. The food, the bars, the exercise facilities . . . His eyes settled on a young woman bench-pressing a few pounds. Black hair, piercing blue eyes, black tights and a slender body that hinted at the faintest touch of substance in all the right places. She reminded him of Jackie, his always-willing assistant. He wished Jackie were there and Penny . . . and Penny someplace else. If Jackie were there with him, the whole thing would be a lot more fun. As it was, it was shaping up to be pure work.

* * *

Chrissie Clark, dressed in a sweater and jeans, stood with her hands on the rail, feeling the wind tear through the air. She watched with relaxed pleasure as the foamy whitecaps chased one another over the blue sea and the mid-morning sun shone down on her. It felt good to be alone for a change. There was no media in sight, and her current boyfriend, Brad, was busy drinking chocolate martinis and playing poker with two very sketchy couples—neither of whom seemed to have any interest in the environment. She looked behind her, noticed an empty deck chair and walked over to it. "Do you mind if I plop myself down here?" she asked the elderly woman in the next chair.

"Of course not, dear. Do soak up a little sun before it's too late."

As the woman spoke, Chrissie saw the glint of recognition in her eyes. Chrissie was grateful that she had the grace not to start the "Aren't you Chrissie Clark . . ." game.

The woman was right, she thought. It was already getting chilly and they said it would cloud over during the evening. She glanced out the corner of her eye at the woman, who was busy talking with the equally elderly man on her other side. She might very well be a somebody, but she wasn't a big-time somebody, a somebody whom Chrissie would be expected to recognize. The realization was a relief. Chrissie had grown tired of big-time somebodies.

Chrissie's trip to the top of the charts had taken longer than those of some of her peers. She'd started in clubs that, during the day, smelled as if they could use a good scrubbing. She'd been spotted by Harold, a slick guy who was better connected than her then-current agent had been. Harold managed to put together a few small shows and she developed a regional reputation. She finally tired of Harold's insistence that her body was part of the deal, and eventually found Buddy, and Buddy managed to do it. Big shows. A contract with a big label. An international following.

Chrissie had been at the top of the charts now for almost five years, but she still wasn't comfortable. She was reconciled to her royalties dropping because everybody was copying her stuff, and she almost looked forward to returning to live shows. Even now, there was for her nothing quite like having twenty thousand people around you, screaming their love for you. And she returned the emotion. When she smiled and waved, both were acts of total sincerity.

But what was going to happen when she finally fell off the top? When Buddy could no longer pull rabbits out of his hat? When people no longer even wanted to steal her stuff?

Nobody just sinks slowly and disappears anymore. Now you fall with a loud, bone-shattering crash. One moment you're the Queen of the Universe, the next you're the worst sort of tramp. And when that happens, the media—and the self-appointed bloggers, most of whom she suspected couldn't tie their own shoes—fall upon you. They tear you to pieces with both beak and claw and then gnaw on your still-living organs.

She'd once had tons of friends—friends who were nobodies. But she'd lost track of most of them. Now she spent her time being seen with somebodies, very few of whom she considered friends.

Chrissie felt an overwhelming desire to speak with the lady next to her, whoever she was. "There's something almost surreal about lying in these deck chairs when we're headed toward the South Pole," she remarked.

The woman looked at her and smiled. "They've become part of the ritual, haven't they? Years ago, Fred and I made a number of passages to Europe on liners and everybody seemed to feel they had to spend hours in the deck chairs. Even in the winter."

On hearing his name, Fred raised his head, smiled at his wife, then at Chrissie and then settled back into his chair.

"We put on every scrap of clothing we owned," continued the woman, "wrapped up in one of those horse blankets they provided and lay there, a brilliant smile pasted on our faces, obviously having the time of our lives."

As the singer listened, she realized the woman was studying her, even evaluating her. Maybe she's trying to decide whether or not to introduce me to her grandson, she thought. She must have one. That might be a real adventure. A change of pace. To have a boyfriend who's not a somebody, who doesn't have a big, gold ring in his ear and an incessant need for attention. Like she once did.

Chrissie lay back in the chair and was soon dozing, lulled by the ship's stabilizer-gentled motion.

* * *

By noon, *Aurora* had crossed the forty-fifth parallel, the wind had increased, and the sky to the south had started to darken. Despite the increasing seas, the ship barely rolled, thanks to the new, cutting-edge stabilizer system installed during the overhaul. And the ship's third engineer, Jacob Rounding, could appreciate the stellar operation of the new system. He could but he didn't because he simply didn't care.

Jake Rounding was born with a chip on his shoulder, and for various confused reasons, it had grown much larger over the decades, until now he was thin, white-haired and stooped under the weight of a very heavy block.

Rounding had drifted into the merchant marine and over the years risen from engineman to his current position. His superiors considered him more than competent and his subordinates considered him okay to work for. But nobody had ever described him as warm or cheerful. There are many more aimless wanderers like him to be found at sea, even in today's world of high-tech navigation.

Third Engineer Rounding was examining an electrical distribution box on the deck just above the boat deck when he first spotted the little girl. She was talking excitedly to an elderly couple—waving her arms and dancing from foot to foot—and the couple appeared to be utterly enthralled. Rounding suddenly felt as if a spear had been thrust into his chest. The little girl looked just like Annie had when she was young.

Well over twenty years ago Jacob Rounding had found himself living with a woman whose essential cheerfulness had seemed, for a time, to be the perfect counterbalance for his own gloom. A child had resulted, a little girl whom they named Annie. And Annie had captured Jake's soul. In time, however, the adults' relationship was destroyed both by Jake's incessant gloom as well as by the constant absences demanded by his profession.

During the first few years after the split, until Annie's eighth or ninth birthday, Jake had managed to keep in touch with her and her mother. As the time passed, a portion of the mother's cheer had become barbed, at least with respect to Jake, but Annie's joy had remained pure, her enthusiasm undiminished. Then the mother had found what turned out to be the right man, for a change, and married. Every effort was made by both sides for Jake to spend time with his daughter, but it simply wasn't the same. He came to feel he was shut out, unwanted. He was driven back to sea—to voyage from here to there, purposelessly and forever.

And yet, his love for, his obsession with, his daughter had grown with every night he spent lying in his bunk, alone in the dark, emotionally lost and going nowhere.

He'd planned to see her again. Time and time again. But, somehow, something had always interfered, so, instead of knowing the real Annie, he dreamed of the little girl who once was, many, many years before.

Then it was too late. She was gone. According to the news she'd joined some half-assed demonstration about something nobody would remember two days later. The weather had been hot, as was the political situation; the cops were cranky, and somebody had given an order that may or may not have been misunderstood. Depending on whom you believed. The fact was that Annie was dead. The system had taken from Jake the one thing, the one person, about whom he cared in the slightest. And with respect to Annie, he had cared with every ounce of his soul.

Trembling, Third Engineer Jacob Rounding forced himself back to the junction box to try to determine why the electricity was off in two of the most expensive suites. He decided he was going to have to send one of the electricians.

* * *

"How's it going, Cagayan?" asked Jake Rounding an hour later as he tried to peer into the tiny space behind the backup generator.

"Good, Mr. Rounding," stuttered Marcello as he returned to wiping up the diesel oil that had spilled from a leak, now repaired, in the generator's supply line.

"Find any other problems?"

"No, sir."

"Good."

Cagayan listened as Rounding turned and continued on his way. He then reached into his right pants pocket and rubbed the cell phone. It'd become for him a fetish, the ultimate symbol of power. Of strength.

Although he had not appreciated it at the time, Marcello had experienced power from even his youngest years. His father, as stern and demanding as any man with too many children, no money and no wife might well be, had required his near total obedience. He had rewarded performance with food, and failure with starvation and beatings.

The boy recognized power and authority, but he had not begun to understand its totality until the day his father, his existing icon of power, had been forced to his knees. There, in the eyes of the soldier, he had seen the pleasure that comes from the exercise of power. And from that day on he had been compelled by the world around him to learn more and more about power, strength and weakness.

The runty, malnourished boy's path to the sea was a long, painful one. It started with unending hours of walking down muddy roads and across fields and through the hot, damp forest, sleeping where he could. Along the way he stole food from farmers just as impoverished as his father. Then one night, one of those impoverished farmers named Pablo caught him stealing a banana and beat him severely. Instead of driving him off into the forest, however, Pablo threw him in an old pigpen behind his house, which was itself little more than a shell of random, rotten planks, flattened tin cans and tree branches—and made a virtual slave of him.

For the next three months Marcello worked Pablo's tiny fields—his bare feet deep in the richly organic mud, his body lashed by the hot, summer sun—while Pablo starved and beat him. It didn't take him long to understand that Pablo beat him not because he had misbehaved but because beating Marcello gave him pleasure. When a man is weak himself, it is always a pleasure to inflict his will on somebody even weaker.

One night Pablo went a little too far—he beat Marcello so severely that the boy's brain stopped working correctly and his left knee, when it finally healed, would only bend with the greatest effort. Believing he'd killed Marcello, Pablo threw his remains over his shoulder and carried him a mile into the forest through a torrential downpour. There he dumped him in a muddy ditch, anticipating that the wild boars would dispose of the meat. And there Marcello would have died if not rescued by some missionaries.

The missionaries succeeded in saving his body but had no luck with his soul. Marcello feared them because he could not understand the power about which they preached. To him, power was a stick, a fist, a gun. As soon as he could, he escaped into the forest and finally out onto another mud road, now limping and stuttering from injuries that never healed.

Over the following years—years filled with hunger and degradation—he tried once or twice to rise up, to be strong himself, only to be brutally beaten down again. Because he stuttered and had to think before he spoke, and was very small and skinny, some called him *mono*—monkey. Others just called him *tonto.* Stupid.

When he did finally reach the sea, he was able to get a job crawling through and shoveling out the truly foul bilges of a hopelessly rotten, dirty inter-island passenger ship. It was the sort of ship that appears occasionally on the evening news having sunk, drowning four hundred people in the process.

Twenty years later, when Omar came across him in a back-street bar in Rio, Marcello had accepted the world's judgment of him and concluded he'd gotten as far as he ever would. He was an oiler, a bilge cleaner, an unlicensed engineman, and that was all he ever would be. His destiny was to do all the mindless shit work. He would always be the *mono*, the *tonto.* He hated everybody around him and he hated himself even more.

Omar had first spotted Marcello because the small, unemployed oiler was sitting alone at the bar, stuttering quietly to himself through clenched teeth. It took Omar less than one beer to determine that the Filipino might well be a surprisingly valuable asset. His rage was sincere, deep-seated and white-hot; he was aimless, despondent, and he was far smarter than even he seemed to believe. Shortly thereafter Omar discovered a bonus quality: Marcello had always made a point of listing himself as a Roman Catholic, even though his parents had been Moslems.

Over the next few weeks they met from time to time. They spoke of oppression and power, hatred and revenge.

They went up into the mountains to drink beer while Omar taught Marcello about rifles. They also spoke of money, but it soon became clear to Omar that power of a much purer, more personal sort was the key to Cagayan. Deep within his disciple burned a long-denied lust to have power of his own. The power to force his will upon, and control the destinies of, others. The power to decide who will live and who will die. The power of the rifle. And the bomb. All Omar had to do was awaken the passion and show Cagayan how to make it real.

As they spoke, long-abandoned furies moved to the forefront of Cagayan's consciousness. So powerful did they become that he seemed to pay little attention when Omar made some suggestions about how to save himself after he'd launched the mini-holocaust.

In due course, *Aurora*'s overhaul was completed and a significant number of new crew members had to be hired quickly. Omar arranged for Marcello to be one of them.

Cagayan rubbed the cell phone again. He could use it at any time. Type in a number and press call and the world would end. He was the strong one. He was the one with the power, and the temptation to exercise it was almost overwhelming. But now was not the time, not the place, for the terror to be the greatest.

He went back to wiping up the oil.

* * *

"Some of these PFDs are beginning to look a little tired," said the chief mate to the boatswain as he looked into a locker near the starboard lifeboats.

"Yes, sir, they are," replied MacNeal, the boatswain. "There's some paperwork headed your way already."

"Good. I must say you've kept right on top of the brightwork. The captain was very pleased at how good the ship looked during the Welcome Aboard Party."

"Thank you, Mr. Mate."

"What do you think of the new men you got in Rio?"

"For the most part they're good. No real bad apples, no real incompetents, although a few are pretty young and green. There're a couple I might like to trade in at the end of this trip, but I don't really have anything to complain about."

"Good," said Winters as the pair continued to walk forward. After they'd gone a few paces, the mate stopped and banged his hand on one of number three boat's gripes—the wire straps that held the boat securely in its cradle. "I see you replaced this one. By this time tomorrow we'll probably be back in the usual shit, so let's take the chance to fix and secure anything else that needs fixing and securing this afternoon."

"Yes, sir." By now both the wind and the ship's motion were beginning to develop a certain edge.

The mate and the boatswain continued their tour of inspection. It was a ritual with which both were very familiar. The mate would comment on things, knowing that in most cases the boatswain was already working on them, and the boatswain would agree, knowing the mate was condemned to return soon to his purgatory of paperwork. The two had now been working together for several years and had developed a comfortable relationship. Anyway, that was how matters have always been handled between mates and boatswains.

* * *

Despite the growing seas, *Aurora* continued to make good time as she sliced her way south toward the fiftieth parallel and the even worse weather that awaited her there.

As midnight approached, a number of the tables in the Masthead Lounge, the larger of the ship's two lounges, remained crowded. While pop music played quietly in the background and three servers made the rounds, the more social among the passengers were able to enjoy themselves or, in a few cases, drink themselves half to death. Thanks to their inability to see anything but their own reflections in the lounge's picture windows, most were blissfully unaware of what the dawn might bring.

At table seven, Senator Alvin Bergstrom held court. In attendance were Babs, Linda Williams and several media persons who were there to get a little "background," having promised to use no direct quotes. Wendell Gardner had also settled there a few minutes before, after managing to wear out his welcome at several other tables, even though the other people at those tables had essentially agreed with his stridently advocated positions.

"I'm still a little confused about the man versus nature argument," remarked one of the news reporters.

"That's no longer a legitimate question," replied Linda, before Wendell could butt in. "Our computer models prove that all significant change is controllable . . . by us."

"But some big names continue to argue the contrary . . ."

"Old has-beens!" shouted Wendell before Linda could cut him off again. "Those characters are stuck in the past . . . and many of them have accepted money over the years from the oil companies. Look, who's getting all the federal grants these days? It's not the old, corrupt fogies; it's the young people who know what's what."

Linda glowered at Wendell while the senator sat, smiling, and Babs squirmed. How much of this would the media end up indirectly attributing to the senator? she worried. Guilt by association was a big part of the game. And how would his backers react? God, she might yet have to find a new job. And all because the old bastard had the hots for a girl forty years younger than he was.

At table thirteen Tim Sanders was exchanging pleasantries with Sam and Alison Parker—a pair of lively senior citizens who looked half their real age—when Dana returned from checking on Katie.

"All well?" asked Alison.

"Oh yes," replied Dana with a smile. "She's sound asleep, and anyway what could happen to her? We know the neighbors on each side and across the hall—Katie introduced us to them. I've already spoken to the night steward and she knows how to ring for him."

"She'll be fine," Alison assured her.

"You know," started Sam, "this is the fourth expedition cruise we've been on—Asia, Africa and South America—but I have a feeling this one is a little different. We're still trying to keep an open mind about this global warming business, and when I attend some of these seminars I get the same feeling I got when we went on one of those long weekends the time-share developers give out. We ended up almost locked in a room for hours while three brokers triple-teamed us to buy a unit."

"We're here for the penguins," said Tim, "and anything else we get to see or do. I mean, Antarctica is Antarctica, whether or not it's shrinking, so when special discounts were offered to schoolteachers in my area, Dana and I decided it would be a great family adventure, especially since . . ."

Dana put her hand gently on his.

". . . especially since what with the cost of college these days it may be a long time before we can have another grand family adventure."

"Bravo!" enthused Sam.

"Are you tired, dear?" asked Tim.

"Not at all. I'm loving every minute."

Tim and Dana had sworn an oath to each other not to mention Dana's incurable cancer while on the cruise. And Tim could well understand that she might have little interest in sleep. She'd have plenty of time for that later.

* * *

Dave Ellison, *Aurora*'s one-man security department, made a final visit to his office before going to bed. He checked to ensure that the security cameras—which covered the public spaces and the passageways leading to the passengers' rooms—were all running. He checked his e-mail. Then he pulled a bottle of Scotch out of his desk drawer, poured himself a shot and leaned back in his chair.

This, he told himself, had to be the cushiest job he'd ever had. Even cushier than being a lieutenant in a small, suburban police department. All he had to do was deal with drunks and make sure nobody stole the passengers' jewels. As it turned out, few, if any, of the passengers ever brought their jewelry to Antarctica—and certainly not their fur coats. And, so far, there'd been no drunks, although he had a feeling the kid with the ring in his ear might develop into a problem before the voyage was over. He was an arrogant little prick and he was a drunk and who knew what else. Cutting him down a little might be a very satisfying exercise.

7

Rio de Janeiro

"I don't like this part of town, Marine. I didn't like it in daylight and I like it even less now." As he spoke, Ted reached into the pocket of his still-wrinkled jacket, just to ensure the Beretta hadn't somehow disappeared.

"I'm totally with you, amigo. I'd feel lonely here with a battalion of combat-ready grunts to keep me company."

Ted grunted noncommittally.

"For what it's worth," said Ray, "this place is undoubtedly as dangerous for locals as it is for us."

"Yeah. Good."

As they spoke, Ray was driving slowly down the once-paved street on which—according to Alex's map—the Bar Tiffany was located. For Ted, the street's transformation was stunning. What had been a row of drab, colorless storefronts during the day, had come to life. With the setting of the tropical sun, it had transformed itself into something that resembled a jungle garden, filled with extravagant, night-blooming orchids of all colors and shades.

"There it is," said Ray, pointing ahead at the "Bar

Tiffany" sign in yellow-and-blue neon. When they were abreast of it, he stopped so Ted could peer into the open door.

"Looks jammed," remarked the SEAL as the beat—a mix of Africa, Iberia and very possibly Los Angeles—blared out at them. Just when the two began to feel themselves moving ever so slightly to the music, the driver of the truck behind them leaned on his horn and the music was forgotten.

"God." Ted groaned as both jumped slightly to the reverberating concussion. "That was shock and awe!"

Half a kilometer down the street Ray thought he spotted a reasonably safe place to park. "Don't lock it," he said as they closed the doors.

"That comprehensive insurance you signed up for cover here?"

"That's Alex's problem."

"Hey, you pay us guard your car?"

The two Tridents looked at each other. "Maybe we should have walked," remarked Ted.

"We may end up doing that yet." As Ray said it, three kids—who couldn't have been more than eight—appeared from the shadows. Praying that this was one of the cases where cash really could buy loyalty, the marine gave each a dollar. "And each of you will get two more dollars if the car's still okay when we get back," he promised.

"Sure thing!" said the leader of the guardians.

"We're too early," grumbled Ray as they approached the Bar Tiffany. Where they stood in the street, the melody of odors—cooking oil, urine, an undertone of rot and a whiff of some flowering plant—was especially strong. "We've got fifteen minutes, at least."

"Let's kill it here," replied Ted, nodding at another garish watering hole a few yards from where they were standing. "We'll be less obvious sitting at a table than standing on the sidewalk, looking like we're trying to pick up some disease."

The bar in question, the Club Travessura, turned out to be a large, open room, decorated in red and green with colored lights flashing and loud music blaring. After edging their way in, they took a battered Formica-and-stainless table as close to the center of the action as they could. Ray ordered each of them a beer. The air-conditioning whirred and rattled, but it was still hot and crowded and smelled of beer, booze, humanity and tobacco smoke. Everybody seemed to know everybody and nobody seemed to pay the two Americans any attention. Not even the very worn girls, some of whom couldn't have been more than fourteen or fifteen.

The Club Travessura was not the sort of place American tourists—or even businessmen—could be expected to visit. It was clearly a local bar for the residents of a painfully impoverished *barrio.* Still, *cariocas* rich or poor tend to be a very cosmopolitan people, and none of those enjoying the action at the Travessura saw any reason to gawk. Ray tried to strike up a conversation with the three men at the next table. They were polite but clearly not overly impressed by the visitors, preferring to continue discussing something they seemed to consider of real importance. All the while the crowd flowed around them—swaying either to the music or to the tune of the alcohol in their blood—as if the two weren't there. Ray thought he recognized one or two men from the yard. Ted thought he spotted one or two who seemed to recognize them. They each finished half a beer, laughing self-consciously as they did. It was then time to move on.

The Bar Tiffany proved to be smaller, darker and dirtier, although just as crowded as the Club Travessura had been. It also had its limited supply of Christmas decorations set up and flashing.

The two insurance investigators took a table right alongside a small, scuffed dance floor and each ordered a beer. And again, nobody seemed to pay any attention to them. Except for one of the B-girls, Ray suddenly realized. She was looking right at him and laughing. Without taking her eyes off him, the girl tapped the girl next to her on the shoulder and whispered something. The other girl burst into laughter.

That, thought Ray, must be Dani. He studied her as she studied him. She was small. Scrawny, he decided. Far too scrawny. Unhealthy. He could well imagine the bitter existence she endured and could see from twenty feet that her teeth looked like hell. What her true age was he couldn't guess, though he felt certain she'd be dead by thirty unless the Agency did something for her. Not that he had the slightest idea what their deal with her was.

Dani was a wreck, yet Ray couldn't take his goddamn eyes off her. It was the smile—mischievous, challenging and commanding at the same time. Dani was in charge and she knew it. And so did just about everybody else in the bar.

A stream of sweat began to work its way down his spine.

Dani started to walk slowly toward them, her face alight with that impossible smile. Ted, having noticed the odd expression on Ray's face, had turned, only to be captivated by that same smile. As she approached, hands reached out from beside her to attract her attention, to hold her. She brushed them all away with a "your time will come" smile. Her progress was something just short of regal. It was as if a queen were passing through the mass of her subjects.

Men continued to follow her with their eyes as she worked her way toward the two obviously wealthy Americans, weaving through the swaying, sweating mob.

"Hi, guys," she said in heavily accented English. "I think I'd like to know you better. Buy me a drink. A champagne cocktail."

"With a cherry?" offered Ray, as he had been instructed by Mike. Before he could even wave, the waitress had appeared at the table with the drink.

Dani smiled. "What do you want to know about Coccoli

and Rojas?" she asked after the waitress had disappeared back in the direction of the bar.

"Whatever you do. What are they up to? Where did they go? Why?"

"I don't know that much. I never sat with either or did anything like that. They come in here from time to time and I've got big ears. Coccoli, he's a big talker. The other one always looks like his wife's hounding him." As she spoke, Dani's fingers tapped on the wood table as if she were playing a piano one-handed.

"You mean Rojas?"

"Yes."

"Does he have a wife?"

"Don't know. Never mentioned her, but a lot of guys who come here have wives and don't mention them."

"When's the last time you saw them?"

"At least a week ago. Maybe more."

"Know where they are?"

"No idea." As she spoke, Ted noticed that her smile, while still in place, had a certain hollowness to it. As if the sense of strange power the girl radiated was a masterful act that might collapse from exhaustion at any time. Not tonight, perhaps, but some night.

"You said Coccoli was a big talker. What did he talk about?"

"Recently? He seemed to think he was on to something big. You know, big bucks. I assume drugs. That's the big business around here."

"There anybody here they talked to who we can also talk to?"

Suddenly, Dani's smile completely disappeared, replaced by an expression as cold and disinterested as the heart of the most heartless terrorist. "That's all I can tell you except they both talked about somebody named Omar. Omar this and Omar that. I'm sure Omar had something to do with their big plan."

Without making any sudden moves, Dani stood and,

giving no warning whatsoever, somehow just disappeared into the crowd. It was as if she hadn't been there at all.

So intent were Ray and Ted on trying to figure out the girl's actions that they didn't notice, until it was too late, the two men who had appeared alongside the table. One, who moved around behind Ted, was short and wiry, much like the SEAL. The other, now standing beside Ray, was seriously overweight. "You are Mr. Anderson and Mr. Fuentes?" asked the fat one.

Ray looked at him without saying anything.

"Show me your identification. Your passport."

"Who are you?" asked Ray, suspecting he already knew the answer.

"Federal police," snapped the fat one, flashing an ID quickly in his face. "Now your passports!

"You are insurance investigators?" asked the fat one after perusing the little blue books.

"Yes."

"You have been asking questions all over the shipyard. Now we wish to ask you some questions. Come with us."

Ted tensed, certain he could overpower the guy behind him but unsure whether or not the two were really cops. The boss had made it very clear he didn't want any incidents. Ted decided to follow Ray's lead. He was, after all, senior.

The two Americans glanced at each other. "These aren't cops," the glances said simultaneously. "Or if they are, they're bent."

Before either could act, both their heads erupted into sharp, overpowering pain. The sort of pain that makes you quiver from head to foot and want to vomit. Stunned by their assailants' blackjacks, neither reacted when the Berettas were stripped from their pockets.

"Get up! We're leaving."

Clutching his spinning, screaming head and on the verge of screaming himself, Ray just looked up at him stupidly.

"Up!" shouted the fat one again, dragging Ray to his feet.

None of the Bar Tiffany's other customers seemed to show the slightest shock at, or even interest in, the proceedings.

The blackjacks had been applied with a high degree of finesse. The blows had been calculated to stun rather than totally incapacitate, and they had done just that. Even before they reached the door, the two Tridents had regained the ability to move under their own power and their heads had cleared somewhat, although the pain continued to throb nauseatingly.

With the fat one walking beside Ray and the other thug behind them, they started down the brightly lit street. The bars and the sidewalks were still jammed with pulsating masses of humanity, desperate to grab a little bit of life and joy from the physical bleakness that dominated their daily existence.

"In!" said the fat one, stopping alongside a van.

While the fat one issued the orders, the smaller one reached to open the door, thereby making the last stupid mistake of his life. Driven by instinct and a totally unprofessional fury, Ted was all over him—knocking his legs out from under him, grabbing and breaking his arm and slamming his face into the side of the van. The fat man, who had overestimated the lasting power of their blackjack work, was stunned himself by the speed of Ted's attack on his companion and was no match for Ray. It took the marine officer another fifteen seconds to force his opponent onto his knees with his arm half torn off and the gun now in Ray's hand.

"Not bad for an officer," hissed Ted, slightly winded.

"Oh shit!" growled Ray, also slightly winded, as he noticed the three men standing in a shadow at a corner about fifty feet away and felt the thunderous crashing of their automatic weapons pound against his mangled head as they opened fire. "God damn it, Ted, under the van!" he shouted. "We've walked into the middle of a turf war."

While the two Tridents wormed their way under the van, wishing they could take their pounding heads off and throw them away, the automatic weapons tore the bodies of their first two assailants to shreds. They then processed the shreds into canned dog food.

* * *

Omar sat in a darkened car two blocks from the Bar Tiffany. He was little more than a shadow as he watched the gang he'd hired to kill the Americans massacred by another gang.

He'd made a mistake. If al Hussein had given him more time to arrange it, he would have been able to check out the gang's current position more carefully. But more important than the mistake was his growing conviction that the operation itself was endangered. The Americans were not part of the plan and neither was this fiasco. Al Hussein was a very precise person—too precise. He'd be angered by tonight's events, maybe even thrown off balance. He might well make a mistake himself, and he'd blame it all on Omar.

Even if al Hussein represented no serious threat, it was still time to move on. Omar was a very sensitive man and knew when an operation had veered out of control and might well blow up in his face. There was nothing more for him to do but leave. Tonight. To drive to the airport and get on one of the first flights out. Despite computers, despite identity chips, despite everything, the world was still a big place and Omar knew how to disappear into it. He'd done it before. And at the right time he'd reappear, although certainly not as Omar.

* * *

"Shit," grunted Anderson just as his arm and head disappeared under the van.

"What?" Fuentes had to shout to be heard above the firing of the automatic weapons and the thunking of their heavy rounds into the van's body.

"The pricks got me in the arm."

"Keep moving. They're going to hit the gas tank any second now. Then across the street and down that alley."

"If this is a gang hit, why do they want us too?"

"Because we're here."

"Roger."

Slithering backward as fast as they could, the two dragged themselves out from under the van. Crouching, they ran like hell across the now totally deserted street. By keeping the van between themselves and their assailants, they managed to make it almost to the alley before their retreat was appreciated by the gunmen.

"Wish to damn I'd grabbed that scumbag's gun," remarked Ted when the two stopped about fifty yards up the alley.

"I've got the fat guy's," Ray reassured him. "How bad's your arm?"

"Nothing's broken."

"You going to be able to kill one of these bastards?"

"It'll be a mixture of pleasure and pain."

"Good. You make yourself disappear behind that crap piled along that wall. I'll hide behind that next pile of garbage. As soon as I can get a good shot, I'll take out one of them. That should make the remaining two concentrate on me, allowing you to slip behind them as they pass and take out another. With luck I can then get the third before he blows you away."

"What if they don't follow us in? What if they just wait for us?"

"Don't think they will. These guys are simple thugs. All of them. They'll either come after us or leave before the cops arrive."

"Can they get in behind you?"

"Looks like a dead end to me."

Without uttering another word, Ted disappeared into the mound of boxes, garbage cans and whatever else was there. Ray sprinted to the next pile and slipped behind it.

They waited in the tropical night, sweating and listening to the rats rooting around them. The air stank of garbage and humanity. Multicolored lights flashed dimly down the alley. Tense and alert, Ray checked over the gun. Even in the dim light he knew it was a cheap one. Probably not very accurate. But, fortunately, it had eight unused rounds.

Then, although Ted couldn't see it, the light from the street dimmed and the shadows of three men became faintly visible to Ray. He tensed even more, a cascade of sweat now pouring down his neck. Long shot. Cheap gun. How long would it take them to respond and how accurate would their response be? If they got him, or if he failed to get at least one of them, he and Ted were dead.

The thugs advanced slowly, looking carefully around and behind anything stacked along the walls. Ray held the pistol in both hands and steadied it on the top of a garbage can filled with something that generated a sharp, nauseating stench. The thugs reached the pile in which Ted was mixed, and one angled over to look at it. Ray squeezed off four rapid shots and one thug collapsed onto the slick, grimy pavement. Cursing, the other two split, one moving to take cover on the left and the other moving unwittingly to take cover alongside Ted.

Despite his injured arm, it was the work of a second or two for the SEAL to break the thug's neck as his victim virtually dove into what he'd hoped would be safety. Without saying a word Ted then grabbed the dead thug's weapon and opened fire on the remaining assailant, dashing as he did across the space between the two piles.

The third gunman didn't stand a chance.

"Okay, ditch that gun," hissed Ray, staring at the small but impossible-to-conceal machine gun, "and let's get the hell out of here. You have the map?"

Ted reached into his left pocket and pulled it out.

"To the car?"

"Yes, but by side streets."

Ted studied the map in the barely adequate light. "Down

this alley then right for . . . three blocks then left and we should come out opposite it."

"Shit! I didn't think the alley had another end."

"One of us is damn lucky."

"You lead."

The pair sprinted down the alley and turned right onto a virtually unlit street, bordered on either side by low, dark concrete block buildings—each hiding behind its own barbed wire–capped fence. Partway down the first block they shrank back into the shadows and crouched, listening for pursuit.

"If somebody is chasing us," whispered Ray, "they know the neighborhood better than we do. They may be ahead of us."

"Roger."

Making as little noise as they could and keeping in the shadows, they worked their way tensely down the street. At one point, Ray backed up against a fence, only to jump halfway across the street when a dog snarled and tried to bite him through the mesh. Frustrated, the dog—which sounded very big—started barking furiously. It was a tune taken up by a number of other four-legged watchmen along the way. Moving a little faster now, the pair reached the third corner, turned right and reentered the street they'd originally left.

"Damn it." Ted groaned at the sight that greeted them. The rental car was right where they'd expected it. But it had been totally stripped. No tires. No wheels. No doors. And undoubtedly very little left inside.

"Somebody must have offered the little bastards more than two bucks each for it," grumbled Ted.

"We're going to find a cab."

"What about this pile of scrap?"

"That's why we've got the Good Witch on our team. She'll just have to wave her magic wand and get us out of town before they find it and trace it to us."

"What if the cabbie doesn't want blood in his car?"

"In this part of town I think they have to put up with that sort of thing. Anyway, I've still got this sidearm."

"The way things are around here he's undoubtedly got one too."

"Then we'll just have to try money. That works sometimes."

"I don't think we'll find one here," observed Ted after scanning the street.

Then they heard the first siren. "We don't want to be here at all," said Ray. "There's a main street about eight blocks to the east as I remember. Let's get the hell out of here and see what we can find there."

"Roger."

"And remember, at the moment, the police are *not* our friends."

"Roger."

* * *

It was barely six in the morning when Mamoud al Hussein's home phone rang. The engineer was already up, preparing for the day ahead.

"I apologize for calling so early, Mamoud," said Roberto Palmeira, "but our two 'insurance investigators' seem to have been involved in a shoot-out a few hours ago between what the federal police believe are two rival drug groups."

"Are they injured?"

"They're back at their hotel and Anglo-Swiss says they're to fly out on a chartered jet in a few hours."

"What more is known?" asked Mamoud, struggling to avoid showing—even to himself—his irritation that Omar's efforts had been so messily unsuccessful. While he still had total confidence in the project, this sort of thing could not be permitted to happen again.

"There was some sort of shoot-out between two groups of drug dealers. Several witnesses mentioned that two foreigners were involved somehow. Knowing how the police feel about these drug wars, I doubt they will make much of an effort to investigate unless we pressure them to."

That's something, thought al Hussein. At least everybody believes it was drug-centered.

"Is it possible they are U.S. DEA agents?"

"That seems very likely to me, but I doubt anybody would ever tell us if we asked."

"Yes, I doubt so too. Of perhaps greatest importance, has Anglo-Swiss indicated they're reviewing or reconsidering our desirability as an insured?"

"They've indicated nothing yet."

"Do you think these two discovered anything that might help us cure our drug problem? As I have said on several occasions, before Tecmar can make it to the next level, we will have to get drugs under control."

"It's possible, but they told me nothing. It's too bad you couldn't meet them."

"Yes, it is. I shouldn't have taken the afternoon off. I might have learned more."

"Mamoud! You can't blame yourself for this."

"It appears there's nothing we can do at the moment, so I would like to move on to all the magical things we told those people in Houston we can do for their LNG carriers. I will see you at the office at nine."

"At nine."

8

The South Atlantic / Drake Passage

Wearing navy blue trousers and a matching sweater, Arthur Covington stood on the port wing of *Aurora*'s bridge and observed the first glimmer of day, a narrow yellow strip that lay briefly on the horizon, only to be swallowed up almost immediately by the low, solid clouds. Beyond the horizon, about a hundred miles to the east, lay the dark, unseen mass of the Falkland Islands—the Malvinas if you favor the Argentine side of the long-standing dispute with Britain. The wind, predictably, was blowing a half gale, and the South Atlantic was responding by heaving itself into seething, hostile masses the size of a two-story building.

The trip so far had been almost a vacation for Covington, but now they were returning to the heartlessly deceptive waters for which he and the rest of the crew were paid extra. Once *Aurora* edged around Cape Horn and started across the Drake Passage, the temperature would continue to drop rapidly. At the same time they would be exposed to the full fury of the Westerlies, monstrous winds that blow continuously, nonstop, round and round the world, with no land to civilize them in the slightest. These were the waters—with their screaming winds and bitterly cold temperatures—that had destroyed countless adventurers and killed a high percentage of the ships that were brave, or foolish, enough to dare them.

Covington was tempted to turn into Ushuaia and hide there for a day or two, but as always, the schedule was tight and the weather people seemed to feel the low-pressure pulse that was working its way from the Pacific to the Atlantic would have blown past by the time they reached the South Shetland Islands, just off the Antarctic Peninsula. The awful truth was that the damn things seemed to come and go with no warning, not even in the satellite age. He grabbed his night glasses and surveyed the angry gray waters. Every summer vast quantities of ice broke loose and drifted north. This year, more ice had been reported farther north than usual. Some was in the form of icebergs, which could be detected by radar. Some was flat pack ice, which radar could easily miss but which could still slice a ship open.

Concluding the time had come to add a coat to his outfit, Covington walked into the pilothouse. The mate of the watch was pacing slowly back and forth, looking out the windows. The helmsman and lee helm were seated behind their long console, keeping their eyes on the hundreds of gauges and lights. The joystick twitched occasionally, obedient to the commands of the automatic pilot. Resisting the temptation to remind the mate to keep a lookout for ice, the captain retired to his sea cabin to rest up for the night.

* * *

"So much for those stabilizer things," remarked Brad to Chrissie Clark as they entered the half-empty dining room. As he spoke, Brad self-consciously fingered the big gold ring in his ear. "Just one more example of this half-assed boat not quite cutting it."

"I guess there's only so much they can do," replied Chrissie as the ship rolled slowly to port, forcing her to grab a table to steady herself. "You should have taken those pills."

"I did."

Then you shouldn't have had so many chocolate martinis, she thought.

In fact, the singer was barely listening to her current, very public boyfriend—an actor who hadn't quite made it yet, despite his PR people's best efforts. Rather, she was studying the little girl sitting at a table off to one side with her parents. The faces she was making as she explained something to them were a riot. She'd seen several kids aboard the ship, but this one had to be the funniest.

"Isn't that guy over there, waving at us, a senator or something?" demanded Brad, breaking in on Chrissie's thoughts.

"He's a congressman, I think. The senator's the old guy." Chrissie had never heard of this particular congressman before boarding *Aurora* and still didn't know to which party he belonged.

"He's waving us over. Should we? It could be a good photo op."

"I suppose so," said Chrissie. "He may need us more than we need him, though. We're a way to prove he's cool and with-it."

"Ms. Clark, I'm Peter Evans," said the congressman, holding his hand out as the singer and her friend approached his otherwise unoccupied table. "And this is my wife, Penny." From the look of it, the politician and his wife were just finishing up a breakfast of bran cereal and fruit.

Penny's got a few years on the congressman, thought the singer as she took his hand. On top of that she's kind of frumpy. A little too much makeup and something's not right about her hair. It's hard to imagine her climbing Mt. Everest, unlike some of the chicks aboard. "Chrissie, please, Congressman, and this is Brad."

"Brad," said Evans, "and let's immediately move on to first names. We're all friends here. Coffee?"

"Sure," said Brad, who was already reaching for one of the cups at an unoccupied setting.

"No, thank you," said Chrissie.

"So what do you think of this voyage so far?" continued Evans as Chrissie and Brad took their seats. "The ship seems very well equipped, although I understand that this nice weather may not last."

"I'm enjoying it," replied Chrissie.

"Have you attended any of the seminars?"

"No, not yet. But we're looking forward to seeing the real thing in a day or two."

"I've attended four," announced Penny Evans, "and they were utterly fascinating." As she spoke, the door to the galley must have swung open to let a waiter through, because the smell of something greasy being prepared drifted across the room. Brad curled his lip but said nothing.

"Penny," said Chrissie, looking directly at the congressman's wife while also looking over her shoulder at Katie Sanders, "everybody knows, or thinks they know, that I live a glamorous life, but to be honest your life seems to me so much more glamorous. I mean you're there, in Washington, where all the important things happen and you know the people who make them happen. All I do is amuse people when they have nothing better to do than listen to me."

"I do love every minute of it, Chrissie," said Penny with practiced brightness, "but you know as well as I do that it's not all fun and games. Being in the public eye so much can be a little stressful. It's worth it, though, to be there with Pete while he serves the people. But you underestimate your own influence. Half the country hangs on your every word. In the end, I'm just Mrs. Evans, while you're the one and only Chrissie Clark."

While Chrissie and Penny chatted, nibbling on the remains of a bowl of fruit as they did, Brad looked bored and uncomfortable and Congressman Evans listened with a polite smile fixed on his face. Suddenly Evans started waving toward the door, in a discreet manner. A media team was just entering the dining room, their eyes roving in search of action. The tall blond reporter spotted the politician immediately and, dragging the video guy with her, headed toward the table.

As the media advanced, Wendell Gardner appeared from nowhere. "Good morning, Pete," he said as he sat down. "Morning, Penny. Did you catch Rod Johnson's seminar yesterday afternoon? Now that was real science! None of that paid commercial propaganda that some people continue to put out."

Before anybody could reply, Jessica, the blond reporter, was there.

"Congressman, Chrissie Clark. What a catch! Do you mind if I get your impressions of the trip so far?"

As the ship rolled, Chrissie sat there, saying all the right things, answering every question the way Jessica made clear she wanted them answered. All the while she was thinking about Penny Evans and Katie Sanders. Penny was very good at sounding happy, but there was a faint, dark aura about her, as if something was missing. She had obviously chosen her role in life, but was it the right one?

Just then, Brad decided to open his mouth—which was generally a mistake. He turned toward the video camera and announced something about mounting a personal expedition to the Amazon to show his support for both the environment and the peoples who lifestyles were being endangered. He added that he planned to start organizing, and fund-raising, as soon as they got back from this expedition, and would Congressman Evans care to be a sponsor? As he spoke, he fingered the earring and smiled, clearly pleased with himself.

With Jessica there, Evans had no choice but to promise to consider it. He then turned the conversation back onto topics which revolved around him, especially his almost single-handed efforts to get a bill passed to regulate the fuel consumption of jetliners.

Chrissie half listened to Evans while she decided she'd had it with Brad. Not only was he making up roles for himself—everybody in the business did that—but he was starting to believe them. He was, without doubt, sexy—the tabloid editors loved to put him on their front pages with headlines suggesting he was, or wasn't, the father of somebody's baby—but he was also a moron. And that ring was driving her nuts. She had no objection to rings, although the only ones she wore were on her fingers, but Brad's was absurd. It was much too big, and then there was the stupid line he kept repeating over and over about it. That it was from a tribe of Amazonian Indians who had died out four hundred years ago. The closest Brad had been to Amazonia was when they flew over a corner of it a few days before. As for the ring itself, she'd been with him when he'd bought it at a tag sale on Martha's Vineyard the preceding summer.

Brad was history! As she made the decision, the cynical side of her moved to the fore. From what everybody told her, romantic breakups made even better copy than did budding romances. And the media, by the dozens, were right here, on *Aurora*. How convenient! But should she do it during the voyage or wait until their return to somewhere? And should it be noisy and messy from the start or should it start as little more than whispered rumors and grow from there? It might all be too confusing now, aboard the ship. She might find herself fighting with the congressman—not to mention that goat of a senator or even the snow, ice and penguins—for attention. She'd have to think about it for a day or two, although she did feel certain that there was an empty stateroom available somewhere in the ship.

* * *

"Captain Covington, this has been fascinating," said Tim Sanders just as the ship lurched to port. "We've all enjoyed it more than I can tell you."

"Yes, Captain," said Katie while she held on and stared at the GPS plot showing the ship's track across the Southern Ocean. "Dad had a little trouble with the idea you don't have a big wooden wheel, but I convinced him the joystick is just as good. I have one on my computer in my room and it works just great for video games."

"I'm very glad you all enjoyed it," said Covington as he guided the three of them across the pilothouse to the door leading down to the public areas. "Tell me, Katie, from what you now know, would you consider being a sailor, like Mr. Winters and me?"

"I think that would be great fun. How do we start?"

"You start by finishing school," replied Covington, caught flat-footed by his own queston.

"You do think the weather's going to improve, don't you?" asked Dana. "We're all looking forward to going ashore tomorrow."

"This particular mess is blowing past. We're well into the Drake Passage and the weather's gotten no worse—which means that it's getting better."

As Covington spoke, he mentally crossed his fingers. Everything he'd said was true, but the reality remained that they were scheduled to land on the Antarctic Peninsula's western side, the side most exposed to the monster winds.

"What about the snow?" asked Katie, never onc to lct the obvious go unexplained.

Covington glanced out the pilothouse windows. Despite the spinning window wipers, it was impossible to see anything through the dense, gray-white air. "That will clear up before midnight."

"That little girl is certainly getting her money's worth," remarked the chief mate after the captain's guests had disappeared.

"You think I'm overdoing it? Perhaps I am. I admit she's a borderline smart-ass, but I find her amusing. She reminds me of one of my two when she was that age. She's an intense finance person now, but back then she was a Katie—all over the place. Are we ready for the Crossing the Line Ceremony?"

"Yes, sir. The boatswain's going to be King Neptune and some of the saner deckhands will be his court of Blue Noses."

"Who will Davy Jones look like?"

"He'll look like me, Captain."

"Very well. The boatswain has pretty good judgment."

"So far, so good, Captain. Except for the weather at the moment."

"You mean nobody's blown us up yet or taken hostages? Yes, and no drunks have picked fights or fallen overboard either."

"Dave Ellison mentioned to me that he's a little worried about that boyfriend of your favorite singer—he drinks too much and has more of a thing about authority than most of us do—and I'm a little worried about Gardner, one of the tour guides the sponsor sent us. He tends to be a little aggressive at times. Seems to have already pissed off some of the passengers."

"We'll keep an eye on the three of them." Covington knew that Winters didn't like Ellison any better than he did. There was something about him. Maybe it was his attitude. Maybe it was nothing. At any rate, they were stuck with him. The owners had sent him.

* * *

"Penny," said Pete Evans quietly and carefully, "you certainly don't have to go ashore tomorrow—or whenever these people finally get us there—if you don't feel comfortable doing it."

Penny finished mixing her drink at the little bar in their suite and turned to him, keeping a solid grip on the bar as she did. "But I *want* to go ashore, Peter. That's why I came. You came for the photo ops—to be seen with tuned-in people doing tuned-in things. I came for some adventure, a vacation from the wasteland that's the life of a congressman's wife. And you're the one who doesn't like boats."

"What about your attacks?"

"Every now and then I feel a little dizzy and maybe lose my balance. It's nothing. This ship has more people ready to help me than that singer, Chrissie, has men ready to die for her.

"Peter, whatever you're here for, I'm here to see the penguins and the seals and the whales and whatever else there is to see. And don't worry, I won't embarrass you. That's really what you're worried about, isn't it? That I'll make a fool of myself and of you in front of the witless TV people."

Peter Evans took a long sip of his Scotch. "Fine! We'll go ashore together."

"Maybe I shouldn't have come along. You could have brought Jackie along, just like Senator Bergstrom brings his PA on trips like this in place of his wife. She's young and athletic. She'd fit right in."

Peter Evans listened to his wife's words and looked at her face and knew what he had suspected for some time—Penny *did* know about him and Jackie.

* * *

What's that son of a bitch doing here? thought Marcello Cagayan as he spotted Hensen using a wrench to open the access hatch to a rarely entered void near one of the ship's fuel tanks. Cagayan was on watch; he belonged there as he made his rounds of the engineering spaces. Hensen was off watch. He wasn't supposed to be in this area until four in the morning. And he wasn't supposed to be screwing around in that void. There was no reason to be opening it.

The briefest flicker of panic passed through him. The son of a bitch was screwing around only a few feet from where two charges—each a combination of C4 and thermite—had been placed in the fuel tank, positioned so that when they detonated flaming diesel fuel would pour into the bilges.

Cagayan stepped back behind a mass of vertical pipes and watched as Hensen opened the hatch and pulled out a bag. Any sound the Filipino's movements might make, any sound of air moving into and out of his lungs, was lost in the ship's almost primal beat—the rumble of the engines and the periodic groans of the hull as it pounded and twisted its way through the living waters. A tremendous tension—a clash of fear and anticipation—had been growing within him the past few hours, causing his muscles to tense. Now it came to a head.

It was drugs . . . Of course! realized Cagayan. The bag was filled with little bags. Hensen was sitting cross-legged on the deck and counting little bags. Hensen was dealing right aboard the ship. The crew? The passengers?

He knew Hensen. Everybody knew Hensen and nobody liked him. It was a miracle he hadn't already been pushed overboard. He had no trouble believing the pig was the ship's dealer.

The ship was rolling, groaning quietly, and the air in the space tasted dead.

Cagayan calmed himself. Hensen couldn't possibly stumble on the charges. They were inside the tank. He was no threat. But he was a prick, one who had gone out of his way to make life miserable for Cagayan. He reached into his pocket and felt the cell phone. As he held the phone, he felt a wave of confidence, of power, run up his arm and into his heart. There was no reason he *had* to kill Hensen, just as there had been no reason the soldier *had* to kill his father. But he *would* kill Hensen, because he was now certain he *could* kill him.

Cagayan reached down to his tool belt and pulled out a short screwdriver. A Phillips head. He stepped out quietly from behind the pipes and in four quiet steps was behind the dealer.

Hensen turned with a look first of surprise and then of irritation. "Oh shit! It's the little monkey," he said with a sneer as he turned back to sorting through the bag. "Get lost!"

A jolt of white-hot anger shot through Cagayan, fusing with his new sense of power and strengthening it. "Fuck you, prick," he stuttered as he threw one leg over the seated drug dealer. Hensen outweighed his attacker almost two to one, and much of the difference was muscle. He tried to stand, to throw Cagayan to one side, but was unable to unwind his legs and move quickly enough. Cagayan used one hand to shove Hensen's head against his leg while he drove the screwdriver into the dealer's temple. Hensen's head jerked back, his eyes full of shock. His mouth opened but nothing came out. Without waiting to determine the result of his first move, Cagayan yanked out the screwdriver and jammed it back into Hensen's ear, only to withdraw it yet again and drive it once more into the temple.

Without even checking to see if his victim was really dead or just unconscious, Cagayan dragged Hensen by his head—using one hand to contain the blood trickling out of the wounds—toward the hatch to the void. He stuffed the body and its collection of magical pills and powders back into its rust-coated crypt. Continuing to move quickly, he used the rag he always carried when on watch to wipe off the screwdriver and clean up what little blood remained on the deck, and then threw it into the void. It was but the work of seconds to secure the hatch again.

Panting slightly, his teeth bared, Marcello Cagayan looked around.

Victory, a newfound sense of power, surged through him, making him tingle all over, making him want to roar. It was an experience he'd never had before. He then looked at his clothes. Blood. Too much blood. His shirt was covered with Hensen's blood. He couldn't just march off to his quarters and change his clothes. He was on watch.

A terrible thought burst through his joy. Was it possible he'd just fucked up? Killing Hensen wasn't part of Omar's plan. The engineman represented no real threat, and now, by killing him, he'd put himself in a dangerous position. An impossible position, covered with blood.

The possibility both scared and embarrassed him. Maybe he *was* a *tonto*. Maybe there was no good reason to kill Hensen. He reached again for the cell phone and started to open it. No, now was not yet the time. His work was barely begun.

And there was a solution. He walked aft about twenty feet, stooped over and opened a round scuttle in the deck. Holding his flashlight in one hand, he climbed down the ladder into the bilges and, careful to keep his shoes out of the inch or two of water, flashed the light around him.

There they were! Two shoulder-high steel beams that had been crudely cut during the overhaul. Considering their location, nobody had bothered to smooth their cutting torch–jagged edges. Gritting his teeth, but without hesitation, he dragged his left arm over the sharp, jagged surface. The pain was sharp, but nothing in comparison with what he had suffered on countless occasions over the years. Blood flowed out all along his forearm. After wiping some on the beam and more on his clothes, Cagayan struggled up the ladder and aft to Main Control, where he reported to the engineer of the watch.

"What happened to you?" the officer demanded the moment he caught sight of the engineman.

"I was checking the bilges, sir, just aft of frame twenty-three, and slipped and fell on the end of one of those beams that were cut off during the overhaul." As he spoke, he held up his gouged arm.

"Did you secure that scuttle after you?"

"Yes, sir."

"Very well. You go to sick bay and have that arm fixed. Then come back here so I can fill out a complete report. The company's very strict about injury reports."

"Yes, sir."

9

En Route to Ushuaia

Mike Chambers took a long sip of now-cold coffee and looked at the clock on his desk. 0300. Damn! Despite the temperate weather outside, the office felt cold and dungeonlike, as offices often do very early in the morning, when the rest of the world is home in their own beds.

A year before, with his rotation to shore duty approaching, he'd promised Jill he'd be home at a reasonable time for dinner, and maybe a movie every now and then, for the next couple years. After almost twenty years of putting up with his extended absences when his various ships had been deployed, not to mention the equally irritating shorter absences when they'd been operating locally, she deserved better. And, frankly, he wanted to be with her. He'd also promised himself he'd be able to spend more time, much more time, with Kenny, his fifteen-year-old son. He didn't kid himself that now was the time Kenny needed him the most. He'd probably needed him more a couple years ago, but there was still time for him to help the boy break some of the undesirable attitudes he'd already developed. At least he hoped so.

That was all then. Now he was sitting in his office in the middle of the night, drinking cold coffee and reasonably certain that he was going to send himself and his group off on a nine- or ten-thousand-mile trip before he even got home again.

The phone finally rang.

"Boss, this is Ray."

"What's up?" asked Mike, letting out a small sigh of relief. He hadn't hesitated to send the pair to Rio, but he hadn't been really comfortable with it. Neither was trained to troll for intelligence in foreign cities, and although Ray could probably make himself comfortable there, Ted—being 100 percent mainland American—might not.

"We made contact with Dani, the girl, and learned a thing or two, although nothing earth-shattering."

"Shoot."

"She's seen and eavesdropped on the pair. It seems that Coccoli's an arrogant little stud—just like the yard workers told us—and Rojas is more timid. She hasn't seen either in a week or two, but before that both were talking as if they were in on some big deal that was going to make them rich. She assumed it was drugs." As the marine spoke, Mike sensed something wrong. It was as if Ray was having to make an effort to speak.

"You okay, Ray?"

"Yes, sir. Winded and a little bruised but okay."

When Ray paused, Mike happened to glance up to find Alex, who had been napping on one of the cots they maintained for long nights, standing at his door. He smiled and waved her to a chair and turned on the phone's speaker.

"Possibly the most interesting tidbit was that both referred to someone named Omar in connection with this big deal of theirs."

"Omar?"

"That's it. Omar. Dani never saw him and never heard of him."

"Ray, god damn it, there's something you're not telling me."

"We had a problem, Captain."

"What?"

"While we were talking to Dani, a couple guys came in. Said they were federal police and seemed to have the IDs to prove it, although now it's obvious they weren't. Before we could do anything, they slugged us with blackjacks, took our weapons and marched us out to a van. Then another crew opened fire on them and us with machine guns. Thanks to Ted we managed to slip away."

"Casualties?"

"Ted's got a hole in his arm and we both have unbelievable headaches. I've cleaned Ted's arm and treated it with antibiotics from the medkit."

"What about your heads?"

"We'll be okay, someday. We've looked into each other's eyes and they seem normal. And no double vision."

"How romantic!

"You are two lucky sons of bitches," continued Mike after a pause. "You sure it wasn't a setup?"

"I think it was, sir. By the druggies. I've now learned not to go around asking questions that even hint at drugs in Rio—or in shipyards."

"Listen up, Captain," said Mike to the marine officer. "What you've come up with is just enough to confirm my desire to do some cruising in *Aurora Australis*. The taxpayers can afford it."

"It might be worth it to go back and talk to some of the other bar patrons who knew Coccoli and Rojas. Maybe they can tell us something about this Omar."

"Forget about it. It sounds to me like nobody's going to be willing to talk to either of you two at this point. They'll probably run like hell the minute they see you. We'll see if Alex's friends can follow through and come up with anything."

"Aye, sir."

"Are you sure Ted doesn't need a doctor now?"

"He's a SEAL, sir."

Mike glanced at Alex and rolled his eyes.

"Assume we're going to extract you in the next twelve hours or less. In the meantime, stay in your room. Are you still armed?"

"One Saturday night special Ted snatched from one of the thugs."

"Don't even go out for food until further notice. I'm going to clear this with Alan and I'll be back to you in a few minutes. Don't turn your phone off."

"Aye, aye, sir." He hung up.

"They're okay, then?" asked Alex, a worried look on her face.

"At the moment. Please listen carefully to what I tell Alan. Most of it will probably be the truth."

Mike then dialed Alan Parker's secure home number.

"Parker."

"Mike Chambers. Are you awake, Alan?"

"Yes." He didn't really sound it, but that didn't matter to Mike.

"Ray and Ted have picked up a little extra intel in Rio on those two shipfitters. Our guys were also attacked. Set up by somebody. I plan to extract them ASAP. I also plan to take the team to *Aurora*."

"All of it?"

"Everybody but Vincent, the new guy. I have to leave somebody to mind the shop."

"And what will you do?"

"Search the ship. Try to spot something."

"I thought you said there weren't going to be any incidents."

"Things happen."

"How're you going to get to the ship?"

"Extract Ray and Ted then fly to Ushuaia and helo out to her."

"That's a long flight for a helo."

"It's doable."

"And the weather?"

"Miserable at the moment but wait an hour."

"You going to use a cover or just let it all hang out?"

"We're performing a random security checkup on the ship at the owner's request. It's a new service . . ."

"I never heard of it."

"Nobody else has either. Yet."

"It does make sense. Proactive. May even keep Homeland Security off our backs. Just as long as we don't ruffle the passengers' feathers."

"Homeland Security?"

"They're beginning to define the American homeland as the entire world. Okay. Dress warm, buddy."

Mike hung up and looked at Alex. "You get all that?"

"A jet to Ushuaia, via Rio. A helo to Antarctica and earmuffs for all. I suppose you want me to explain our new service to the ship's owners."

"You're always more convincing than I am."

"You care whose jet?"

"Try your friends."

"And the helo?"

"Try the civilian contractors first. I don't want to spend time explaining what we're doing to some Argentine admiral."

"Weapons?"

"Glocks, automatic rifles and Tasers for everybody . . . a riot gun and a dozen flash-bangs."

"I'm on it, Boss."

An hour later Mike was back on the phone to Rio: "We're scheduled to fly out of Tampa at zero four hundred in a CIA jet which should reach Jobim about eleven hundred. You wait at the hotel until it's time to check out and take a cab. When you get to the airport, go to the general aviation section, to the Aviaos Sul facility."

"Were both ready, Captain."

"How's Ted's arm?"

"Still bleeding. Minimally."

"Will he be any good to us?"

"He just killed a man armed with an automatic weapon, sir."

"I'll round up a corpsman and bring him or her along. Alex is arranging for Anglo-Swiss Re to inform Tecmar that you two seem to have gotten into the drug business a little deeper than you were prepared for so they pulled you out. They can deal with the federal police, I hope. Is there anything else anybody expects you to be doing while you're there?"

"We were supposed to meet this morning with Mr. al Hussein, the owner's representative. They say he's the moving force there."

"One hell of an engineer, from what I read. I'd love to sit down and have a beer with him sometime. Anglo-Swiss will have to include a special apology to him in their message. Anything else?"

"No, sir."

"See you in a few hours, then."

* * *

At shortly after eleven fifteen in the morning a twenty-passenger executive jet marked "Liberation Airways," landed at the Antonio Carlos Jobim International Airport. After slowing and turning off the runway, it taxied promptly to the Aviaos Sul hangar, where it stopped, leaving both of its engines whooshing gently as they idled. Ray and Ted, who were standing next to the hangar, had sprinted out to the plane before the door even opened.

"Okay, you two," shouted Mike as he lowered the ladder, "in the plane. I've got a doctor here. She'll check you both over on the way to Ushuaia. After she's looked at Ted, I'll decide whether he goes on with us or goes back with the doctor. Now find some seats and secure your seat belts."

Before either could answer, Mike was pulling up the

ladder and closing the door behind them and the jets were screaming again as the plane turned and headed back toward the runway. Fifteen minutes later, thanks to Alex's magic wand, they were airborne again.

Leaving Ted in peace for a few moments with the doctor, Mike took Ray aft to an empty row of seats. "How's your head feeling?"

"Pretty good. We both got some quality sleep."

"Okay. Your eyes look normal but we'll let the doctor decide. Now, about your attackers. Do you think the CIA stringer was in on it?"

"I've been thinking about that, Captain. The way she broke off the contact makes me think she was both scared and surprised. I don't think she was in on it. In fact, I'm a little worried about her."

"Is she cute?"

"That's not quite the word, Captain. She's pretty beat . . . I think she may be sick . . . But you can feel an aura, a sense of life surrounding her."

"You let yourself get distracted too easily.

"Is there a lot of fallout?"

"Damn well bound to be, but Alex's got some of her friends busy confusing the issue so nobody can pin it on us. She's still trying to learn more about Coccoli and Rojas."

"Was she able to come up with anything from the crew's records?"

"The majority are Latin Americans, the rest from all over. A dozen felons, maybe. Many more with unclear backgrounds, but that's how it is aboard every merchant ship if you really look closely."

"Any seem involved in radical politics?"

"I'm sure a number are unhappy with their various governments, but none appear to be on the run. All sorts of vaguely possibles," summed up Mike, "but nothing that sets my alarms ringing. Nothing we can focus on. And, so far, nothing has happened to pin on anybody. Alex is going over the passengers. Criminal records, radical politics and odd connections to foreign governments. Now let's see how Ted is."

Both Ted and Ray were fully fit for duty according to the doctor, who, Mike suspected, had never issued a sick pass in her life. That's why he'd selected her.

* * *

"These plans are screwed up," remarked Ted as he studied his copy of the *Aurora Australis* plans Mike had passed out. "Some of them don't match."

"I've noticed that too," remarked Chambers. "She's old and she's been overhauled and altered a number of times. It's more than likely some of the details on these plans are wrong. The good news is that Alex has also managed to come up with a set of the job orders from the overhaul. In some cases they even indicate who worked on the job or at least signed it off."

Ted screwed up a smile. "At least that's a starting point. Any mention of Coccoli or Rojas?"

"About a dozen, but we all know that there were undoubtedly some little projects the captain or the chief engineer finagled that didn't make it into the records. Still, this data should be very useful."

"Sir," said the plane's copilot as she stepped through the cockpit door and headed toward Mike, "this message just came in for you."

"Thanks," said Mike, taking the message and reading it. He then handed it to Alex.

"Interesting," said Alex as she pulled her laptop out of its case and started to open it.

"According to this message," explained Mike to the rest of the team, "an engineman named Sven Hensen is missing aboard *Aurora*. They're searching the ship and have also turned around to search their track. It may be nothing, of course, or maybe not. If he's gone overboard, then we might not ever know more."

"Boss," interjected Alex as she looked up from her laptop, "Sven Hensen had a possession of a controlled substance conviction about four years ago."

"I'm afraid, sir," remarked Ray, "that twenty percent of the American electorate would have one of those if they'd only gotten caught."

"I'm not sure how much this really helps us."

"Maybe, maybe not," mused Alex. "There is a correlation between his sort of record and violent acts, especially if it's violence for hire."

* * *

The Southern Ocean is a fickle place. It's known for having, during the austral summer, the most gentle, although far from warm, weather. It is also known for having the most awful. Weather so terrible that few who haven't experienced it can even imagine it. Finally, it is known for the blinding speed with which its weather changes. It is a speed that neither the North Atlantic nor the North Pacific can possibly match even on their nimblest, most unpredictable days.

The Southern Ocean also has a queen city—Ushuaia. Tacked on to the southernmost tip of Argentina, Ushuaia is a city of about fifty thousand, a small, low-profile place at the very end of the world. It is surrounded by snowy mountains and the blue-gray waters of the Beagle Channel, fields more often brown than green and an abundant crop of rocks and lichen. While beaten and abused continuously by the weather, the city is far from humble. Its architecture is clean and varied, its people sturdy, and its traffic jams equal to any in the world. Ushuaia even has its own yacht club, a fact which should not be surprising since, thanks to its winds, it is the best possible location for those hard-core sailors who want to really sail.

Ironically, despite its lack of glamour, the city's air terminal was undergoing a modest expansion—in order to better serve the growing numbers of affluent tourists who seemed to yearn for just such ends of the world.

"Beautiful weather," remarked Anderson as he climbed out of the jet into the dark, wind-maddened sleet.

"Isn't it," agreed Fuentes, rubbing the bruise on his temple as he did.

"Listen up," barked Mike Chambers, "our next ride is that helo over there." As he spoke, he pointed at a big, twin-rotor civilian supply helicopter parked in the same dimly lit corner of the airport where the jet was. "So grab the gear and let's get to it!"

Shouldering their large and very heavy duffel bags—which were filled with clothing, weapons and a variety of sensors—the Tridents hurried quickly through the slush, leaving the doctor and the jet crew gratefully contemplating the first-class meal and warm beds they would soon be enjoying in Ushuaia's glitzy new tourist hotel. "Whoever the hell they are," remarked the doctor, "I'm damn glad I'm not one of them."

"Welcome aboard." The middle-aged Argentine pilot grinned as, one after another, the team climbed up and into the helo.

"How often do you fly in this shit?" asked Jerry.

"Hell, this is summer. We service some of the Argentine research stations down south—we have half a dozen, you know—and now we even fly in the winter. You should see that."

"Going to be like this all the way?"

"No. It's a little clearer to the south, but the wind's beginning to work itself up."

"If you're not worried, we're not," said Ray Fuentes.

"I worry all the time," replied the pilot, "but don't let that worry you. We figured you'd be hungry, so we've got something for you. We considered sandwiches but then decided to give you a cultural experience, so we're serving tapas tonight. Who knows, some day we may be a real airline." With that he opened a large insulated box filled with about fifty smallish plastic containers, each of which contained a snack-sized portion of food—a couple brazed beef ribs in sauce; artichokes stuffed with chicken salad; cooked chicken livers wrapped in bacon. The selection seemed endless, and three or four portions made a good meal.

"Estupendo!" murmured Ray. The food on the beat-up helo looked better than what the CIA had served on its snappy jet.

"Here's some bread," continued the pilot, "and those thermoses contain coffee, tea and cocoa. Sorry, no wine on this flight. So choose a seat, strap yourself in tight, put on the headphones, sit back and enjoy the flight.

"Whoever the hell you are," he added under his breath as he banged twice on the side of the cabin and headed forward to the cockpit.

Even before he reached the door, there was a short whine then a growing shriek as the copilot lit off the forward rotor.

No rest for the weary, thought Ray as he tried to make himself comfortable in the icy, pounding space. Just then a blast of torchlike air erupted from the heating vent, making him wonder if frying was preferable to freezing.

10

The Drake Passage

"Where the hell's Hensen?" demanded Mr. Acosta, the second engineer.

"Don't know, sir," replied his assistant. "But he's not here."

The officer looked out the window of the relatively quiet Main Control into the booming, thudding, shaking madhouse that existed in the Main Engine Room. That was where Hensen was supposed to be. But he wasn't. He couldn't see him, and none of the men out there could see him. "This isn't the first time that fucker's been late. A month or so ago he didn't even show up at all. Claimed he was sick. I still don't know where the hell they found him."

Shaking his head, Acosta turned and studied the watch bill posted on one of the bulkheads. Just to make sure it hadn't been changed since the last time he looked at it, twelve hours ago. "Call his quarters."

"This is Main Control. Is Hensen there?"

"No," replied an electrician named Swaboda, one of Hensen's two roommates. "He's supposed to be on watch."

"He damn well is, but he's not here and the second's pissed."

"He may have swapped with somebody," offered Swaboda. "He's a little odd. He's always doing what you don't expect." In fact, both Hensen's roommates knew just how odd their third roommate really was—how he supplemented his income—although neither spoke of it.

"He didn't swap with anybody. He's just not here, so cut the crap. Any ideas where he is?"

"No. No ideas. Sorry."

"What was that all about?" asked Ivan Singh, the other roommate, as Swaboda hung up.

"The miserable bastard hasn't shown up for his watch."

"Not only is he a miserable bastard, he's also a stupid bastard," replied Singh as he rolled over to try to get back to sleep. "Maybe this will be enough to get him canned."

"Or even better, maybe the fucker fell overboard."

"That's not very charitable."

"You don't agree?"

"Of course I agree."

Ernesto Montalba, the chief engineer, was informed within ten minutes that one of his men was missing. He immediately reported the situation to Arthur Covington.

Damn it, thought Covington as he swung his legs over the side of the bunk in his sea cabin and reached for the light switch with his free hand. In all probability the fellow—who the chief assured him was not always totally dependable—was lying drunk and passed out somewhere. Or sleeping with one of the passengers. Or God knew what else! He'd seen it all over the years and so had Montalba. "When was he last seen, Chief?"

"A little before midnight, Captain. He was in the crew's lounge."

"When he left, did he tell anybody where he was going?"

"No. He just up and left."

"Very well. Keep searching."

Covington then called Dave Ellison, the security guy. "Dave, we've got a missing engineman named Hensen. He was seen a little before midnight in the crew's lounge and not since. He hasn't shown up for his watch."

"Yes, Captain?"

The son of a bitch didn't sound very alert. Probably hungover, thought Covington. "Unless you already know what he looks like, I want you to look him up in the ship's records. Then I want you to review your video records for the past eight hours to see if you can spot him." The surveillance cameras only covered part of the ship, but it was worth a try.

"You've got it, Art," replied Ellison without enthusiasm.

Covington hung up without replying. That was the third time he'd addressed him as "Art," and, stuffy as it might seem, Captain Covington didn't appreciate it. The slug had been some sort of a cop. Undoubtedly the type that liked donuts by the bag. Ellison's position was one of the few aboard the ship about which he had no say when it came to hiring. The owners reserved that privilege strictly for themselves.

With a sigh, he called the bridge and directed the mate of the watch to stop the ship and to pass the word for Engineman Hensen to contact the chief engineer immediately. He then slipped on a shirt, trousers and bedroom slippers and hustled to the bridge, where he temporarily disregarded the mate's questioning look and leaned over the GPS plot of the ship's past and future tracks.

"This isn't the best night to fall overboard, sir," observed the mate.

"No, Mister, it's not. None are." The officer was young, thought Covington. Alert, hardworking and reasonably competent. If only he could be cured of the tendency to point out the obvious at the wrong time.

Despite having had to dodge several large chunks of ice, *Aurora* had been able to maintain speed and had made excellent progress cutting across the Drake Passage. They were now closing in on the Antarctic circle and the cove scheduled to be the first eco-landing. The temptation, considering the foul nature of the Southern Ocean, was to write the man off and continue on before the weather came up with another nasty trick or two.

The fellow might well have fallen overboard right after he was last seen, about four hours ago, thought Covington, his fingers tapping on the keyboard. In that case he'd have fallen overboard over a hundred miles ago. Or he might have fallen fifteen minutes ago. Either way, the chances of his surviving without an exposure suit were absolutely nonexistent. Still, he had to try, even if it meant nothing more than going through the motions. He owed it to the crew, and to the owners and to himself. And to all the other seamen, past and future, who had ever run the risk of falling overboard. He continued tapping rapidly on the navsystem keyboard, correcting the ship's track for the past six hours for prevailing wind and current, thereby generating a course to follow to retrace their path.

He looked at his watch. Another hour or more to dawn. Should he start north now and run the risk of passing the man in the dark, or should he wait and run the risk of not finding him when he'd gone overboard only a few minutes before?

"Ah, Mr. Winters," he said to the shadow that had appeared beside him. "I want you to call all hands and station them along both sides of the ship and turn on the spotlights. Then we will head north."

He then sent out a man overboard report.

* * *

"Mr. Rounding," squawked the walkie-talkie in Jake Rounding's hand.

"Yes, Chief," responded the third engineer.

"Where are you?"

"We've just finished searching Storeroom Three Alpha. No sign of him."

"Okay, Jake. Keep going and keep alert."

"Okay, Chief."

Jake Rounding barely knew Sven Hensen, but the engineman's disappearance had the third engineer on edge. He thought of Annie, shot to death by the police in a stupid, meaningless demonstration, and knew that what he had done had to be done. And Hensen had nothing to do with anything. All the same, he felt somehow as if a noose were beginning to tighten around his neck; as if the world were beginning to close in on him.

"What next, Mr. Rounding?" asked one of the men with him.

"The Auxiliary Pump Room."

"Hensen's a shit, sir."

"I've heard that before. We've still got to search for him."

* * *

"This is it, Mister," said Covington to Winters shortly before noon. "If he's still alive, he's someplace behind us so we're going to turn and run down the reciprocal of the course we've been running and zigzag a little as we go."

"He can't possibly be alive, Captain," said Winters as he watched an Argentine search plane head south along the track they'd just covered.

"I'm well aware of that, but we have to head south anyway, so we might as well continue looking as we go."

The captain then walked over to the public-address system: "Ladies and gentlemen. Several hours ago I informed you that one of our crew may have fallen overboard and that we were going to retrace our track north in the hope that we might find him. We have now completed our retracing and, unfortunately, have failed to locate him either aboard the ship or in the water. Accordingly, we are about to turn south again and head for our first destination on the

Antarctic Peninsula. Along the way we will continue to search, so please keep your eyes open."

* * *

"What are your thoughts, Chrissie, about this man who's fallen overboard?" asked the brunette with the microphone in her hand. "Absolutely tragic, wouldn't you say?"

Chrissie, wearing her thoughtful smile, looked at the media person a moment, thinking that she was like all the others, almost exclusively interested in interviewing herself. "I'm with you there, Jen. An absolute tragedy."

"And whadaya think of the way the captain's handling it? Some people are saying that he's wasting everybody's time by searching as long as he is, while others want him to keep trying. Congressman Evans is in conference with him right now. He's going to make a statement later."

"Fact is," answered Chrissie, feeling that by even talking to the brunette she was playing a fool's game with yet another clever fool, "I'm with the captain and I'm looking forward to hearing what the congressman has to contribute." That, she thought, should end the reporter's efforts to put words in her mouth.

* * *

"Ladies and gentlemen," boomed the public-address system, which had been set to override so it was audible even where it had been turned off locally, "this is Congressman Pete Evans. As many of you know, I represent the tenth district of Connecticut."

Evans paused, then continued, "As we all know by now a tragic event occurred sometime last night. One of the ship's crew fell overboard—I can only say that the man was a hero, a credit to merchant marines everywhere, and our prayers go out to his family. I want to assure every one of you that I am monitoring the situation minute by minute. I have just concluded a conference with Captain Covington and fully intend to ensure that everything possible is done and is done right. You may count on me to keep you informed and to keep your interests my top priority."

Pete's a damn ambitious sucker, thought Senator Alvin Bergstrom as he lay in bed, listening to the speech and fondling Linda Williams's left breast. So, for that matter, was Linda. Perhaps even more so. He knew she had less than no real interest in his hairy, warty, tired old body; that what she really wanted was sponsorship of and votes for legislation. Well, she wasn't going to get it. A little bit, maybe, but not all of it. Not from him. He'd undoubtedly dance around praising the noble intentions of those who did sponsor her legislation, but somehow, he would never end up voting for it. Because it cost too much. Because it conflicted with a better bill he was working on. Because any halfway plausible reason. If necessary he'd be sure to be out of town investigating some mega-disaster or other. Sometime, after the cruise was over, she would be told. Not by him, but by Babs. That's what Babs was for. To clean up things like Linda. In the meantime Linda would simply have to settle for his hairy, warty, tired old body.

The senator leaned over and licked that which he had been fondling.

* * *

Arthur Covington sat at his desk and reread the message. Then he looked up at Mr. Winters. "You *did* read this?"

"Yes, Captain. The company wants us to head north across the Drake Channel again and prepare to receive a helicopter full of U.S naval personnel who are going to conduct some sort of courtesy security inspection."

"Yes, very gracious of them."

"Does it mean that they know something solid that we don't?"

"I wish I knew. We don't seem to have any choice but to go along with it."

"What are you going to tell the passengers?"

"That at the owners' request the United States Navy has arrived to give us a routine courtesy inspection and that there is absolutely nothing to be concerned about."

* * *

"What's this all really about?" demanded Congressman Pete Evans shortly before midnight, when he found Mr. Winters standing on the boat deck looking aft through the light but wind-driven snow at the brilliantly lit fantail.

"As the captain explained, sir, this is a routine security audit that the United States now conducts at the request of shipowners." As he tried to soothe the congressman, Winters wondered just how successful the operation was going to be. Between the wind's violent and unpredictable gusts and the ship's rolling and heaving, he had trouble imagining a happy ending. But, presumably, their midnight visitors were all trained in this sort of thing.

"I never heard of any program like that."

"I understand it's very new. Maybe they are doing a few trial runs before announcing it."

"Wendell Gardner tells me there's more to it than that."

"I can't speak for Mr. Gardner, sir, he works for the sponsors of the voyage, but I'm sure the captain will tell you more—if there is more to tell—when he knows more. As it is, he's satisfied these people are on legitimate official business."

Before Evans could express more displeasure, a big, orange helicopter appeared out of the night astern and slowly approached, dragging its static wire below it. "Now please excuse me, sir," said Winters as he started down one of the ladders. "I'm needed on the fantail."

Feeling both intensely irritated and also a little nervous, Evans looked around. There were maybe a hundred or so other passengers standing there, watching and looking both confused and concerned. He might have expected more, but then it was almost midnight and the weather absolutely sucked. Even Penny had chosen to stay in bed. He did, however, count all three media teams on station.

Evans continued to watch as the helo made its approach. Its static wire clunked on the rolling, heaving deck then slid over the side as the helo was blown away by a ferocious gust. Back it came, lower this time, trying to line itself up over the ship's rolling, pitching deck, only to be shoved away yet again by another gust, from the opposite direction.

On the third approach, a dark figure—Evans would later learn that it was Mike Chambers—in an orange survival suit and with a large duffel bag, could be seen swinging below the helo.

The gust that had been holding the Trident Force leader off the ship disappeared just as the helo had worked its way back over, and Mike swung forward as he dropped rapidly toward the deck. With what must have been a painful crash, he slammed into the rolling steel and stumbled. Even before he could gain his footing, the helo drifted off again, dragging him toward the side. Only at the last minute was Mike able to trip the quick release on the harness.

It was time, decided Congressman Evans as he exhaled the breath he'd been holding, to get over to the nearest media team and provide them with some informed commentary. As he walked along the rail and watched, the helo's pilot—who was gritting his teeth and praying as he hadn't prayed since he was six—returned and managed to deposit another package—Ted Anderson—on the deck safely before once again being blown downwind.

The helo came in again, this time to deliver Alex. The approach was from the starboard side of the ship. The altitude was about two hundred feet, and the wind seemed to have steadied for a moment or two.

With her duffel strapped beside her, Alex stepped out into the raging night, supported by the hoist wire. The helo's crewman started to lower her until she was swinging about seventy-five feet below him.

Congressman Pete Evans watched in renewed shock as

a downdraft slammed the helo. The black figure plummeted, almost in free fall. He grasped the rail even harder as he realized that whoever it was dangling at the end of the wire was either going to slam into the ship's side at fifty miles per hour or disappear into the raging black-and-white madness below. And the helo was going to crash right on top of her.

He glanced at the media team, which was still fifty feet away. Maybe this wasn't the sort of thing he wanted to be involved with.

Of course it was! It was high-impact news.

* * *

When Alex had stepped up to the open door and looked out into the screaming cold night, she'd come to the sudden conclusion that taking the next step, the big one, was not a particularly smart thing to do.

Maybe it was a lack of sleep—she'd spent the entire trip from Tampa to Ushuaia on the computer and not even a dead man could have slept in the helo. Maybe it was the bitter cold—she'd never experienced anything like it before. Maybe it was because she'd just turned thirty-two and might even be getting a little smarter.

She'd jumped out of aircraft at least fifty times before. On wires, with a parachute, and even to execute low-altitude free fall. All the same, on this particular pitch-black night, with the wind screaming and the Southern Ocean boiling as it slammed against the side of her tiny target, she felt an almost overpowering desire to be at home in her own living room, doing practically anything other than what she was about to do.

Stop screwing around and do it! She checked to make sure her crash helmet visor was locked up—so she could see what the hell was happening—then turned for one last look into the helo. The crewman—over whom Alex felt she towered—grinned, revealing his two missing front teeth. He gave her the thumbs-up sign, and she stepped out into the shrieking void. She returned the okay and he started to lower her rapidly, to get her clear of the bouncing helo. The survival suit was stiff but comfy, she thought, although her nose began to feel brittle almost immediately. But everything was fine. She'd trained for this sort of thing endlessly and was totally qualified.

Once clear of the helo, Alex began to recover her sense of adventure. The sensation of hanging between raging sky and boiling, barely visible sea was thrilling. Liberating. It was also, a little voice pointed out, stomach-turning. As she swayed in the gale, she looked ahead and down. There, visible through the spotty snow, was the lighted white form of *Aurora Austalis* glowing in the dark as she pitched in the nasty seas.

Alex had already concluded that the helo's pilot and crew were good. Not only had they managed to survive countless trips in this impossible region, where horrific weather was considered run-of-the-mill, but she'd just seen them deliver two of her teammates more or less intact. If they could do it with them, they could undoubtedly do it for her. It was no more than a matter of faith, and faith was essential to people who jumped out of aircraft. She'd probably end up with a bruise or two—she tended to bruise easily—but that would be the end of it.

All of these cheerful preconceptions disappeared and Alex's stomach rocketed several feet up her throat when a horribly powerful and totally unexpected downdraft slammed into the helo, causing her to plummet to within a few feet of the hungry Southern Ocean.

There she dangled. Rising a few feet then falling back. At one point a wave actually kissed her foot. And then she looked ahead and forgot about the presumptuous wave. A hundred feet or less away, the high white side of the ship was racing at her at an impossible speed. She assured herself the pilot was doing everything he could to prevent her imminent extinction, but somehow she didn't feel much better for it. She tried to swing the duffel bag around to act as a bumper when she hit, but was unable to hold it in place. It was ridiculous to even consider trying to climb the hoist wire. There was no time, and she obviously couldn't do it, anyway. Not with the duffel filled with two hundred pounds of weapons, sensors and clothes.

Oh shit! she thought. There was nothing else to say or think about the situation.

She felt a slight, grinding vibration through her left hand, which was wrapped around the life wire. She looked down and could have sworn she was rising. Then she looked ahead at the great, white wall, now maybe fifty feet away, and allowed herself to believe that it was no longer approaching but rather drifting off to one side. A gust of wind grabbed her and dragged her off to the left. Her tether, she realized, was now tending up at a sharp angle.

God! she thought in relief. The pilot was allowing the helo to be blown downwind from the ship, and the toothless one was cranking her up. She tried to keep from holding her breath as she waited to see what was to come, well aware that she was no longer a player in the drama—not even a bit player. She was merely a package.

Alex watched as the helo drifted astern of the ship and off to one side. At the same time the glowing white phantom hull slowly dropped below her. Wasting no time, the pilot worked his way upwind and alongside the ship and then charged in again. In what seemed but seconds Alex found herself looking down at *Aurora*'s deck as she descended toward it. She flexed her knees as she landed and tripped the harness's quick release with desperate speed. As she did, the ship rolled, and she found herself stumbling toward the rail, dragging the damn duffel behind her. Four arms grabbed her and held her in place—which was good since the duffel would have made a fabulous anchor.

"We're all damn glad you decided to join us, Alex," said Mike, a big smile on his face.

Alex, momentarily speechless, responded with a thumbs-up sign, thinking of the toothless helo crewman as she did.

She hoped he and the pilot would make it home in one piece. But they couldn't leave quite yet. They still had to get Ray, Jerry and Ted down. They still had a chance to kill themselves. It also occurred to her that the time might well come when this sort of bullshit was no longer fun.

* * *

"The proud men and women of our military are not only brave," intoned Peter Evans to Jen, the brunette, "but they have the best training in the world. I doubt there's another force on earth that could carry out the sort of operation we're now watching."

As he spoke, Evans gripped the rail tightly, afraid that the ship's increasingly violent behavior might throw him off to one side in a humiliating heap.

"Can you tell us, Congressman, exactly why this force has arrived? There are all sorts of rumors flying around—drugs, terrorists, environmental enforcement actions . . ."

"I'm sorry, Jen. I'm afraid I'm not at liberty to disclose the precise reason for this operation. I can only join you in applauding its execution. Not only by the party itself, but also by that fine helicopter crew of ours. They're all doing a fantastic job."

11

The Drake Passage

Jacob Rounding leaned on the fourth deck rail and watched as the dark packages descended from the sky, his slender, stooped frame hidden in one of the ankle-length thermal coats favored by engineers in all climes, when leaving the Venusian heat of the engineering spaces to view the outside world. Around him clustered half a dozen other engineers, all equally warmly packaged.

"This is insane," remarked one of the enginemen. "They almost killed her then!"

"Her?" demanded another. "What makes you think it was a girl?"

"I can always tell. It was the way she ran when she almost went over the side as the ship rolled."

"Are you in love again, Dobbs?"

"Probably. She's got guts."

"She can probably also break your neck with a flick of her wrist."

"That doesn't necessarily make her a bad person."

Rounding listened to the chatter and was briefly tempted to remark that young Dobbs should fall in love just as often as he damn well pleased. At least that way he would be living. But he decided the subject of love was something he didn't want to get into.

"Mr. Rounding," asked one of his companions, "do you have any idea why these hotshots are coming to visit us? Really? I mean is it drugs or terrorists or are they here to arrest somebody?"

"We'd all like to know," replied the third engineer carefully. "They said it is a courtesy inspection to check on the ship's antiterrorist security."

"You mean like carding us and checking our references and searching us every now and then?"

"Something like that."

The announcement that a party of U.S. naval personnel was being delivered to the ship had set off an alarm in Jake Rounding's highly stressed brain. While he couldn't be *precisely* sure why they were coming, he did know they weren't tourists who'd missed the ship's sailing. What they were was authority. United States government authority.

And Dobbs may well have guessed right—they probably were there to arrest somebody. He hunched over in the howling wind, his stomach churning, and watched as the show continued.

They'd discovered it was him, he reproached himself, and now they'd found him. He'd begun to hope it had been so long ago that they'd forgotten about it. Or lost interest. He'd hoped that being on a ship a million miles from nowhere would protect him. The more he thought about it, though, the more he realized that instead of protecting himself he'd trapped himself. He was here and they were here and he had no place to run or hide.

Beginning to shake, Jake rested his forearms on the rail and looked down at the deck. Poor Annie! He'd been such a shit father for her! He'd been a shit non-husband for her mother! His whole life had reduced itself to shit. Just as he'd known it would even back when he was in junior high school.

It was all too late now. There was nothing to do but wait. They would summon him—or maybe they would show up at his cabin, kick in his door and shoot him right where he stood. Or, if he was really unlucky, they might not shoot him right away.

What he couldn't understand was why here and why so many? There'd been five of them. Five to arrest a worn-out old bugger like him? But then he knew the procedure; he'd seen it on TV. Five big officers to arrest one ninety-year-old in a wheelchair. Cuff the felon and run him in front of the TV cameras. Give the onlookers a jolt of shock and awe to remind them who's in charge. And, in the end, if it began to look as if the bastard was innocent, remind the judge that one can never be too careful in this day and age.

* * *

Arthur Covington sat at the head of the table in his small conference room and looked up when Mike Chambers walked in, dressed now in a set of blue coveralls with "United States Navy" embroidered over the left breast. "Captain Covington," said Mike as he offered his credentials, "I'm Captain Michael Chambers, United States Navy."

Chambers stood, accepted the credentials and studied them a moment. He then gave them back and offered his hand. "Welcome aboard, Captain Chambers. Please sit down."

"Thank you, Captain."

Like many other merchant mariners, Covington viewed the navy, any navy, with mixed emotions. In times of war they could be damn useful, but the rest of the time they had an irritating habit of descending on you shouting orders, screwing up your operating schedule and generally making your life miserable. Frequently for no discernible reason.

"To what do we owe your visit, if I'm allowed to know? The owners said it's some sort of new, random security checkup that you Americans are now offering your friends . . ."

"I'm afraid we don't offer it to just anybody, and it's not totally random."

"Oh?"

"To begin, you have a high-profile passenger list, a very tempting target to anybody with terrorist ambitions."

"That has occurred to me."

"What I doubt you know is that two shipfitters at the Tecmar yard, along with the girlfriend of one of them, disappeared shortly after your overhaul was completed. We have since learned that they seemed close to a person named Omar, about whom we know absolutely nothing except that the shipfitters seemed to have some sort of big plans and this Omar was central to them. We don't even know at this point if Omar is his real name. Finally, not to be indelicate, there's the matter of the yard's ownership . . . and this man of yours who seems to have gone overboard."

"You were undoubtedly already on your way to us before Hensen disappeared."

"Yes, but our data searches had already turned him up. He had a drug conviction."

"You've got my attention, Captain, although I'm afraid a number of my crew have been in trouble from time to time. Are you really telling me we have terrorists aboard or an explosive device or some other such thing? If so, then I'm fully prepared to turn north immediately for Ushuaia to offload passengers. Or do you think this is all about drugs?"

"I don't know what it's really about, and no, not yet. Unless you feel it best. I don't think we have enough to abort the voyage."

"And I don't particularly like jumping just because some terrorist bastard decides to amuse himself by dropping a few hints. What, then, do you have in mind?"

"My people and I will search as much of your ship as we can, using your crew's eyes and our sensors, and see if we can come up with anything. We plan to start with a list of likely locations along with a description of the work orders executed during your last overhaul."

"You're starting with a damn long list."

"I know. We hope to shorten it by talking to some of your crew—and, I'm afraid, some of your passengers. The ones with either criminal records or radical political connections."

"All this without any real proof there's anything to look for."

"I'm not going to say you can never be too careful, because it's all too easy to go overboard. We're working on a hunch, at the moment."

"We'll be crossing the Antarctic Circle soon. Do you have any objection to our holding a Crossing the Line Ceremony?"

"None whatsoever. It might help distract the passengers from us."

"We're also scheduled to effect a landing a few hours later on the Antarctic Peninsula, to give the passengers a look at the local wildlife. May we do so, or do you wish to keep the ship in quarantine?"

"Please follow your itinerary. In fact, if you're anchoring, that will be an excellent chance for us to perform an external hull inspection. I'll have our most experienced diver, Chief Andrews, do that with me. We're a little more familiar with ship bottoms than the rest of the team."

Covington glanced at Chambers's wedding band. "Does your wife know about this thing you have for boat bottoms?"

"Yes, and it's fine with her just as long as the kids don't find out about it."

Covington chuckled, deciding that he and Chambers would probably get along. "I'd be more comfortable if you'd call me Art."

"Only if you'll call me Mike."

"A pleasure."

"We've brought our cold water regulators and I understand you have a fairly extensive dive locker."

"We do. I'm sure Kim Ackerman, she's the ship's diver, can outfit you with everything you need. Now, how is that man of yours who was injured when he landed wrong?"

"Fuentes? He has a badly sprained ankle, but your doctor seems to have wrapped him up pretty well."

"My hat's off to the man who delivered you. The Argentines are good, damn good, if you ask me."

"That they are, Art.

"About the media . . . ," continued Chambers.

"I'm in no position to confiscate any footage they took of your arrival. Greenpeace, the sponsor, is very touchy about censorship."

"I understand that. They've probably already transmitted it. I was hoping you might come up with a method of distracting them from my people. Even a little."

"The best I've been able to do is keep them out of the operating spaces and crew's quarters. When do you want to meet with Congressman Evans?"

"I was afraid of that. What about the senator?"

"I don't think he could care less. But the congressman wants to keep control of things and he wants everybody to know that he's keeping control of things."

"I'll meet with him in an hour. No media, if possible. May I use this room?"

"My pleasure, just as long as I don't have to be here. And at some point I'm sure Rod Johnson's going to want to talk to you."

"Who's he?"

"The Greenpeace on-scene rep."

* * *

Marcello Cagayan found the arrival of what was clearly a military force of some sort as worrisome as did Jake Rounding. His first impulse was to detonate the charges right that very minute, before anybody could find them or take him. But this was the wrong place—too close to land. Omar had said to do it farther east, where the nearest help was thousands of miles away.

As was so often the case, Cagayan's head started to throb as he tried to think it all out. Did they know about the charges? Did they know where they were? Did they know about him? And how did they know? Had they taken Omar? Or whoever had placed the things if it hadn't been Omar himself?

He took a deep breath and patted the cell phone in his pocket. The contact made him calmer, made his thinking clearer. He had power now. He was in the big leagues. He no longer had to panic at the first sign of others who thought they had power too. Hadn't Hensen proved that? These people who had come down from the sky were just part of the challenge now. If necessary, he could trigger the charges in five seconds, but in the meantime he had plans. Plans that went beyond those laid out by Omar.

* * *

"What's the plan, Boss?" asked Ray Fuentes, his damaged, grapefruit-sized ankle up on a chair, after Mike had assembled the team in one of the three large, surprisingly plush suites Captain Covington had assigned to them.

"First, I want to remind you of the very delicate position we're in. Many of the passengers are VIPs. Neither the ship nor the crew's American, and we're not even sure there's a problem. On top of that, the video footage they got of our arrival has already hit prime time and some of the news commentators are already going into hysterics, which means some of the passengers may follow."

"What do we do about them?" asked Ted Anderson.

"Who, the passengers or the media?"

"The media."

"Avoid them the best you can. They're prohibited from the ship's operating areas, so try hiding there if they get too intense."

"What do we tell them?"

"Nothing for the moment. Not even name, rank and serial number."

"What about the guy they lost overboard? You figure he was a terrorist or just some sort of druggie?"

"Assume both, if that's any help. How's your arm?"

"At least ninety-five percent, sir."

"Very well. I want you and Jerry to go to work with the crew searching. Work from those two lists Alex has generated. You're looking for anything that doesn't belong. The ship's people should know very well what belongs and what doesn't. You're going to back them up if and when they find anything suspicious. Start in the engineering spaces and other working spaces, then the crew's quarters and then the passenger accommodations."

"You think we can cover the whole ship, sir?"

"No, of course not! We're going to do our best. If there is a device and if there is somebody aboard controlling it, our searching may cause him to make a mistake."

"Like detonating it?"

"We run that risk."

"Aye, sir," replied Jerry after a brief—but pregnant—pause.

"While you're doing that, Ray and I will be talking to the crew members on Alex's other list—the ones with sketchy pasts. Alex is going to go over the crew list again and also the passenger list."

"I've already made a preliminary run on them, Boss," reported Alex.

"And?"

"Among the passengers we've got four with securities fraud convictions or prejudicial settlements; six who've made false statements; four tax evaders; six spouse abusers; ten convicted of possession of cocaine; twenty-five felony DUI convictions and three convicted of ecoterrorism."

"Along with a congressman and a senator," added Ray, trying to be helpful.

"What about radical politics and questionable connections?"

"Nothing obvious. The crew's from all over, so some may be out of favor with their own governments, but we really have no way of knowing. Same for the passengers. None of them are on the Homeland Security Watch List."

"We'll add the felons to our list."

"What do we ask them, sir?" asked Ray, grimacing slightly as he moved his foot.

"How they like the trip so far. What they think of the ship and its crew. How they feel about the ship's security. Have they seen anybody else behaving strangely. Use your imagination."

"And the crew?"

"The same . . . but be sure to ask if they know or ever heard of Coccoli, Rojas or Omar."

"Aye, sir."

"And one more thing. The ship's scheduled to anchor to let the passengers go ashore. While she's anchored, Jerry and I will conduct a bottom inspection. Alex will relieve Jerry on the search team."

The rest of the team, thinking of the bitterly cold water, smiled at Jerry. He gave them the thumbs-up sign.

* * *

Mike knocked on the door to Linda Williams's stateroom and waited. He knocked again, wondering if she'd decided to make him drag her out of the senator's stateroom, where he'd finally managed to locate her by telephone a few minutes before. The door finally opened. "Mr. Chambers?"

"Yes," replied Mike, flipping open his wallet as he did.

Linda studied the credentials for what seemed like several minutes. "Okay, come in but leave the door open."

Mike walked in.

"So what can I do for the navy?" she demanded.

"I'm surprised you're not at one of the seminars."

"Those are to educate the customers. I'm here on business, not as a tourist. I'm working with Senator Bergstrom to put an end to all the shit. To clean up after people like you. So what do you want?"

"According to our records you have been convicted of an ecoterrorist act."

"Clever little people, aren't you? A couple friends of mine decided to stop the destruction of an endangered marsh, so they torched some houses being built there. Nobody was hurt."

"And you?"

"I was driving the car. But that was a long time ago. Most people now appreciate the wisdom and reasonableness of our actions. Getting back to you, what do you want?"

As he studied her, Mike suspected she was older than she looked.

"We're conducting a random security evaluation of *Aurora* at the request of her owners."

"That's bullshit and I don't care what you told Pete Evans. So why do you come to me?"

This is what those bastards at the FBI do every day, thought Mike as his irritation increased. "Doesn't it make sense, even to you, to go to a convicted terrorist when one suspects terrorism?"

"You think I'm involved in some sort of terrorist plan aimed at this ship!"

"I think you might, or might not, have noticed anything, or heard something, that might point us in the right direction."

"I think the senator would advise me at this point to consult a lawyer. Are there any aboard who are willing to work pro bono? Do you know what that means?"

"Thank you for your time, Ms. Williams," said Mike as

he turned to go. There was no way he could continue talking with the woman without drawing his sidearm and shooting her right between the eyes.

It's a matter of not enough sleep, he thought. But there was no time for sleep. He stepped out into the passageway and right into a news team. "What can you tell us, Mr. Chambers? Have your people found anything? Is there really a bomb aboard? Does the woman in that cabin have anything to do with it?"

"Get lost!" he said without thinking.

* * *

"Ladies and gentlemen," announced Captain Covington. "In a few minutes the ship will be crossing the Antarctic Circle. As is customary, we will stop briefly to allow King Neptune and some of his Red Nose aides to board the ship. Following his arrival, the king will welcome us to his southern kingdom and initiate those of us who have never visited before into the Order of the Red Nose. Everybody is encouraged to actively participate in the ceremony. If not, please do come watch. Following the ceremony, everybody will receive a certificate attesting to their having crossed this chilliest of lines."

Chrissie Clark, who was sitting with Brad at a table in the lounge, digesting her breakfast, looked up at the speaker as the captain clicked off. "That sounds like fun."

"Sounds idiotic to me," replied Brad.

Still smiling to herself, Chrissie studied him. He was looking worse by the second, and it wasn't just a matter of her having kicked him out of bed. "Still haven't been able to find the guy who's supposed to sell you dope?"

"No, god damn it. I told you, the guy was the guy who disappeared overboard."

"So I guess you're going cold turkey." As she said it, Chrissie thanked God that she'd never gotten past grass and a few other relatively minor odds and ends.

"Fuck!"

"You don't mind if I take part in this Red Nose thing, do you? You don't even have to watch."

"Sure. A little publicity will never hurt you."

He was right, she thought, but he was also wrong. The fact was that she just wanted to do it, and really hoped the media would be so busy with the politicians—and Lloyd Llewellyn—that they'd barely notice her.

About fifteen minutes later *Aurora* coasted to a stop in the eastern portion of the Bellingshausen Sea. To the east lay the Antarctic Peninsula, their first port of call—if you could call a shingle beach on an ice-covered pile of rocks a port. With its predictable capriciousness the Antarctic weather had changed radically. While it was still cold, the snow had stopped, the sky had cleared, and the wind had dropped to a gentle breeze, causing the seas to also lose much of their power.

As soon as the ship stopped, there was a great splashing and commotion under one of the boat landing platforms that had been extended over the side. Suddenly, almost as if he had been standing on another platform below the visible one, a tall, almost regal, figure appeared and started to climb up a ladder onto the platform. The figure—blessed with an immense red nose—was dressed in a nineteenth-century admiral's uniform and covered with long strands of dangling kelp. Just as Captain Covington, who was standing on the platform, saluted King Neptune—for that is who the kelpy figure was—another figure appeared. It was Davy Jones, the king's prime minister and grand vizier.

With Captain Covington leading, the party proceeded up to the fantail, where an old barber's chair had been set up. Surrounding the barber's chair were eight veteran Rednoses, each with a big red nose and a long fake turtle flipper attached to one hand.

After settling onto his throne, King Neptune, who bore a strange resemblance to the ship's boatswain, welcomed all to his domain. He then ordered the polliwogs to form a line for their initiation.

The first batch of initiates was composed of the younger members of the ship's crew—those who had never crossed the line before. Dressed in their oldest, rattiest work clothes, they were ordered to run toward the king while being thoroughly hosed down with cold water. They were then directed to slow down and walk a gauntlet between two rows of Rednoses, who thwacked them with their flippers. Once they were past the gauntlet, their noses were painted red with face paint and they were sent below to dry off and warm up.

Predictably, the first passenger at the head of their line was Katie Sanders, followed by her parents. Before anything happened, each passenger participant was interviewed by Davy Jones—who bore a faint resemblance to the chief mate. Being the youngest person aboard, she was assigned a special initiation fee—instead of running across the deck, she had to walk like a penguin while a fine spray of chilly water soaked her. When she reached the gauntlet, giggling uncontrollably, she was greeted by a multitude of pats on the back from the Rednoses. When that ordeal was over, King Neptune touched her on each shoulder with a very dead fish of some sort and pronounced her a genuine Rednose, at which point her nose was painted. With a tremendous smile of pride, she turned to watch her parents jog side by side across the deck under the now-familiar spray. Once Dana's and Tim's noses had been redecorated, the show continued.

"Ms. Clark," asked Davy Jones when Chrissie reached the head of the line, "how much of this would you like?"

"Everything, Davy, everything."

Peter Evans and Penny insisted on the same, although Peter made a point of ensuring that the video cameras were running when he started.

Some passengers wanted more water, some less, and only about one-half participated, but all, participants and spectators, seemed to enjoy the event, and many a red nose was still visible at midnight.

As soon as the ceremony had been completed, King Neptune and his court returned to their kelpie realm and *Aurora* turned southeast, toward her first stop.

* * *

Jerry Andrews stopped next to the main reduction gear behind one of *Aurora*'s two monster diesels—piles of metal so big that they didn't even look like engines—and looked forward. The engine room was incredibly noisy and hot as the two huge steel beasts pounded, causing the deck to quiver slightly, driving the ship forward and expending monumental amounts of energy in the process. The room was three stories high, ringed by catwalks, and every level was filled with things—the engines themselves, motors, pumps, boxes, tanks, lockers and an infinite number of pipes, conduits and wires. And between and behind every one of those things were spaces—spaces in which other things could be hidden.

As Jerry watched, twelve of the ship's engineers worked their way slowly through the space, looking between and behind things—looking for anything that they knew didn't belong there and then making check marks on lists. Then he watched Ted lowering a small transducer into a tank of pneumatic fluid. The transducer was connected to a specialized sonar unit that scanned the tank's inside wall so they could see if it matched the outside.

He and Ted had initially hoped they would be able to speed up the process by using their sensors for a preliminary survey, but problems had developed. Jerry's radiation detector had done its job by not sounding off once except when he'd first calibrated it. Unfortunately, Ted's sniffer—designed to detect a variety of molecules given off by various explosives—had proved utterly useless for surveying. There are an almost limitless number of oils and other solvents used aboard a ship. And the air in the engine room was full of them. Not only did many give off volatile molecules similar or identical to a variety of known explosives, but many could be used to make explosives themselves. Until something was found, neither the sniffer nor the small X-ray machine they'd brought would be of any use, reducing their high-tech arsenal to the Geiger counter and the sonar.

Despite the challenges, they'd already come across several items of interest—all of which turned out to be contraband. Three bottles of rum and half a dozen little caches of marijuana. Then one of the enginemen found a parcel wrapped in brown paper carefully hidden under a fixed air flask.

"Chief Andrews, I've found something," shouted the man, waving as he did to get Jerry's attention in the cacophonous engine room.

Jerry hustled over, knelt down and studied the parcel for a moment. He then reached under the flask and pulled the parcel out. With a chuckle he opened it, revealing somebody's collection of pornographic magazines.

"Why the hell'd they bother to hide that?" asked one of the enginemen to nobody in particular.

Jerry just shrugged his shoulders

"That tank's clean," shouted Ted as he walked over beside Andrews, still carrying the sonar unit. "You think this is getting us anywhere?"

"I think I wish we had more to go on."

"Yeah. I'm with you. You think we'll be home by Christmas? Hannah's really going to be pissed if I miss another."

"I sure as hell hope so. I think we all believed that since this counts as a shore-duty rotation we might be home from time to time."

"Even Captain Chambers?"

"He got suckered along with the rest of us. Anybody look under the reduction gears?"

"I did. First place."

"Just for the hell of it, let's take a walk down the shaft

alley. See if we can find anything. If these guys find anything, the second engineer will beep us."

"Why not!"

With Jerry leading, they walked behind the reduction gear and stepped onto the catwalk that led to the long, narrow space through which the propeller shafts made their almost two-hundred-foot trip to the propellers. As they followed the catwalk aft, they could sense the icy waters flowing past the steel plate on either side of them, as well as the churning under the stem as the propellers rotated, forcing the water to flow aft. Every now and then they stopped to look under or behind something. All the while the two eight-inch counter-rotating propeller shafts, their oily surfaces glistening slightly, spun on either side of them, making a very faint whirring sound as they passed through the bearings that supported them.

Suddenly Ted stopped.

"You got something?" asked Jerry.

Ted knelt down and shined his flashlight behind a bearing support.

"Hell no. It's just an empty beer bottle."

* * *

Mike was sitting in his shared suite, eating a sandwich, when there was a knock on the door. With a twinge of irritation he put down the food and opened the door to find Rod Johnson, complete with plaid shirt, standing there, a look of anger on his face. "Mr. Johnson, please come in."

Johnson nodded and entered, then came right to the point. "I understand you interrogated Linda Williams an hour or two ago. Gave her a hard time. Why?"

"Does she work for you?"

"Not directly. She's an ally."

"She also has a conviction for committing a terrorist act."

"That's open to debate."

"As we discussed before, my people and I are here

because there are hints, strong hints, that something is wrong aboard this ship. It may well be drugs—which is not of significant interest to us. It may also be terrorism, which is."

"We're very sensitive with respect to terrorism. Remember, it was our ship the French government blew up about forty years ago, and it's our inflatables the whalers and tuna fishermen keep trying to sink. But what you're doing is beginning to look like harassment, an effort to torpedo this educational cruise. With every passing day, we have more and more friends in Washington, but we still have enemies. The Department of Defense, to name one. I think it would be best if you cleared it with me before talking to any of our people—or close friends."

"Mr. Johnson, although I personally agree with much of what you people are pushing, I insist upon conducting this operation as I see fit."

"By whose authority?"

"Captain Covington's."

"I'll talk to the owners, then. They're very sympathetic to us."

"I doubt they will interfere with their captain in a matter like this."

"We will see," snorted Johnson as he turned and walked out.

12

The Bellingshausen Sea

Using a cane borrowed from the ship's doctor to keep from toppling over, Ray Fuentes hobbled into the crew's lounge, looked around and spotted his target. "Ivan Singh?" he said as he approached a small, thin young man sitting in a corner, watching a soccer match on TV.

"Yes?" said Singh.

"May I see your mariner's card?"

"You one of the American navy guys doing the security check?"

"Yes," replied Ray, thinking the blue coveralls must not be as self-explanatory as they seemed to him.

"Sure," said Singh, standing and taking out his wallet.

Ray studied the card. It looked in order. For that matter, Singh had shown up on none of Alex's lists, except the crew list. And the list of Hensen's roommates.

"You're not a United States citizen," observed Ray.

"No, I'm Argentine."

"And you're an electrician?"

"No, an electronic tech, actually."

"How long have you been on this ship?"

"This is my first trip. I joined her in Rio." As he spoke, Singh's eyes returned periodically to the soccer match.

"How well did you know your roommate?"

"You mean my late roommate? Not very well, but well enough to know he was the ship's drug merchant."

"Did you buy from him?"

"No. Of course not. But everybody knew that Hensen was the man."

"What about your other roommate?"

"Swaboda? Hell no. He's young, like me . . . has a family and likes to think he has a future too."

"You knew what he was doing but you didn't report it to Mr. Ellison or any of the officers?"

"I try to mind my own business. At least when it comes to other people fucking up their own lives. Anyway, talking about things like that can be dangerous."

"Have any idea where he kept his inventory?"

"Not the slightest."

"Not in your room?"

"I don't see how."

"We'll have to look."

"Of course, amigo."

"Have you ever been in trouble with the law?"

"Whose?"

"Anybody's"

"A couple speeding tickets."

"Did Hensen ever say anything about politics?"

"You mean did he talk like a terrorist? No, I don't think so. His only interest was money as far as I could tell. That's why I always kept my locker locked."

"Did he have any special buddies?"

"Only his customers, and I don't imagine even they liked him. He was greedy and he liked to push people around just for the hell of it."

You joined the ship in Rio. Did you know anybody at the Tecmar shipyard?"

"No, the ship had moved down to a commercial pier before I joined her."

"How about Coccoli? Rojas? A guy named Omar?"

"No. Never heard of any of them. Your Spanish is very good."

"I'm Puerto Rican. Just slumming with the gringos."

"Sorry," said Singh, smiling for the first time. "I shouldn't be so defensive. If you're here to check on security, then that must mean that we have a problem, and I haven't the slightest desire to be a victim. As I said, I've got a wife and kid and I still like both of them."

"Can you think of anything you've heard, seen, smelled or even imagined that might help us determine if there is a problem and what it is?"

"No, I really can't. I mean, there're all sorts of oddballs in the crew—half of them, I'd say—but I wouldn't know where to start. A lot of the Latins think I'm a little strange with my turban and long hair. In India there're a lot of Singhs who the government suspects of being terrorists because they're Sikhs. But then there are millions of Singhs in India."

"Okay. Thanks. If anything occurs to you, no matter how harebrained, please find me. I'm Fuentes, Ray Fuentes." As he spoke, the marine pointed at his name on his coveralls.

"You can count on me. As I told you, I like things the way they are."

* * *

Wrapped in a purple ski parka that might have been a little too large for her, along with a PFD on top, Katie Sanders held her mother's hand almost as tightly as she was holding her breath. "Hey, Mom, this is great," she managed to whisper without seeming to exhale. "I think I can see them already."

Aurora Australis had anchored in the lee of a low, rocky

islet about five hundred yards off the rocky, snow-covered, western shore of the Antarctic Peninsula. The temperature was well below freezing, but thanks to the islet, the sea was reduced to a nasty chop. Despite the waves' shrinkage, Captain Covington had twisted the ship across the wind to create an even greater lee on the port side. None of this mattered in the slightest to Katie. What mattered to Katie was that there were penguins ashore. And all sorts of other great and wonderful stuff.

"Okay, People," shouted Wendell Gardner as a forty-foot hard bottom inflatable boat bounced over the chop and surged up next to the landing stage built into the ship's port side. "Before we board the HBI, I want you all to note that there is no pack ice in sight. None. This is what we've done to ourselves. Take a good look! Now let's board the boats.

"Hi, Pete," said Wendell to Peter Evans as the first group of twenty passengers emerged from the big cargo door in the ship's side and out onto the landing. "Hi, Penny."

"Good to see you, Wendell," responded Evans with an extra large smile pasted on his face, just in case one of the camera crews had him in their sights.

"Hi, Wendell," said Penny cheerfully. And Penny was cheerful, anticipating the adventure almost as much as Katie. "I can't wait to get ashore and see the sights." The fact that her husband didn't share her enthusiasm didn't bother her a bit. In fact, she was beginning to enjoy his hidden discomfort. She'd long known he disliked water almost as much as he feared making a fool of himself in public. Or his wife's making a fool of him.

Thanks to the chop, the boat was rising and falling despite Arthur Covington's best efforts. And the stage was a little slick and the water looked terribly cold. Much to Evans's relief, however, both Wendell and the stony-faced Ecuadorian deckhand working with him were well practiced at getting passengers, including Penny, off the landing and into the boat with surprising grace.

Once aboard, Pete Evans still didn't feel comfortable. In addition to pitching and rolling, the damn inflatable twisted, buckled and sagged. And nothing felt truly solid. It was as if the damn thing were made of Jell-O.

While the first boat pulled away and the second approached, the Ecuadorian deckhand scanned the next batch of passengers. His eyes settled for a moment on the Sanders. They struck him as unusually close, yet the adults also emitted the faintest hint of deep pain. The condition was all-too-familiar to him—the mixture of happiness and intense pain. He'd seen it in countless friends, relatives and neighbors over the years. He'd felt it himself.

The man who was obviously the father nodded at him and smiled. He nodded back. Then his eyes returned to the little girl in the purple coat who was occupied blowing puffs of steam into the thin, icy air. His own daughter would adore a purple coat like that. He'd have to get her one just as soon as he got home.

"Okay, Chris, you're number one," said Wendell as the second HBI pulled alongside. Chrissie, who'd been talking with Dana Sanders, turned and nodded. With her, but not really with her, was Brad. He was standing to one side with the expression of a whipped dog on his face.

After Wendell had taken great care to ensure Chrissie's comfortable transfer—and considerably less care with Brad—Tim was boarded with almost mechanical efficiency.

When Katie stepped forward, Wendell paused ever so slightly. He really didn't like kids, especially this screaming advertisement for mandatory Ritalin therapy. Leaving personalities aside, he was of the opinion that educating children was a waste of time when what was really needed was a massive reduction in their numbers. Children humans grew up to be adult humans, and it was humans who were trashing the world.

The Ecuadorian deckhand didn't pause in the slightest. Replacing his chronic expression of Andean angst with a glowing smile, he reached down to Katie and swung her up and over the side. "*Arriba, niña,*" he said, half to himself, as he transferred her safely to her father's custody. And the smile remained as he and Wendell helped the mother, after which it immediately disappeared. He had learned early that smiles, like every other valuable commodity, are not to be wasted. As for the missing engineman, about whom he'd been thinking for no particular reason, good riddance! Either he had enemies or he had a competitor even more vicious than he was.

* * *

"Damn it, Mike, this thing is getting out of hand and nothing's even happened yet," snapped Alan Parker. "It's those continuous news broadcasts—they're already tired of talking about global warming, so now they're pushing the terror bit. I'm getting calls from members of Congress demanding to know why you're really there and when you plan to get some results. We need closure on this and we need it damn fast!"

Mike, dressed in a layer of thermal diving underwear below a dry suit, stood at the open cargo door in the side of the ship. He listened to Parker on the satellite phone as he watched the last of the HBIs head ashore with its load of passengers. "I'm going to say it again, Alan, we're doing everything we can. Jerry and I are about to perform a hull inspection. We've got to get going now before the passengers return."

"You trying to hide it from them?"

"No, there're technical reasons that I don't have time to go into. I'll call you in two hours."

As soon as the last HBI was well clear of the ship, Captain Covington stopped the shafts. The ship swung back to a heading somewhere between the wind and the wind-generated current along the peninsula shore.

"You ready, Chief?" called Mike across the bay.

"I'm ready, Captain," replied Andrews as he stuffed his head into the wet suit hood and then let Kim Ackerman, who was also in a dry suit, lift the air bottle assembly up and strap it on his back.

They were, thought Kim, a real Mutt and Jeff team. The tall captain and the stocky chief, both dressed in black.

Andrews looked out at the cold, dark water with distaste. Because of his age, he'd needed a special dispensation to continue active-duty diving. He was beginning to wonder why he'd bothered to get it.

"This your first polar dive, Captain?"

"Yes. Yours?"

"Up till now I've always managed to avoid them."

* * *

Congressman Peter Evans stood alone on the slippery, rocky shore of the Antarctic Peninsula and looked around him at the utter bleakness. Gray sky, gray rocks, gray-blue sea—all highlighted by icy, off-white snow. The only color he could find, besides the clothes of his fellow passengers, were the here-and-there orange blobs on the flightless birds. At least, he comforted himself, he wasn't in that damn rubber boat. Not at the moment, anyway.

Most of the other passengers—including his wife, the Sanders and that singer—were still with the birds, seemingly mesmerized by them. He'd taken one quick look and decided that was enough wildlife for him.

Although he could still hear Wendell Gardner explaining the life cycle of penguins and their role in the environmental chain of life, he tried to concentrate on more important matters. His image, specifically. To clear his head, Evans turned and looked out into the Bellinghausen

Sea, at the dark water and the white hints of ice far off to the left.

"Desolate, isn't it, Congressman? Off the record, the attraction this place holds for some people mystifies me."

Evans turned to find James Ives, CEO of Universal Solutions and Systems, standing beside him. "Yes, it gives us all a taste of what our Planet Earth will be like if these abuses aren't brought under control."

Evans knew Ives slightly. Both were from Connecticut, although Ives had backed Evans's opponent in the last election. But, Evans reminded himself, there was always the chance, if he handled it right, that he might get Ives aboard for next year.

"Pick that up right now!" Wendell's bark cut through Evans's calculations. "The rule is that you carry out everything you carry in."

Both the congressman and the businessman turned to see a startled, and undoubtedly remorseful, Katie bend down and pick up a Kleenex that had fallen out of her jacket pocket. Had they been closer, they might have noticed the near-murderous fury that erupted from Dana's eyes as she put her arm around her wayward daughter's shoulders.

The two men watched the scene for a second in silence then turned and resumed looking out over the Bellinghausen Sea, which at the moment looked as dead as any body of water can possibly look.

"Pete," said Ives finally, "I'm very concerned about how this expedition is being handled."

"Yes, Jim?"

"From the very start I've had my doubts about the captain and crew—Covington strikes me as a bungler, and the crew, as far as I can tell, is almost entirely made up of poorly educated foreigners

"Don't get me wrong! Some of the best minds at Universal are foreigners, but these people . . . Then, all of a sudden, a pack of armed navy types appear in the middle of the night and wander around cross-examining people. I—we, all the passengers—are very concerned. Is there a bomb aboard? Or terrorists? I know what Covington has said, but I have no confidence in the man. What's the real story?"

Evans took a moment to formulate his answer. He had to be careful what he said. He started to open his mouth then realized they were surrounded—two video cameramen, a sound girl and a reporter had appeared from nowhere. They must have also tired of learning more about the penguin's life cycle. "It's a very delicate situation, Jim, but let me assure you I'm doing my very best to keep on top of it."

"Does the government have reason to believe there's a bomb aboard *Aurora Australis* or not, Congressman?" demanded the reporter, breathlessly. "These military people won't tell us anything."

"I'm afraid I can't say any more about it at this time," said Evans as he took Ives by the arm and started to walk away. "I'm sorry I can't do more to relieve your concerns at the moment, Jim, but would you join me for a drink after we get back to the ship? We have a number of things we might fruitfully discuss. I, for one, feel strongly that Washington isn't directing enough resources to Connecticut, specifically to cutting-edge organizations like yours that can make a real contribution to solving the nation's many problems."

As he pitched himself, Pete struggled to hide his own growing discomfort. He was uncomfortable enough just being aboard the ship, and now the low-level contagion of unease about the navy's presence that was spreading slowly and insidiously through the passengers was making his edginess all the sharper.

* * *

By the time Mike and Jerry had completed suiting up, the ship was lying at an unfortunate angle across both current and waves, the seas were beginning to break over the landing, and the wind was starting to howl again. "I'll tell you, Captain," said Jerry before stuffing his mouthpiece in, "I've never envied those guys who dive into holes in the ice, but at least the water's calm for them. This is a mess!"

"Lets move our butts, then. We don't have that much time." With that, Mike led the way to the mid-sized HBI that was tied to the stage with its engines running and two men seated in it.

"Hit it, Chief," said Mike when the HBI was alongside *Aurora*'s bow. Each diver grabbed a bundle of two lines, one of which led down from a boat boom rigged out from one of the ship's bows and the other from a boat boom rigged out from the other bow. Clutching the lines, they rolled over the HBI's side into the heaving mess. After the briefest of surface checks, they disappeared into the rolling gray waters.

Once they were all the way under the ship, where the surface waves were barely noticeable, the current—and the need for the two lines—became much more obvious.

No matter how different they may look above the waterline, there is a basic sameness to ships when viewed from below. They are, in general, a reddish black mass that hangs over you and, even if not moving in the slightest, gives the impression of preparing to crush you any second. They are also essentially smooth, except for a few easy-to-identify features such as water intakes and outlets and domes for the depth sounder transducers. In *Aurora*'s case, thanks to just having come out of overhaul, the bottom was also squeaky clean. The search should have been a piece of cake.

Under more civilized circumstances Mike would have inspected by swimming from bow to stern, along the keel, then moved outboard about twenty feet and reversed direction. After two or three trips fore and aft on each side, the inspection would have been completed in an hour. Unless, of course, they found something. With the current running as it was, they had to do it the hard way—using the lines, and their legs, to move back and forth sideways across the ship from waterline to waterline, then dropping back and repeating the process.

"I'm already getting cold," griped Andrews, primarily to himself.

"We're going to have to pick up our pace if we want to live to see the end of this dive," said Chambers sympathetically.

At that point, Kim's electronically distorted but still recognizable voice came over the voice communicators: "Lead diver, this is Kim. The weather's really making up fast, so the captain's recalling the boats. He says he's going to have to start turning the shafts in about five minutes. Do you want the HBI to pick you up on the port side, where it's a little calmer?"

Damn, thought Mike, the temptation of Christ! He was freezing, Jerry was freezing; it was all they could do to keep their arms and legs moving, and they hadn't found a damn thing. There was nothing he would have liked better than to surface and get warm, but the inspection had to be completed. Especially the stern area, where it was easiest to hide things. "Kim, tell Captain Covington to go ahead and turn his shafts and recover the passengers. We're going to keep going until we get too close to the screws for comfort. Then we'll surface on the port side and come back down again for a few minutes after all the passengers are aboard."

"That's not very safe, sir."

"No, it's not, but it has to be done."

"Yes, sir. I'll tell the captain and we'll be waiting for you on the port side. Amidships."

"Roger."

The two divers had rearranged their lines and prepared to pull themselves to starboard, into the current, when something big and dark flashed past the corner of Mike's eye. "What was that?"

"Looked like a seal to me, Captain. A damn big one."

The shape reappeared and rocketed toward them, although its course was somewhat erratic. "You're right, Boats, that's the biggest I've ever seen." The beast continued on at them. Then, about ten feet away, it turned on its side, reaching out and snapping at them as it did. "Damn big teeth," remarked Mike.

"You notice the spots on its sides?"

"Yes. Leopard seal, you think?"

"Look at that fin. Looks like something bit it off. Screws up his swimming."

"And his hunting, probably."

"Don't they say crippled predators are most likely to attack people?"

"But this is a seal, Boats," said Mike as a trickle of icy water snuck in between his mask and his hood. "If it were an orca or a mako, I'd have been more concerned."

As he spoke, Mike glanced at Jerry. Was the chief getting a little jumpy? Might well be. The mission was beginning to get to all of them—no sleep, not knowing what they were looking for and not even knowing if there was anything to look for. Just endless circles.

They worked their way across the bottom, keeping an eye on the visitor, which was itself swimming in erratic circles around them. Without warning the seven-hundred-pound beast suddenly swerved in to within five feet, reached out and snapped again.

With mounting concern the two divers continued to kick and pull and scan the bottom of the ship. There was a rumble all around them followed almost immediately by an almost painful pounding sensation that filled the water.

At the same time the current became even more confused. "Captain Covington's begun to twist," remarked Mike as the propellers began to turn in opposite directions, one going forward, one in reverse. As they did, they created a boiling mass of water under the ship's stern and added an element to the current that threatened to carry them into the spinning, twelve-foot meat grinders that normally propelled the ship.

* * *

Two or three feet above Mike's head, Marcello Cagayan crawled slowly through *Aurora*'s bilges, attempting to avoid drinking from the foot or so of water that had accumulated along either side of the keel. As he twisted and squirmed, he flashed his light beside and ahead of him, looking for anything that didn't belong there.

The portion of the bilges which he was searching, the thirty or forty feet that ran from the huge diesels to the reduction gears, was jammed with at least a dozen large pipes. It was an area in which work had been done during the overhaul, when several motors had been removed and some of the surrounding deck plating had been torn up to provide access. Accordingly, it was one of the first areas Ted and Jerry had searched using their mini-cam—a device similar to that used by doctors when they want to see inside you.

The results of the mini-cam survey had been inconclusive, so Marcello Cagayan was specially selected, because of his small size, to search the area in person. And there was a portion, fifteen or twenty feet long, that was so jammed that not even the tiny Filipino could get through.

Determined to play the role to perfection, Marcello continued to squirm and squeeze his way forward until his shoulders were totally jammed. He could feel the steel all around him vibrating as the engines pounded and the shafts turned. He flashed the light ahead of him on the mass of piping. From where he lay he couldn't even see, much less count, all of them. A dozen, at least. He backed off a little, jammed the light between two pipes and reached down into the water. There they were—the two at the bottom, down near the hull itself. The pipes that didn't belong there.

It had to be them. They were exactly where he'd been told they would be. They'd been added during the overhaul and were filled with long, shaped charges of plastic explosive, wrapped in two layers of gas-proof plastic and then inserted into steel piping which had been intentionally weakened along one side. When detonated, the charges were calculated to cut a long gash in the ship's bottom. A gash that would be next to impossible to reach to repair, especially if a wave of burning diesel oil were flowing aft from the ruptured fuel tank.

Satisfied that he had seen everything it was possible to see, Cagayan squirmed backward, out of the space and up into the engine room. After reporting to the second engineer that he had found nothing, he walked aft to the reduction gears. There he dropped down into the bilges again and started to squirm forward, alert for anything that didn't belong.

* * *

Arthur Covington stood at the remote steering and engine controls on the port wing of his bridge and looked down at the small flotilla of HBIs returning from shore jammed with tourists. "On the forecastle," he said into the mouthpiece of his headphones as the wind blew through his thinning, gray hair, "how's the anchor chain tending?"

"Forward, Captain," reported the man posted in the bow. "Everything looks good."

"Very well."

Covington was very unhappy with what he was doing. Loading passengers from HBIs while the ship was held across the wind with screws turning was not standard procedure, although he and other captains did it from time to time. The weather was simply so unpredictable, he reassured himself. There'd been occasions when he'd landed parties in a dead calm and picked them up three hours later in conditions just like this. And as for the naval persons, they shouldn't be swimming near the screws. But then, they were paid to do that sort of thing, so he couldn't worry too much about them. He turned and looked a little farther astern than he had been. God damn it! "Kim," he snapped into the mouthpiece, "tell the boatswain to instruct boat number seven to keep farther away from the stern."

"Yes, Captain."

"This is the bow, Captain. The anchor chain is beginning to droop."

"Roger," replied Covington as he increased the number of revolutions on the port shaft, which was backing.

But, he realized, HBIs and turning propellers were the least of his worries. His ship might very well be in danger, and he bore the ultimate responsibility for her well-being. And the passengers were beginning to get restive. Three had been in that morning, demanding that he "do something." Although no new evidence had appeared, the passing of time seemed to be increasing their fear of bombs and terrorists. Perhaps he was being too stubborn. Perhaps he should have turned north to Ushuaia as soon as Chambers and his gang had dropped down from the sky.

No, damn it! He needed more. Just leaving the pier was dangerous.

He remembered that Chrissie Clark had volunteered to perform again after dinner tonight. He liked her singing, he liked the mellow glow she generated. Her performance would undoubtedly take some of the edge off the customers' nerves. And his own.

* * *

Oblivious to the action on the surface, where the HBIs were hurrying from shore to the landing platform and back, pounding over the increasing chop and trailing foamy white wakes as they went, Mike and Jerry continued their increasingly dreary sweep of *Aurora*'s bottom. Kicking and pulling, they forced themselves from side to side, growing increasingly cold and tired as they did. Both were also beginning to develop headaches from the powerful harmonic waves generated by the ship's screws churning in different directions. One shoving massive volumes of water forward, the other forcing only slightly less in the opposite direction.

Suddenly, while Mike was examining a large cooling water intake, he felt something slam against him. He turned to discover that it was Jerry. "You okay, Chief?"

"That goddamned seal just bit off most of my right fin."

Only half believing, Mike twisted to look at the fin. It was almost totally gone! The beast had missed Jerry's toes by less than an inch.

"That's it, Chief," said Mike. "If we don't knock off, we're going to be two dead sailors in no time."

"I may already be dead, Boss. I won't know until I warm up a little."

"Kim, this is lead diver. We're going to come up and warm up and wait for the captain to finish twisting. Stand by to pick us up about three-quarters of the way aft on the port side. And be advised that a very hostile leopard seal is swimming around here. It's not only challenged us, but has even taken a bite of Chief Andrews's fin."

"Roger, lead diver. There have been one or two reports in the past of this sort of behavior."

Despite their frigid condition and strong desire to get out of the water, the two divers executed their ascent slowly and carefully, back-to-back, alert for the passenger-filled HBIs racing around. Not to mention the leopard seal, which continued to circle them with what Mike had to assume was a look of hunger and frustration on its doglike face.

13

The Bellingshausen Sea

Forty minutes after the HBI crew had dragged them out of the water, Mike and Jerry were sitting in the cargo bay, out of the wind, drinking hot coffee and watching as the last of the passengers reboarded the ship and the deck force started to recover the HBIs.

"Captain Covington says he's stopping the shafts," reported Kim after listening intently to a walkie-talkie.

"Thank you, Kim. You have those bang sticks ready?"

"Right here, Captain," said the girl, handing him a yard-long aluminum pole with a ten-gauge shotgun shell and contact trigger at one end and a handle and lanyard at the other. "To take it off safe, pull out that pin just ahead of the handle."

"Roger. Chief, ready? Now we get to the juicy part."

"Aye, aye, sir," replied the chief boatswain's mate as he stood and groaned, accepting his bang stick. While he felt no personal animosity toward the seal, neither did he wish to lose a foot, or anything else, to the beast.

After rigging new air supplies, Mike and Jerry grabbed their guy lines, jumped over the side and drifted down and aft. Although both were still chilled, they were no longer totally frozen. That, combined with the absence of the turning screws' head-pounding harmonics, allowed them to work much faster than they had on their first dive.

Predictably, now that they were prepared for the seal, there was no sign of it.

"Boss, this is Alex," said the communicator a few minutes after they'd reentered the icy, clear waters of the Bellinghausen Sea. "I've just learned from a contact at the FBI that the third engineer of this ship, a man named Jacob Rounding, had a daughter killed by police about twenty years ago in a political demonstration."

"What was she doing?"

"Not much as far as I can tell. Waving a sign and shouting. In all, half a dozen were killed or wounded."

"Anything else on his record?"

"Not a thing we can find. Something of a loner and may have had a drinking problem in the past, but his last couple ships were unhappy to see him leave."

"Why'd it take so long for this to come up?" asked Mike, drifting off to one side despite his efforts to remain stationary.

"Apparently Rounding never married the mother and abandoned them both, and the girl used her mother's maiden name. The mother never cooperated much with the media, and since some of the other families did, they got all the press and she just fell between the cracks."

"Shit! I can imagine that might be more than enough to give a guy a grudge. I want you and Ray to find this Rounding and talk to him, right away. A grudge, assuming he has one, doesn't prove anything, but it's as good as any other lead we've gotten."

"Roger."

"You get all that, Chief?"

"Yes, Captain."

"Let's try to finish this up quickly without overlooking anything."

"I thought that was our objective all along."

* * *

"Do you know where Mr. Rounding, the third engineer, is?"

Jacob Rounding, walking with his customary stoop down a passageway toward the Auxiliary Machinery Room, heard the words from around a corner and didn't recognize the voice. He paused, his heart beating.

"No, sir," replied the voice of an engineman he did know. "He may be in the Auxiliary Room, through there."

The third engineer peeked around the corner of the passageway and saw two figures in blue coveralls disappear into the Auxiliary Room. He stepped back from the corner, half-paralyzed by fear and guilt. After all these years it had come back to get him!

It was such a stupid thing to do—writing three letters to the president saying he was an asshole, an asshole vampire, and that when he got the chance he'd drive a stake through his fucking chest. He'd been between ships then—his sour personality seeming to mask his basically high level of competence—wondering if he'd ever get another and drinking heavily. It was about five years after Annie had been murdered, and he'd been so terribly lonely and discouraged. That was back when he could still feel lonely and discouraged, instead of just numb. Then he'd sobered up and concluded that the president gets thousands of letters like that every year and that there was no way they could track down each and every one of them.

The relief had been great but far from complete. The sharp fear that he would be detected and apprehended receded, but a lingering unease had remained, along with his burning anger and cancerous feelings of guilt. Both had continued to smolder, slowly burning out his soul, over all the intervening years.

Now, what the hell to do? He could turn himself in to them—but he was undoubtedly now classified as a terrorist, and everybody knew what they did to suspected terrorists! He couldn't face that. A wave of abject fear, of terror if you will, swept through him.

He could turn himself in to Captain Covington and ask to be turned over to the Ecuadorians since the ship was flagged there. That would probably be worse. Anyway, the American government would take him no matter what Covington said.

He would return to his cabin and shoot himself. He didn't really want to die, but he couldn't bear the thought of spending the rest of his life in a cell, beaten and tormented. His mind now settled, Rounding turned and walked rapidly back down the passageway, up two ladders and into his cabin. Trembling, he removed the small automatic from the lower drawer of his desk, sat down and studied the weapon. How do you do it so it hurts the least? he wondered. Through the temple or through the top of the mouth?

He knew damn well he didn't want to die, but what choice did he have? His life was shit, but he didn't want to end it, either. But neither did he want to live the nightmare the government would force him to endure.

Maybe he could escape. No, that was stupid. To Antarctica? There were a bunch of foreign research stations within fifty or so miles. One of them might be Russian, he thought. He could claim to be a political prisoner. They might go for that.

Without putting down the automatic, without even thinking more about what he was doing, Jake Rounding grabbed his heavy thermal jacket and dashed out the door. He paused as he pulled the cabin door shut behind him. He heard voices coming from his left, from the direction of the Auxiliary Room. He turned to his right and ran as quietly as he could down the passageway. He came to a watertight door, which he stepped through and slammed behind him. Then he jammed the dogs so it would be impossible to open from the other side.

As he ran through the twisting corridors, up and down ladders, he passed various other crew members, some of whom noticed the look of alarm on his face. “What’s going on, Mr. Rounding? Is there trouble? Did they find a bomb?”

The third engineer didn’t reply. He just charged on past them.

“Mr. Rounding,” boomed the PA system, “Mr. Jacob Rounding, please report to the bridge. Anybody knowing the whereabouts of Third Engineer Rounding are instructed to report this information to the bridge and, if possible, detain him.”

Jake paused for a second and then continued on toward the cargo bay. When he burst into the big, open space, twenty startled eyes turned in his direction.

“Stand back,” snarled the fugitive, drawing the automatic from his pocket as he dashed across the space, knocking down Marcello Cagayan, who was helping flush the outboards with fresh water.

Cagayan landed on the deck with a thump. Startled and shocked at first, he quickly reached into his pocket for the cell phone. While everybody else watched Rounding dart over to the ramp down to the landing stage, Cagayan took out the phone and examined it carefully, terrified that it might be broken.

It seemed okay.

“Get that HBI back into the water,” snapped Rounding, pointing the gun at Kim Ackerman. Understandably, nobody was interested in arguing with the automatic, so the HBI splashed back into the water almost immediately. Without saying another word, Jake Rounding jumped into the boat, lit off the two big outboards and, after backing away from the stage, roared off into the Antarctic afternoon, headed south.

* * *

“It should be on the passageway that branches off to the right, up ahead,” said Ray as he hobbled along, trying to keep up with Alex. “There’s a nameplate on the door.”

"Roger," said Alex. She was tempted to slow down a little for Ray, but at the same time, she knew she shouldn't. Their job was to find this guy and Ray was able to take care of himself. Just as they reached the place where one passageway branched off from the other, they heard a muted *thunk*.

"What was that?"

"A watertight door being slammed shut," replied Ray, drawing his sidearm as he did and starting to hobble faster than Alex would have ever believed possible for someone in his condition. They sprinted around the corner and past the door that said "Jacob Rounding." They came to a screeching halt at the watertight door at the end of the passageway. Panting and sweating, Ray grabbed the dogging wheel and tried to turn it.

"Shit, he's jammed it."

Alex threw her long, thin frame into the fight, but between them, they still couldn't get the wheel to budge.

"Okay, we've got to backtrack," puffed Alex.

"Backtrack to where?" asked Ray. "Where do we think he's going?"

Alex pulled her walkie-talkie out of her pocket and called Captain Covington. "This is Alex Mahan, Captain. We finally tracked this Mr. Rounding down—he was leaving his quarters—but he ran and has managed to lose us. Would you pass the word again for all hands to report if they see him and, if possible, try to detain him? We have no way of knowing whether he's armed or not and why he's running."

"Very well, Ms. Mahan." Covington didn't sound very happy, she thought.

No more than three minutes after the second announcement boomed over the ship's PA system, Alex's walkie-talkie came to life again. "He's in the cargo bay, Ms. Mahan. He's armed and is in the process of commandeering an HBI."

"An HBI? Where in God's name can he go?"

"The man's always been a little strange . . . maybe he thinks he can reach one of the research stations, although I can't see what good that would do for him. What, precisely, do you suspect him of doing? Is there an explosive device?"

"That's the worst part of it, Captain. All we know is that he had a daughter who was killed in a political demonstration fifteen or twenty years ago."

"If you want to try to catch him, you'd better get down to the cargo bay."

By the time they reached the bay, Rounding was long gone. Fortunately, Captain Covington had thought to order another HBI put back in the water. While they were waiting for the almost empty fuel tank to be topped off, Alex called Ted. "Where are you?"

"In the forward storerooms. What the hell's going on?"

"Ray and I went to question the third engineer, whose daughter, it turns out, was killed fifteen years ago in a political demonstration. Instead of talking to us, he's run. He's grabbed an HBI and headed off to God knows where. Ray and I are going to follow in another HBI. You get up here so you'll be available when Captain Chambers pops up."

"Roger."

* * *

Jake Rounding stood behind the HBI's steering console, braced between it and the helmsman's seat, while the boat pounded, skidded and twisted over the choppy seas—flying at times into the sharp air and then crashing back onto the cold, hard water. Suddenly, with absolutely no warning, he burst into a laugh of true joy. Where it came from he neither knew nor cared, but a great weight had been lifted from his shoulders and for the first time in over twenty years he felt alive. Totally alive.

He hadn't the slightest idea where the nearest research

station was. Neither did he know which country operated it. The whole idea had been stupid, foolish, but it had indirectly saved him by driving him to take the HBI. Now, all the dreary years of empty wandering were over. He knew exactly where he was going—Fiddler's Green as the real oldsters still sometimes called it—and he eagerly looked forward to his arrival.

He'd deserted his little daughter and allowed her to be shot down in the street. He'd treated her mother like trash and had done penance for it all by not allowing himself to live for so much as thirty seconds over the intervening years. But his penance was now over.

He looked back at *Aurora* and saw that another orange HBI had left the ship and was following him. It was at least half an hour behind him. He had half an hour to live a lifetime and he intended to do just that. He felt and tasted the icy wind; he absorbed the stark beauty of the pitiless, icy land lying to his left and the gray waves breaking all around him. He thought back to Annie when she was four. He relished it all and made it all part of him. Yesterday disappeared, as did tomorrow. Only today mattered. Only this particular instant, which now seemed a lifetime. He felt his heart pounding and his blood flowing and the cold air flowing in and out of his lungs. He found himself standing up straight after decades of stooping.

Driven by its twin 350-horsepower outboards, the HBI charged up and over another wave, taking wing in the process.

Oh my God, I'm flying, thought Jake with delight as the boat, its engines screaming, hung suspended in the air for what seemed to him an eternity.

* * *

"Can you see what the hell he's doing?" asked Mike over the radio as he looked at the radar screen on the console of his HBI.

"He's still headed south," replied Ray. "We're not close enough yet to see any more than you can on your radar."

"You seem to be gaining on him."

"I think the HBI rides a little better with two people in it."

"Remember, we need him alive."

"Roger."

"And he's armed."

"Roger."

Mike continued to chase the other two HBIs with both throttles jammed full ahead. Bending in the middle, the boat's bow drove up and over a wave, tossing the HBI into the air, where the wind blew it off to one side. It landed on the crest of the next wave and flexed again as the bow tried to dive into the trough, only to be forced skyward once more. And again it lunged off to one side. Driving one of these things, he thought, is like riding on the head of a snake hunting for a rat. Thanks to the dry suit he was still wearing and his mostly dry undergarments, he was at least beginning to warm up. His body, that is, not his soul.

What had the man done that caused him to run? Left an explosive device? Poured arsenic in the potable water supply?

Shit! He had to find out before it was too late.

He picked up the radio again. "*Aurora*, this is Captain Chambers."

"Roger, Captain, this is the mate of the watch."

"I want you to get hold of the ship's doctor and have her test the water supply for every possible poison she can think of."

"She tests the water once a day, sir."

"For bacteria. Now please forward my request to her. I'm sure Captain Covington will approve."

"Roger."

* * *

"Congressman Evans, Congressman Evans!"

Pete Evans, who was standing with about fifty other

passengers on the boat deck, watching the HBIs race across the gray waters, turned to find Jen, the brunette, with her video person.

"Can you confirm that the man they're chasing is a terrorist?"

"I'm sorry but I can neither confirm nor deny that," replied Evans, his face ashen as he squirmed inwardly. It was becoming clear to him that an icy death was an increasingly real possibility.

"Does that mean that there definitely is an explosive device somewhere aboard this ship?" The mention of an explosive device elicited a gasp from some of the nearby passengers, many of whom had turned their attention from the now-distant HBIs to the interview.

"I'm really not at liberty to go into details at this time."

"Why haven't the FBI or Homeland Security been called in?"

"You can rest assured they will be if necessary."

In hope of getting something a little more newsworthy, Jen turned to a female passenger standing bundled up against the weather. "Can you tell me what you think? Is that man a terrorist? Are you satisfied with the authorities' response?"

The woman looked confused, her eyes as big as saucers. "I don't know what to think . . . Nobody is telling us anything."

* * *

Now there're two of them, thought Jake as he looked aft over the two big outboards. And the first was getting close, close enough to start shooting very soon. If they did shoot, they might only wound him.

He looked around at his desolate surroundings and continued to feel an overwhelming joy. The glow of the past half hour still warmed him through and through, like the mindless buzz of too much rum. The universe was a big place, he told himself. Much bigger than he had ever imagined before.

Everything was possible, all regrets washed away. Anticipation was folly and fear irrelevant. Now was now and that was it. Now was the wind screaming through his hair, the pounding of the boat, the sense of flight, of freedom. He had sinned and he had done his penance, and now he had been permitted to live out what was left of his life in a state of near ecstasy. So great was the universe, he told himself, that he might yet get a chance to see his Annie again.

The time had come. He felt no fear, no hesitation. Off to his right lay a large, rocky islet, faced with high cliffs. He turned and headed for the highest cliff, locking the steering wheel as he did. He then sat back in the chair, drew the pistol and pushed the barrel against his temple.

There wasn't a tremor in Jake Rounding's body, not the slightest hesitation in his mind, but the HBI was pitching and shaking wildly. Fearful that he might only injure himself, Jake placed his left hand on the barrel to steady it and then fired. So great was the roar of the engines and the howling of the wind that the *crack* of the pistol was inaudible fifty yards away.

* * *

Mike drove his HBI over and around the curling waves, keeping one eye ahead and one on the radar. "What the hell's he doing now?' he snapped into the radio.

"He just turned right, Boss, and is headed for that islet," replied Alex.

"I can see that. What's he *doing*?"

"As far as we can tell, he's just sitting in the driver's seat, driving the HBI into the rocks."

"God damn it! That makes no sense," growled Mike into the wind.

* * *

"Jeez, Ray!"

"I don't believe it! You'd better tell the boss."

"Boss, this is Alex," she spoke into the radio. "Rounding

just drove the HBI right into the rocks. A wave picked it up and slammed it into the cliff . . . it did a backward somersault and now it's lying upside down, tangled in the rocks at the base of the cliff with the surf breaking over it."

"Get in there and get him."

"Aye, aye, Boss," replied Alex, a note of asperity in her voice. "He's wearing the dry suit, isn't he?" she added to Ray.

Ray throttled back and cruised slowly back and forth along the rocky shore, looking for any sign of life, any hint of ambush. The man did, after all, have an automatic with him. Meanwhile, Alex rooted through the HBI's lockers. "Here's one," she finally almost shouted. "I knew there had to be at least one. In fact, here's a second."

"What?"

"Emergency thermal survival wraps. In case somebody gets soaked and doesn't have any dry clothes."

"How fortunate we found them," said Ray, dryly. "Now the boss won't have to feel guilty about us. You see any sign of him ashore?"

Alex studied the islet. "No. And I don't see where he could hide. He must have been pretty badly beaten up when the HBI went ashore."

Ray slowed and turned in toward the wrecked HBI.

"How deep is it up forward?"

"About four feet where there aren't any rocks."

"Good. We're going to do it the way Jerry would."

"It's too bad Jerry isn't here to demonstrate."

Gunning the two big engines, each billowing clouds of blue-white smoke, which were immediately blown away, Ray backed into the waves. The waves returned the favor by breaking furiously over the transom and pouring cascades of icy water into the boat.

"Okay," Ray finally said when they were about a hundred feet out, "let go." Alex, who was up to her knees in water, pushed the largest anchor they could find over the side.

With the backing engines throttled way down and Alex

keeping a strain on the anchor line, the boat drifted forward. "Okay," she reported, "I think it's set."

"Good. Now you come and take the helm."

Once Alex was at the controls, Ray worked his way forward—his eyes still scanning the islet for any sign of movement—as the HBI pitched and rolled and twisted, until he was hanging over the bow. By now, both were totally soaked and shivering.

"Stop the engines and raise them," shouted Ray, his teeth beginning to chatter, as he tumbled over the bow with the HBI's painter in his hand. "Shit," he gasped as he landed in the water, his heart stopping for a beat or two and his legs going numb almost instantly. At least his ankle didn't hurt anymore. "Go, Alex!" he shouted again as he turned and, placing the painter over his shoulder, started to march in place toward the rocks.

Alex finished securing the anchor line so the boat was held stern-to the breaking seas. She then paused a second, observing the waves just as Jerry would have insisted she do. When one wave had broken and partially retreated, she slipped over the bow with as much grace and balance as she could—only to immediately trip on a loose rock and disappear underwater.

Oh God! She tried to think and found she couldn't. Her brain had seized up, leaving only the most basic of instincts to drive her. Her body stiffened and a mouthful of icy water threatened to be her last.

Hearing her splash, Ray looked back over his shoulder. "You okay?"

Alex floundered for several seconds—although at the time they seemed like hours to her—and was almost overrun by the HBI as it was driven forward by the next wave. After gasping and stumbling, Alex finally got her footing. "No," she was able to stutter, "but I'll make it."

Both of their words were now clipped, forced, breathless, due to the near impossibility of getting the muscles around their mouths to move the way they wanted them to.

"Good," cheered Ray as a wave rose to his neck, "because in a few minutes we'll both be dead."

Alex forced her way through the violently churning water until she reached what was left of Rounding's HBI. She quickly realized the boat was firmly anchored by the mass of its two big, and now very dead, engines. Without pausing—because pausing takes time, and neither she nor Ray had any—she forced her near-paralyzed lungs to gulp in a breath of razor-sharp air and felt them burn. She dropped to her knees, then her hands and knees and looked under the wreckage.

Without a mask her view was both fuzzy and confused by the roiling water, and at first she saw nothing of interest. Just as the pain in her lungs became unbearable, she spotted what could be Rounding—wedged between the console and the seat. When her lungs screamed loud enough, she dragged herself out from under, stood up and took several deep breaths, her brain too numb to even curse. The second time under she was able to grab one of Jake's legs and pull. At first the body moved, then the other leg jammed up against the side of the HBI. Somehow, in a fury, she grabbed the wayward foot and pulled it over beside the other. She then pulled again and the body slipped partway out from under. Standing, she pulled the body the rest of the way out and—pummeled by the waves—headed for their HBI, dragging Rounding by the collar. With every shuddering breath, her lungs felt as if they were being massaged with a lighted blowtorch.

"Well done, Alex." Ray tried to say it, but it came out an almost incomprehensible jumble of sound.

Alex and her prize reached the HBI just when a wave was ebbing. As the boat dropped and the water roiled around her, Alex shoved the body half over the gunnel, only to collapse herself. She found it amazing how low the HBI's gunnels appeared when you were in the boat and how high when you were in the water.

Ray turned and, while keeping a strain on the painter, stumbled back to the HBI and gave Alex the biggest shove he could muster. He then did the same to the body, and with Alex pulling, they got Rounding into the half-swamped boat. Then it was Ray's turn to collapse, barely able to hang on to the line rigged along the gunnel.

Alex grabbed the soggy, frozen marine under his arms and, with a heave so mighty it surprised her, got him over the side and into the boat. They looked at each other a second, oblivious to Mike's HBI, which was now about two hundred yards away. Alex stepped over to the console and turned the ignition, praying that the electrical system wasn't soaked, while Ray started to haul on the anchor line. Both were on the verge of completely losing control of their bodies. It was only by the most strenuous acts of will that they succeeded in doing anything other than shudder.

One after the other the engines started with a growl, and Alex lowered them while Ray continued to pull on the anchor line, the breaking waves fighting his every effort. "Okay," he said finally, tossing the anchor line as far from the boat as he could, "we're under way." Alex spun the HBI and headed away from the islet.

"You leaving the anchor?"

"Hell yes. And the wreck too. What do I care if somebody gives SECDEF a ticket for leaving garbage in an environmentally sensitive area?"

Alex had to smile, despite the throbbing numbness that scorched her every nerve.

"You have Rounding?" demanded the radio as they struggled to wrap themselves in the thermal blankets. And to hold them in place.

"Affirmative, Boss," replied Alex finally. "He's dead, I'm afraid. Can't say what killed him and we're too busy trying to avoid joining him to look carefully,"

"Well done, the two of you. We'll work out the details when we get back to the ship. I'll escort you."

"Roger."

"So, *chica*, no matter what the boss says, we have not had such a good day today," stuttered Ray a few minutes later above the growl of the engines.

Chica! There were few men Alex would allow to get away with that . . . and Ray was one of them. "No, *chico*, today has not been our best."

"You think this guy was really a terrorist?"

"Either that or he was utterly insane, and I can't honestly guess which. So much of this mission doesn't fit together."

"If he was, what did he leave for us to find?"

"Let's leave that to the boss to worry about for now. We've still got to get back to the damn ship and warm up. I hurt now more than I ever have in my entire life. I can barely steer this damn boat I'm shaking so hard."

Ray, his face an unhealthy mixture of blue and pasty white, just nodded as he hung on for dear life and balanced on his one good leg, desperate not to be tossed over the side as the HBI bounced, skidded and slid across the choppy gray waters.

14

The Bellingshausen Sea

"I don't like doing it one damn bit, but the media has forced our hand. According to the owners, Jen and Jessica and what's his name have managed to convince the entire world that Captain Chambers's people identified and killed a terrorist who was an officer of this ship. We're going to Ushuaia and offload the passengers."

Covington paused to look around the conference table at Mike; Ernesto Montalba, *Aurora*'s chief engineer; the purser; the chief mate; and Dave Ellison, the ship's security officer.

"Arthur," said Montalba, "I still find it difficult to believe Jake was a terrorist. Strange, yes, but not a terrorist."

Mike, who had been frowning, looked especially sour when he heard the chief engineer. He didn't really believe Rounding was a terrorist either, and he was furious that the media was attributing his death directly to Ray and Alex. He was certain Alan had fanned the flames, and he resented it. There was nothing the bastard would like better than a dead terrorist to point at. One who had been identified and neutralized by Mike and his people.

"Is there a plan yet for the passengers?" asked Winters.

"More or less," replied the purser. "The owners are arranging for several charter flights out of Ushuaia, and we're going to offer them three choices—a three-day trek through Patagonia, three days more in Buenos Aires or a direct flight home and a modest refund."

"This is going to cost a fortune," observed the chief mate.

Yes, it is, thought Covington. And it will probably also cost me my job.

"What about the sponsors . . . Greenpeace?"

"Publicly they're totally supportive and Rod Johnson seems to agree with the decision. Privately, some of their people have been whispering to the press that the American government has engineered this whole thing to screw them up," reported Covington. "If all goes well," continued the captain, "we'll be safely anchored in Ushuaia in two to three days. In the meantime, Captain Chambers intends to continue searching. Jim," he nodded at the purser, "will have his hands full and so will you, Dave. In addition to ensuring that nobody steals the passengers' jewels, you're going to have considerably more upset passengers than usual."

"I've already noticed an increased level of irritability among them since Hensen disappeared," Ellison said.

"You haven't found anything new about that, have you? Something that Captain Chambers's people may have missed?"

"No."

Covington sighed. He hated having to abandon his schedule. He hated having people die—even suspected terrorists—and he hated mysteries.

* * *

"Well done, Mike, well done to all of you." Alan's satisfaction, and even relief, was totally clear, despite the electronic mangling of his voice. "You and your people identified and neutralized the terrorist—before he could act—under the most trying of circumstances. It's on all the networks, complete with interviews with some very relieved passengers. They're also suggesting that the man who was lost overboard was killed because he was interfering with the scheme. All we need now is for you to get your stuff together and hold a press conference. You and Alex. Keep it simple; we'll fill them in later with all the details."

Mike was standing in the suite he shared with Jerry, dressed in a borrowed bathrobe and drinking a double shot of brandy, hoping it would make him at least feel warm, even if he wasn't. As he listened to Alan, he wanted to throw the phone on the deck. "Alan," he finally growled, "you're so damned worried about your turf war with Homeland Security you're not thinking straight. We have absolutely no evidence this Rounding was a terrorist. All he did was run—he didn't attack anybody. And there seems plenty of evidence that he's been highly unstable for some time, although nobody really paid much attention to it. The five of us, along with Captain Covington and his chief engineer, are still inclined to believe he was just nuts. That he lost it for some reason—possibly the circumstances of his daughter's death. We'll probably never know. Furthermore, we didn't kill him. He killed himself. And the guy who went overboard was the ship's drug dealer."

"The media seem to think that Fuentes and Alex killed him."

"They didn't."

"There were no witnesses."

"They didn't even fire. The round that killed him came from his own automatic."

"By the time that's established nobody will care. None of that disproves my case, which, Captain, is now policy!"

"Roger," replied Mike, after pouring the rest of the brandy down his throat.

"Keep me posted."

"There's more."

"What?"

"Even though we can't find a terrorist or anything else, both Covington and I have had enough. We're going to head northwest for a few hours to get clear of the peninsula then turn northeast and go to Ushuaia. The ship's owners aren't happy about it since they agree with you, but they're making arrangements for the passengers."

"I have no objection to aborting the voyage at this point. Like I said, keep me posted."

"And one more thing—the stabilizer system has crapped out, so you may see a lot very unhappy passengers on TV soon."

"Rounding!"

"No, a gasket on the hydraulic system. They figure it will take four to six hours to repair."

"Keep me posted."

As Mike switched the phone off, Jerry stepped out of the bathroom, freshly showered and looking almost alive. "You look pissed, Captain. That must have been Alan Parker."

"You want to do a press conference—tell the world how we tracked down and killed a dangerous terrorist?"

"Pleased to take care of it, sir, but Parker won't be happy with the result."

"I guess we'll forget about the press conference. Instead, we'll go back to looking, just in case Rounding or somebody else did leave us a present after all."

* * *

"Okay, Cagayan, take a break," one of the engine room supervisors shouted down into the bilges. "Get some chow and some rack time and be back in six hours."

"Okay," replied Marcello. He worked his way back to a hatch and popped up and out. After using a solvent to clean off much of the oil and other crud that had accumulated on his hands and shoes, he trudged up two ladders to the passageway leading to the crew's mess. Bilges, he thought.

They were his destiny, his whole reason for existing. Up till now.

When he reached the mess, he collected a bowl of stew and bread and sat down to eat while he watched the TV. The stew was good, so he got a second bowl, figuring he would need it that night. Once done, he started to leave, but found he couldn't take his eyes off the TV. Especially now that the media people had taken over one of the ship's channels and were providing almost nonstop coverage so the passengers could see what interested them most: themselves.

He knew he should hit the rack and get some rest because he had a very busy night ahead of him—almost certainly his last night—but watching the drama unfold was simply too enthralling to miss. Contrary to Alan Parker's calculations, the passengers—all eager to be interviewed—were becoming increasingly nervous about who and what Rounding might really have been and seemed angry and frustrated, convinced that somebody was hiding something from them.

Many were certain the culprit was Captain Covington. Others seemed to think it was the United States government. One, some guy named Ivy—or maybe it was Ivory—was shouting he was going to have the captain arrested and sue the owners. Marcello could see the fear behind his threats and enjoyed the theater. The jerk thought he was a "big man." He had no idea how small he really was in comparison with Marcello Cagayan. Marcello reached into his pocket and stroked the cell phone gently.

"Hey, man, lots of excitement today!" said Vido, the young Ecuadorian deckhand, as he sat down next to Cagayan and put his iPod on the table.

"You're right there, Vido," replied Cagayan in Spanish. "It's the devil's own work. Makes me wonder sometimes why I signed on."

"It's the money, man. And the adventure."

"Must be."

"You're an engineer. You know anything about this Mr. Rounding? I mean, you work for him, don't you? Did he kill himself or did the American navy guys do it? What's that all about?"

"Rounding?" said Cagayan as he reached into his right pocket for the cell phone. "I don't know. He wasn't a bad guy." The truth was that Rounding's behavior had Cagayan dumbfounded.

"You really think there's a bomb aboard?"

"It worry you?"

"Of course! You're not worried?"

"Whatever happens, happens."

"There's a rumor we're going to go back early because of him. They think he was a terrorist."

"Yeah?" Cagayan started paying closer attention.

"At first I thought they were talking about going back to BA, but now I hear its Ushuaia."

"That's good for some people."

"Those that have their families stay there during the summer."

"I guess I better get some rest before I go back to looking."

"See ya." Vido plugged himself into his iPod and was instantly lost to the surrounding world.

Cagayan walked down the passageway to his room, rubbing the cell phone as he went. With every step his sense of personal power grew, until it was about to explode. He was the most powerful man on the ship. More powerful than Covington. More powerful than that navy guy. The lives of over six hundred people were in his hands. They would live as long as he wished for them to live, and they would die when he chose to kill them. It was becoming intoxicating. As so many men have found throughout history—some much more worthy than Marcello Cagayan—it is terribly, terribly difficult to set power aside.

Tonight was to be his night, he told himself again and again as he walked to his quarters. Tonight had to be the night. Everything was ready. He rubbed the bandages on his arm. So much blood, he thought, and so little pain. Tonight would be better. Much better.

Except all the shit about old Rounding worried him a little. Was it possible the guy really had been a terrorist? All the newscasters said he was. So what had he planned and what had he done? Was he going to steal Cagayan's glory from the grave?

It worried him but he knew it shouldn't. If it happened, it happened, but his plan was set. Tonight he would prove the "*mono*" was really a giant. When he reached his room, he took out the cell phone and opened it. He then dialed 1111 and set the device where he could easily reach it.

Cagayan lay in his rack, dozing. When he heard the grating and clanking of the anchor windlass one deck above his head and the thumping and banging of the anchor chain in the hawse pipe, he picked up the phone and pressed call.

* * *

The process of raising and housing a ship's anchor is a mundane necessity of the ship's operation. Without its being done, a ship cannot perform her function. But that same act has an almost mystical dimension for most seamen. Once the anchor is lifted clear of the bottom, the ship is under way. Once under way, the ship is considered infinitely more at risk than when at anchor, and the rules change. The ship is now at sea, fulfilling her destiny. Adventure beckons, even if the voyage is only from one anchorage to another in the same harbor, and the crew knows it is doing what sailors are meant to do.

Mike Chambers was not overly romantic, but he was sensitive to the mystique of the anchor ritual and made a point to take a break and watch. He would have preferred to be on the bridge, to pretend *Aurora* was his ship, but he didn't want to get in Covington's way, so he settled for the forward rail of the third deck.

On the forecastle, Boatswain MacNeal stood all the way forward in the prow. After looking over the bulwark at the growing seas attacking from ahead, he signaled the man on the windlass control. With a clank the windlass started to turn slowly and the anchor chain, composed of thick, foot-long links, jumped then started to slowly come home. Meanwhile, a deckhand hosed the chain down at the hawse in order to remove any muck and other crud that might foul the boatswain's carefully tended decks.

A brilliant flash suddenly erupted like a fountain from the windlass motor housing, followed immediately by a tremendous *boom* and a thick cloud of black smoke. The windlass stopped and the hand on the controls was blown back ten feet.

"Shit!" MacNeal groaned. "You two," he grated at the two men standing close to him, "slap that pelican hook on the chain and stop it just in case the windlass lets go." He then noticed the windlass operator lying on the deck and ran over to him. He was alive but he didn't look good. He looked as if he'd been shot by a cannon filled with scrap. MacNeal knelt next to him then shouted into his walkie-talkie: "One of my men is injured. Get the doctor here quick."

"I think we've got trouble, Boss."

Chambers, his stomach beginning to churn, turned to find Alex standing behind him.

"Tell Jerry and Ted to get forward and find out what's happening. You and Ray stand by. I'm going to the bridge."

Even as Mike spoke, *Aurora*'s general alarm burst to life. Several moments later, while the crew ran to their emergency stations and automatic watertight doors slammed shut throughout much of the ship, the alarms were muted.

"Ladies and gentlemen, this is Captain Covington. An explosion of unknown origin has occurred on the ship's forecastle. I'm not totally certain of the explosion's extent, but the damage appears to be limited to the area around the anchor windlass. As a precaution I must ask all of you to do the following: Get your personal flotation device and then report to one of the following public areas. Those of you whose last names start with A through J, please report to the main dining room; those of you whose last names begin with K through S, please report to the main lecture hall; and all those whose last names start with T through Z, please report to the main lounge. Try to make yourselves comfortable and please be considerate of the feelings of your fellow passengers. I expect to be able to give you more information by the time you have arrived at one of these gathering places."

"It happened," said Covington to Mike as the latter arrived.

"I'm afraid so. Motors explode but not that way. I'm going to establish some security for the passengers."

"Please do."

Mike then called Alex and instructed her to collect up Ray and Dave Ellison and each go to one of the gathering places to provide security and maintain order.

"Bridge, this is MacNeal," squawked Covington's walkie-talkie.

"Bridge, aye," replied Covington.

"The windlass is totally destroyed, Captain. I'm going to have to buoy and cut the chain and slip if you want to get under way."

"That's what we're going to have to do. We can't just sit here and wait for something else to happen. How's your man?"

"He's a mess but he's conscious and seems alert. There's a lot of blood but . . . Here comes Dr. Savage."

"Have her call me as soon as she knows something. And you get going on the chain. Advise me as soon as you're ready to slip the anchor."

"Roger.

"Sam," snapped the boatswain to one of his more experienced hands, "you and, ah, Dawson get a sledge and a chisel and get down to the chain locker. Find the next split link," he continued, referring to the special chain link that was split the long way and used to connect the separate ninety-foot shots of chain, "and split it. And be goddamn careful. Don't get tangled in the chain, just in case something up here carries away. I don't want you going through the hawse."

"Okay, Boats."

"The anchor windlass?" said Covington to Chambers. "You think this is all of it? Some sort of message?"

Chambers looked at him and shook his head. "What other ships are in the area?"

"Several other cruise ships—one's an old Russian research vessel—and an Argentine supply ship, but they're all well to the east of us, dodging drift ice. Anyway, they're all smaller than we are. One's not any bigger than a mid-sized trawler."

"Nothing to the west?"

"An American supply ship returning to New Zealand from McMurdo, but she's over three thousand miles away and I suspect having more than enough troubles of her own."

"So we're on our own until we get to Ushuaia?"

"Once we get partway across the Drake Passage, somebody might be able to reach us from Ushuaia, but I'm not sure what they'll be able to do. Especially if the weather keeps deteriorating. All the same, I'll request that any of the larger vessels that might be there get under way to meet us as soon as possible."

* * *

Marcello Cagayan felt the thump then heard the alarms. Phase one of his mission had been executed. He jumped out of his rack and dashed down the corridor. Mumbling a loud "What the fuck!" he joined the stampede and headed for his emergency station at switchboard number one in the electrical Auxiliary Room.

"What the hell's happening?" he demanded of the electrician in charge.

"Some sort of explosion in the anchor windlass. Roberts—he's there—thinks it was a bomb."

"A bomb! Anybody hurt?"

"One deckhand. Roberts doesn't seem to think it's caused much damage, though. Except to the windlass."

"That's fucking strange."

"Yeah, that and Mr. Rounding."

"You think he did the bomb?"

"What else can I think?"

* * *

"An explosion, Dad? Like a bomb?"

"I suppose so, Katie. Something like that. We're just going to have to wait and see."

"Isn't there something we should be doing to help?"

"At the moment I think we should leave it to Captain Covington and those navy people, so keep moving. We're supposed to go to the lecture hall."

"Yeah, I guess you're right. You think they'll have any food there? I'm starved."

"Tim," said Dana, starting to laugh, "you've come up with a real adventure for us this time."

* * *

"This is Jen Harris broadcasting live from the long-troubled cruise ship *Aurora Australis* a few miles from Antarctica." As she spoke, the reporter and her team stood in the opened door of a cabin, facing a passageway filled with passengers headed toward the Main Dining Room. "For several days now, there has been rising concern that the ship is a target for terrorists. Today, those concerns have proven all too accurate. Not six hours ago, American military personnel, after a long boat chase across the stormy, bitterly cold Bellingshausen Sea, shot and killed a member of the ship's crew who was suspected of being a terrorist. Then, not fifteen minutes ago, what was almost certainly an explosive device went off on the ship's foredeck, seriously injuring at least one member of the crew, maybe more. As of right now the passengers have been ordered to assemble in certain safe zones. Although there is little sign of panic yet, everybody is very much on edge.

"Pardon me," she said, reaching out toward a woman with very wide eyes, "would you mind telling us just how dangerous you believe this situation really is?"

* * *

Mike Chambers stood in the pilothouse and rubbed the back of his neck. What a fuckup! Two men inexplicably dead, one seriously injured, one explosive device, six hundred very unhappy passengers and crew, and he was still no closer to the core of the problem than he had been back in Tampa. Should he assume Rounding was a crazy son of a bitch with a grudge who left a device in the windlass as some sort of feeble protest? Had he left more? Or was Rounding not involved at all? Were there other devices? He'd found no evidence of them. Should he encourage Covington to remain anchored here, where shore was only half a mile away? No, that was impossible. It was a lee shore. A deadly mass of ice-cold rock and rock-hard ice. With the weather building the way it was, the ship would be driven onto it by midnight and many would die. The most logical solution he could see was to run for Ushuaia and pray.

* * *

"This is Captain Covington. I can now confirm that the explosion in the anchor windlass has done absolutely no significant damage to the ship except making anchoring more complicated. *Aurora* is as seaworthy now as she was when we left Buenos Aires. It is safe for all of you to return to your normal activities. Please be sure to re-stow your PFDs in your staterooms."

After replacing the PA microphone, Covington told MacNeal to slip the anchor. With a rumble and a cloud of rust dust the anchor chain flew up out of the chain locker, across the deck and out through the hawse hole. Then, with a splash, *Aurora* was under way.

* * *

"If it ain't one thing, it's another," mumbled Brad to nobody in particular. He tossed down the remains of his fifth orange martini as he sat alone in the Masthead Lounge, at a table intended for six, his oversized gold earring glinting.

James Ives, CEO of Universal Systems and Solutions, heard the remark and stopped, clutching his wife's arm as he did. He knew who the kid was; he was the singer's stud. And he could also spot him as a loser. But he was scared now and he had an overwhelming impulse to sound off. "I wouldn't be so damn blasé about it, kid. There's a very good chance we're all going to get blown to hell. I'm going to see the captain right now. The man's a bumbler. Demand he and those damn navy people do something. Get us the hell off this ship!"

"Damn right," slurred Brad. "Hasn't the fucking faintest idea what he's doing."

Ives looked down at the kid and realized he didn't feel any better at all. Finding himself in agreement with this fool was no more satisfying than being in agreement with his simpleminded wife.

As Brad watched the unknown-to-him puffed shirt walk by, he thought about Chrissie, the bitch! She wouldn't let him go with her to the Main Dining Room, where the Cs were supposed to go, and she wouldn't come here, where the Ws like him were supposed to gather. He'd had it with her. Absolutely had it!

* * *

"Yes, Alan," said Mike into the satellite phone, "Jerry's convinced it was a bomb and not just the winch motor exploding."

"Do you appreciate just how difficult it is for SECDEF to see these things on TV before I can give them a heads-up?"

"Alan, there's nothing I can do about the media. They're crawling all over the ship so they see things happening. And there's no way I can arrest them."

"Lean on the ship's captain to do it."

"He won't. We've discussed the problem. They're not the ones threatening his ship."

"How many casualties were there really?"

"One, a deckhand, and he'll probably be okay. Most of the blast was directed upward . . . and both the senator and the congressman are fine. That's the odd part about this whole damn thing: I get the impression it wasn't planned to necessarily injure anybody. That it was just a show. Hasn't somebody claimed credit?"

"No, not yet. At least you got the guy who planted it."

"Rounding? I'm still doubting he did it."

"Of course he did. That, Mike, is the official word!"

Chambers didn't answer.

"What's your plan now?"

"Same as before. Keep searching until we reach Ushuaia and get rid of the passengers. Then, with luck, we can turn the mess over to the Argentines. Let their bomb squad share some of the glory."

"First solid thinking you've come up with. We get credit for killing the terrorist and getting the ship back to port in one piece."

Mike hung up and looked around at the team, which was assembled in the suite.

"You think there's another aboard?" asked Jerry.

"We have to assume that, Chief, and we've got to find it—or them—and also whoever controls them."

"You don't think it was Rounding?"

"I don't know."

"I can't swear there weren't a few scraps of timer in that mess," said Jerry. "I've secured what I could, but the lab's going to have to go through it all."

"Let's hope you're right and that if it *was* Rounding he didn't leave any others aboard."

"What about the life capsules?" asked Ray, his face drawn and his swollen and tightly bandaged ankle up on a table, precisely were the doctor had told him *not* to put it.

"Launching boats in this sort of weather will be a nightmare," replied Jerry.

"We've got our work cut out for us," said Mike.

"We'll still be hunting for a needle in a haystack, Boss," contributed Alex, who looked only marginally better than Fuentes.

"Thanks for reminding me."

* * *

As soon as he was released from his emergency station, Cagayan returned to the crew's lounge, along with a number of others. Suddenly nobody seemed interested in sleep.

Because he was a nobody, nobody paid much attention to the small Filipino. He was free to look and listen, and what he saw delighted him. His shipmates were scared. All they seemed able to talk about were bombs and fires and how the bombs would be in their work space and if the ship sank most of them would die.

The passengers were even more entertaining. He was in no position to mingle with them, but the media crews did it for him. All he had to do was look at the TV to see the fear, and the resulting anger, in the eyes and words of the somebodies who were being interviewed. Despite their own fear, Jen and the other interviewers fanned that fear through their carefully posed, hopelessly leading questions. “How do you think the captain is doing?” “What about the U.S. Navy?” “Were sufficient precautions taken in the past?” “What should be done now?” “Do you think the engineer was the only terrorist?”

And it was he, Marcello Cagayan, the “*mono*,” who controlled it all!

15

The Drake Passage

"Boss," said Alex into the walkie-talkie a little more than an hour after the ship had gotten under way, "Alan wants to talk to you again. He says it's urgent."

"Roger, I'm on my way" replied Mike, who was in the galley, supervising the search among all the cooking gear. "Continue searching," he said to the food service manager as he clipped the walkie-talkie to his belt. "Keep looking for anything that doesn't belong, anything that nobody can identify. If you spot anything, keep away from it! Call me or Ms. Mahan in the captain's conference room. As soon as you finish here, go on to the pantry and then the storerooms." As he gave the instructions, he hoped that Alan wasn't calling to continue micromanaging the operation. He simply didn't have time for that.

"What's up, Alan?" said Mike five minutes later, after grabbing the phone from Alex's extended hand.

"I wish to fuck I knew. Somebody, using what appears to be a totally untraceable e-mail, has claimed credit for your current mess . . . and threatened even worse."

"Read it to me, if it's not classified."

"Classified! It was sent to Reuters! I'm willing to bet the media morons you have with you already know what it says."

"So what does it say?"

"I quote: '*Aurora Australis* and all aboard her are doomed. Free the Faithful to Dream. Free the Faithful to Believe. Allah Akbar.' "

"Who took credit?"

"The Brotherhood of Faith."

"The Brotherhood of Faith? Who the hell are they?"

"Nobody here has the slightest idea."

"Alex?" asked Mike, half covering the mouthpiece.

"Never heard of them."

"At least they did us one favor," observed Alan.

"You mean telling us there's another bomb? I'm not sure how much good that's going to do."

"Well you're going to have to do something, Old Buddy. You've got what, about a thousand people aboard? Do you have a plan?"

"Six hundred, Alan, don't get carried away. At the moment we're headed northwest in the middle of what everybody would describe as a major hurricane if it weren't so far south. We're almost two thousand miles from anybody who might help us."

"That's not the *Titanic*, is it? You've got lifeboats."

"Yes, Alan, and I'd say they're first rate . . . But if we had to abandon ship right now, in the middle of this meteorological nightmare, at least half the passengers and crew would end up dead. There are limits, you know."

"Limits or not, I've got to tell our mutual boss something so he can tell the president what to say to the media. Nothing much else has happened the past few days, so they're in a feeding frenzy about this."

"Same as before. We're going to continue searching the ship and talking with people who seem a little sketchy. And Alex is going to keep digging, to see if she can come up with anything your people have missed."

"That's not going to go over very well!"

"What the hell else do you suggest!"

"You're the on-scene commander, but The Man isn't going to be happy to hear that's all you can come up with. Americans expect more dynamic and imaginative solutions from people in your position."

"Such as?"

"More of a kick-ass, boots-in-their-faces approach."

"On whom?"

"That's up to you to decide. Lean on the sons of bitches. Especially the foreigners. This is war, god damn it! Do what the American people pay you to do."

"Good night, Alan. Sleep tight. I think I'm about to be seasick."

He then called Covington to give him the good news—hoping to beat the media to the punch.

* * *

Even before Arthur Covington had slipped *Aurora*'s anchor and turned to the northwest, the weather had been deteriorating, and it continued to do so with increasing rapidity, causing Covington to reduce speed twice. With the stabilizers still out of commission, the huge waves were totally free to toss the ship around to their hearts' content, forcing her to buck and plunge and roll and groan—and to cause a number of passengers to do the same.

Having awarded himself another break, Mike appeared on the bridge. The scene that met him was hellish, although his view was limited by the surrounding darkness. The wind was screaming, driving a gravel-like snow before it, and waves almost as high as the bridge were rising out of the depths and breaking over the bow as the ship drove into them.

"You're just in time," said Covington as soon as he saw the naval captain. "We're far enough north to weather the Peninsula. I'm coming around to the northeast in a few minutes and heading for Ushuaia, though the ship's going to yaw like the devil with these huge seas on her quarter."

Mike stared at Covington a moment. In the red light of the bridge the man looked washed out, pasty, exhausted. And he'd undoubtedly look the same even if a tropical sun were shining on him.

Mike just shook his head as he walked over to a window and looked out into the raging darkness. He could see practically nothing—except the huge, gray hills just a moment or two before they slammed into the ship—but he could feel, sense, the storm's awful fury. Thinking back, this was probably the worst weather he'd ever experienced in his life. The wind was now thundering on them at close to ninety knots, and the seas, which at this latitude had a clear fetch all the way around the world, were pounding in on them from the west, sixty feet high and breaking against and over the port bow with a thundering, ship-shaking boom.

He'd never tried to turn a big ship across the wind in conditions like this. Or any ship, for that matter. The whole situation scared the shit out of him. Hopefully the passengers had little idea of what Covington was about to do. "What choice do you have?"

"None that I can see. You?"

"She's your ship, Captain."

"If it *was* Rounding," said Covington, changing the subject, "and he *did* use timers, we may be in luck. If we'd continued on our schedule, we wouldn't be in our most helpless location for another two or three days. As it is, we just might be in Ushuaia by then."

"How long do you think this is going to last?"

"It might blow over in three hours, or it might very well last three weeks, even in the summer."

"How far north do we have to go to get out of it?"

"The weather satellite claims once we get a hundred and fifty miles due north we'll be basking in fifty-knot winds and twenty-foot seas, but as I'm sure you've learned, everything down here is subject to change."

"That's an understatement."

"I'm going to execute the turn in about half an hour. You'll have to release my stewards from their searching duties to warn the passengers who sleep through my announcement and help those who don't hold on hard enough."

"I'll go take care of it right now."

"Thank you."

* * *

Boatswain MacNeal forced the door open and stepped out onto the wind-lashed port boat deck, conscious that he was now probably the only person on a weather deck, except maybe a member of the watch on the bridge wings. The deck chairs, the HBIs down in the hold—everything under his control had been stowed and secured against the howling wind and wild seas. But the turn Captain Covington was anticipating would test his most careful preparation to the limit, and he felt a compulsion to check the ten-ton lifeboats just one more time. Without them, if anything else went wrong, they would all most certainly be dead.

Walking carefully on the slippery, rolling deck, he forced his way to boat number two. Hanging on to anything he could find, he checked the gripes—the wire straps that secured the boat into its cradle. All was in order, as it was for the remaining two port boats.

MacNeal then walked back through the superstructure to the more sheltered starboard side. Again, all appeared to be in order. Mentally crossing his fingers, he returned to the shelter of the superstructure, settled into a small public sitting and viewing room and waited.

* * *

Aurora's bow plowed into and over an exceptionally large, nearly invisible wave, driving a sheet of icy spray high into the air and back over the ship. The wave then passed under and the bow pitched down into the trough, making the ship shudder violently and drawing Covington out of the shallow reverie into which he'd slipped. He pounded his gloved hands together to restore circulation as he stepped over to the public-address system.

"Now attention, this is Captain Covington. In a few minutes we will experience very heavy rolls when I turn across the seas and downwind toward our destination at Ushuaia. These rolls will be much more dramatic than we are experiencing now and must not be taken lightly. All hands are to prepare for heavy rolls and secure as much gear as possible. As for you passengers, please secure everything you can and sit or lie down immediately when I pass the word that I'm commencing the turn. Please help the crew secure anything that might break loose and prepare to hang on."

Wondering how much would really be secured and knowing that it was never enough, the captain then walked out to the windward wing of the bridge, raised his binoculars and started to count waves. A few minutes later, confident that the time had come, he put the rudder far right and backed the starboard engine. Given a hard push by the screaming wind, the bow fell off to the right and the ship started to spin across the gale.

* * *

Ray Fuentes was just about to hobble into the Main Dining Room to get some coffee when Captain Covington announced he was beginning the turn across the sixty-foot waves. Grabbing the door frame with both hands—and with most of his weight on his good leg, the one that wasn't throbbing like hell—he felt the ship's bow rise as it attacked yet another wave. Instead of continuing up and over the wave, however, *Aurora* lurched to the right and fell into the trough. He'd expected all that. What he hadn't expected was the violence of the sudden roll to starboard that sent him shooting into the dining room, dragging his damaged foot, totally out of control. An instant later he found himself lying on top of a very pretty girl in a tangle of several people as crockery of all types flew over him and shattered on the deck and the bulkhead. He immediately recognized the girl as the singer Chrissie Clark. Alex had mentioned that she was aboard. The others in the pile were passengers and one of the stewards.

"Sorry," he mumbled as a white-hot pain shot up his leg. "Excuse me."

"You must be one of the navy guys," remarked Chrissie, looking at his blue coveralls and sidearm.

"Marine Corps, actually, but yes."

"That was a spectacular entrance."

"I do my best." As he spoke, he had to fight back a groan. Somebody else in the pile had just started thrashing around, trying to get up. In the process, the impatient and misguided individual twisted Ray's already damaged ankle.

"Is the ship going to roll back upright again?" asked Chrissie, her sparkling hazel eyes boring into his own. "Ever?"

"Undoubtedly. They always do." Except when they don't, Ray added silently to himself.

"You really think there's a bomb somewhere? The captain didn't come right out and say there's another, but everybody still seems to be looking. And a lot of passengers are afraid there is."

"It's very possible."

The ship paused for a second, as if about to recover, and then continued its alarming roll, tossing a chair into the tangled mass of bodies, bruising Ray and several others.

"Was it that man who raced off in one of the boats this afternoon?" She paused a moment. "That must've been you who chased him. You and that tall girl. You look terrible."

Ray almost said he felt as terrible as he undoubtedly

looked, but then he remembered he was a marine and she was a taxpayer.

"We've all been under a lot of stress the past day or two."

There was a crash nearby then a scraping sound and a cry of pain. Only then was he able to escape Chrissie's eyes and look around. Despite the stewards' best efforts, another barrage of crockery had launched itself and two more chairs had shot across the deck, cutting terrified passengers down at the knees. And the ship continued what was now one very long, slow roll.

* * *

Arthur Covington stood on the port wing of his bridge and hung on to the rail as he stared up at the huge, gray-black mountain of water that seemed certain to roll over both him and his ship. Every muscle in his body was clenched—his jaws, his arms, his guts, his toes. As the ship continued to roll, he could feel his feet slipping on the deck.

Turning anything in this sort of weather was a bitch. Turning a middle-sized, underpowered cruise ship was even more difficult. He tore his eyes away from the wave and looked down at the remote controls. The joystick was all the way to starboard. So, therefore, was the rudder. The starboard engine was backing while the port was ahead full. The monster wind had done its job by forcing the bow off to the right, and the rudder and propellers had done their part. *Aurora* was now across the wind, lying in the trough, parallel to the monstrous mountains on either side. Would she continue to swing, to get her bow downwind? Or had he blown the maneuver? Were they now trapped in the trough, just waiting to broach? To roll their guts out until something finally gave way?

He'd done everything he could and the ship had done everything she could and the wind had done its part, only now that same wind might have locked them into a fatal position. On many ships the superstructure is significantly larger either fore or aft. This added windage at one end makes it possible to use the wind to help turn the ship. In *Aurora*'s case, the windage varied little from bow to stern. The difference had been enough to blow the bow off the wind, but now all it was doing was driving the ship farther over on her side and pinning her down there.

Once he'd started the turn, there was no turning back. He'd never felt so alone in his life as he did at that moment.

* * *

Pete and Penny Evans sat on the couch in their suite, drinks in hand, and waited silently. They could feel the ship's motion begin to change, and then they were thrown against the back of the couch as the ship lurched. They both had fear in their eyes, although Peter was in far-the-worst condition. As he felt the couch rolling backward and sinking beneath him, he imagined the ship going over completely, trapping them until they drowned. His chest tightened and he suddenly found it almost impossible to breathe.

"Are you all right, Peter?" asked Penny, who had taken his hand and was clutching it.

"I don't know," replied Evans as he grimaced and reached for his chest. Then he slumped over.

"Is it your heart?" asked Penny, on her knees now, crawling toward him. Without waiting for a reply she grabbed his legs and pushed them up on the couch, then swung his chest around so he was lying flat. "It's going to be all right," she said after putting a small pillow under his head and noting gratefully that his eyes were still open and moving. "Try to breathe, to relax." She then crawled over to the phone and pressed the emergency button. "This is Mrs. Peter Evans. I'm afraid my husband is having a heart attack. Will you please send somebody as soon as possible?"

"We'll get somebody there just as soon as we can, Mrs. Evans, but you do understand our situation."

"Yes, of course. As soon as you are able."

* * *

Six decks below Congressman and Mrs. Evans, Ted crouched on a catwalk in the main engine room and held tightly to a rail. The more the ship rolled, the higher the port engine seemed to climb, until he couldn't see why it didn't break loose and crash down on him. He looked around at the men near him. They were all scared. Even Chief Engineer Montalba, normally one of the most self-controlled men he'd ever met, was strapped into a chair in Main Control and looked as if he were praying.

* * *

His knees slightly flexed, his sleet-reddened face square into the screaming wind, Arthur Covington continued to stand at *Aurora*'s controls, alert for the slightest sign of salvation, the slightest hint of something more he could do. He waited, gauging the wind's direction on his face and feeling the ship's heart and soul through his hands and feet. She was still pinned on her side but she was fighting, he could feel that. Once he'd done everything he could think of, he allowed himself to think of his late wife, now five years dead from cancer. Then, for a few moments, he thought of nothing.

Another monstrous wave slammed into *Aurora*'s steeply angled port side, making her shudder. But she didn't roll any farther. He glanced at the inclinometer. Fifty-five degrees. Another few degrees and something big would break loose or some of the lower windows might shatter, letting in the icy black waters. The wave passed and the ship started to sink into the next trough. But this time there was a corkscrew motion as *Aurora* started to right herself. The stern sank while the bow crept across the back of the passing wave. Covington glanced at the compass, holding his breath. The stern started to rise while the bow fell slowly into the trough. As the next wave passed under them, the corkscrew motion continued.

Covington waited a momentary eternity, the fate of all those who find themselves in similar situations. He then clapped his hands once in delight and relief when he was certain his ship was continuing to turn, that she had won over the waves. He eased the rudder and signaled for the starboard engine to stop backing and then to go ahead. The ship was already almost back on even keel, although with the waves now slamming against her port quarter, she was yawing and wallowing in an utterly sickening fashion.

Once the ship was settled on her new course, he turned and looked back over the deck. The boats were still there. Nothing major, in fact, appeared to have broken loose. He hurried through the pilothouse to the other wing and found the same, reassuring sight.

The ship had handled the maneuver well, but the ride was not going to be comfortable, he thought. Even after the stabilizers were returned to service. Something more for the passengers to be unhappy about. And the ship must be an utter mess below. Winters and the purser were going to have their hands full. And so were Chambers and his people. He walked back into the pilothouse. "I've set the autopilot at zero five three," he said to both the mate of the watch and the helmsman. "Keep it there for now and maintain this speed."

"Aye, Captain," replied the two men, both of whom were still strapped into their chairs, their faces pale.

* * *

About an hour before he was scheduled to return to the bilges, and a few minutes before Covington was scheduled to start his turn, Marcello Cagayan had torn himself away from the drama on TV. He had work to do. He returned to his room and lay down for a few minutes to wait for the turn to be completed. He awoke when his body alerted him that he was in the process of tumbling out of his bunk. He grabbed the bunk frame and waited. Once he could feel the turn was complete and the ship settled on her new course, he dragged himself out and stood up. He wanted to have the next act well under way before they started to miss him in the engine room.

Omar's smart, he thought, but I'm smarter. I have the power now, not Omar.

He reached for the cell phone in his pocket. To make sure it was still there.

He felt the ship yaw and pitch, rolling from side to side as it skittered down the fronts of the huge waves in a sickening motion. It was hard to stand, even for him. Vido had said it was fucking awful cold on deck, which meant that it was really cold, since Vido came from some place high in the mountains where it was very cold. Forewarned, Cagayan grabbed the multilayered thermal undergarment and coveralls the owners had issued to all hands and put them on. He topped them off with a thermal jacket and gloves. Before he put the right glove on, he took out the phone and tapped in four numbers—4444. That was the code that would trigger the two main charges. Just in case something went wrong, all he had to do was press call and the ship would be history. He folded the phone closed and put it back in his pocket.

Cagayan moved quickly out of his quarters and into a short maze of access ladders and passages—the "back staircases" used by the crew to get around, and not generally known to the passengers. Six ladders later he stepped out onto *Aurora*'s fourth or highest deck, tugging at his insulated parka as he did. He still hadn't seen a soul, although that would soon change.

Gritting his teeth, he took a few steps aft, the wind threatening to pick him up and blow him over the stern. When he got to the base of the funnel, he pulled out a set of keys and opened a door into the largely hollow structure. After closing the door behind him, he paused again and looked down. He was out of the wind and out of sight and might soon be warm again. He was standing on one of the blower flats, the little mezzanines built onto the inside of the funnel to provide a space to mount the blowers, which forced fresh air into the main engine room. Running up the center of the funnel were the two diesels' exhaust risers. The space around him was all in shadow, although he could look down and see the brightly lit engine room almost fifty feet below. Where they would be expecting him in another forty-five minutes.

Cagayan sat next to the blower as the heat and roar of the engines flowed up and past him. Shaking, he opened the front of his jacket and took off his gloves, hoping to let the heat in.

After about ten minutes he zipped his jacket closed and put on his gloves again. Standing, he turned and grabbed the rungs of a ladder welded onto the funnel's inside. Then he started to climb.

It was a long, tiring, nerve-wracking climb as the ship's violent motion was multiplied the higher he went. On several occasions it threatened to flip him off the ladder and into the air, through which he would inevitably crash down into the engine room far below.

Beginning to sweat, he paused to catch his breath, hanging on for dear life as he did. He reached into his pants pocket and rubbed the phone.

The phone was his ultimate power, but he now understood it was an impersonal power. True power, to be satisfying, had to be personal. He had to be able to see the fear and awe in their eyes. Just what the army officer had seen in Cagayan's father's eyes before he killed him. Shock and awe at its most personal level. It was something Omar had not mentioned, but it had now become as important to Cagayan as the basic mission.

When he reached the top of the ladder, he opened a

round hatch through the funnel's cap and continued to climb. The bitter wind returned, tearing at him, and the hot, acrid diesel stack gas made him gag.

He looked down at the ship below and the chaos that surrounded it, and the bitterness of the stack gas, and of his whole past life, blew away in the gale. He was above it all now. He was a god.

He reached out and grabbed a long, soot-stained, plastic-wrapped package that had been secured about two feet from the hatch. Using his pocketknife, he cut the lashings that held the heavy package and pulled it toward him. On one end it had a rope loop, which he put his arm through. He stepped back down the ladder, closed the hatch and continued down, back to the blower flat. There he opened the package and checked the AK-47 that it contained. All looked in order. As did the two hundred rounds of ammunition.

After stuffing the waterproof plastic wrappings in a space behind the blower and laying the gun on it, Cagayan opened the door in the side of the funnel and stepped out onto the weather deck. At the moment the weapon would be a hindrance.

* * *

When Mike made it back to his command center in Captain Covington's conference room, he found Alex still propped in a chair in the corner, holding herself in position with her feet jammed against a bulkhead and a bookcase while she tapped furiously on her laptop.

"That the sort of thing you guys do in the real navy?" she asked with a brightness that contradicted the worried expression on her face.

"Captain Covington did a good job. I don't think I could have done it. Maybe we should try to recruit him."

"How many casualties?"

"Three or four broken legs, a mild concussion and a lot of bruises. And Congressman Evans."

"Did he die?"

"A few minutes ago."

"Alan wants to talk to you. He called a few minutes ago and got pissed when I told him now was not the time for anybody here to be accepting phone calls. He said call back pronto—or else!"

Mike returned the call.

"You got the situation under control yet?" demanded Parker.

"Nothing's changed, Alan, except that the captain succeeded in turning the ship and now we're headed directly for Ushuaia."

"That means what, another thousand miles?"

"More or less."

"Another two days?"

"More like three if the weather stays like it is."

"Now listen very carefully, Mike. Thanks to the media this whole thing has become highly politicized. The other side has attached itself to this like a flea to a dog. We have to be seen to be *doing something*! It's obvious that somebody aboard that ship knows something! You're going to have to detain those people—the ones on your list—and sweat them. And make sure the media's there when you take them into custody. Cuffs and all."

Mike wiped his hand across his face. He was fully prepared to admit he hadn't succeeded in his mission, but he was certain Alan's demand would contribute nothing to the well-being of *Aurora* and her passengers and crew.

"Okay, Alan. We'll work on it. I've got to run now—somebody said Senator Bergstrom wants to meet with me," lied Mike.

"Calm him. Reassure him. He's bound to have something to say to the media afterward. How's Evans, by the way? It was on the news along with the other injuries."

"He died a couple minutes ago."

There was no denying that Alan was close to SECDEF and that the media had identified him as one of the DOD's top naval experts, but Mike found it extraordinarily easy to not listen to his advice at times. Alan had never actually served in uniform, as he assured everybody he would have liked to do. His manly libido had driven him to an early fatherhood, and everybody who did wear a uniform was damn well aware of it. He was, however, an avid hunter of small game.

* * *

"Boss, it's Jerry. He has to speak to you." As she spoke, Alex shook Mike's shoulder.

"What? Oh, yes." Mike woke up, but not as immediately as he prided himself in doing normally. He'd fallen asleep in one of the conference chairs. He'd fallen asleep while both Alex and Ray, who'd been even more beaten up than he was, were still hard at work. He stuck out his hand, not wanting to look Alex in the eyes.

"It's okay, Boss. I've been sneaking catnaps when nobody's looking, and Ray landed in Chrissie Clark's lap during that turn and is now so in love he could stay awake forever."

"He's got a wife and daughter . . ."

"Who he loves dearly, but he's a very impressionable guy."

"Captain?"

"Yes, Chief?"

"We've found the missing engineman."

"Where?"

"In a void next to the number two fuel tank."

"Dead?"

"Yes, sir. We haven't touched a thing, but it looks like somebody did something to his head."

"Anything else obvious?"

"A lot of Baggies, some with various colored pills, then some with white stuff and some with brown."

"No indication that he might also be in the bomb business?"

"Nothing obvious."

"Very well. Don't touch a thing and keep everybody away. Especially the media. I'll call Captain Covington and have Dave Ellison and Dr. Savage join you. Where's Ted?"

"He's on his way from the forward storerooms."

"Good. Alex and I are on our way."

"Roger."

"Sounds like we've solved one mystery without solving the big one."

"Sounds that way. Bring the camera. We did bring one, didn't we?"

"Boss!"

16

The Drake Passage

The scene of Hensen's death was at the end of a narrow passageway that led to the Main Engine Room. Mike and Alex arrived to find Captain Covington, Dr. Savage, Dave Ellison and Mr. Acosta, the second engineer, all standing talking quietly. Off to one side stood a very young oiler named Rodriguez. From the expression on his face he knew that whatever he'd gotten himself involved in was not good for him and wished he could just disappear into the bulkhead.

Mike went immediately to the opened void and looked in. The body was lying on its side, almost in a fetal position. There was blood smeared around near the head and a bloody rag lying next to it.

"Who found it?" asked Mike.

"Rodriguez, here," answered Covington.

Mike turned to the young oiler. "Is this how you found it?"

"Yes, sir."

"But," spoke up Patti Savage, the ship's doctor, "I moved the head an inch or two to examine the wound."

"Your conclusions?"

"That he was stabbed repeatedly in the temple and the ear with something sharp. There appears to be a little bit of gray matter mixed with the blood."

"A marlinspike? A screwdriver? An ice pick?"

"A small marlinspike, maybe. Or a screwdriver."

"Must have been bloody, yet I don't see any blood around."

"Must have cleaned up after himself. Makes sense."

"How long's he been dead?"

"A couple days . . . That's really little more than a guess."

"Since he was reported missing?"

"That seems very likely."

"What's on the other side of the voids?"

"The number two diesel tank, sir," replied Acosta.

"What was Rodriguez doing here?"

"Reinspecting, sir. On my orders."

"Who inspected it originally?"

"I can check, sir." Acosta raised his walkie-talkie and asked Main Control to check the inspection records.

"It looks to me like Rounding was our man," offered Dave Ellison. "This would explain why he ran."

"But why did he do it?"

"Hensen must have seen him doing something or maybe he knew something."

"Jake Rounding didn't do this," said Patti Savage with a sigh. "He was a troubled man, but I'm certain he wasn't this troubled."

Ellison gave her the sort of look cops give you when you suggest they might be wrong.

"Damn!" mumbled Acosta as he listened to his walkie-talkie. "The original inspection was done by an oiler named Cagayan. M. Cagayan. I sent him myself, now that I think about it. He's small enough to get into some of the smaller voids and the bilges."

Savage looked slightly sick. "Cagayan came to me the

day Hensen seems to have died with a very bloody arm injury. His shirt was soaked, but the injury really wasn't that serious. I bandaged him up and sent him back to his duty station."

"That's right." Acosta nodded, a look of distress on his face. "I sent him to Dr. Savage. He was on sound and security patrol and came back bleeding. Said he'd hurt himself in the same damn bilge we're standing over now."

"Is Cagayan on watch or searching now?" asked Mike, tension in his voice.

The second engineer again called Main Control. "No, sir," he finally replied. "He's due to report in fifteen minutes."

"Rodriguez, do you know Cagayan?"

"I've spoken to him, sir. I don't really know him. I don't think anybody does."

"Do you know where his quarters are?"

"Yes, sir. They're next to mine."

Mike raised his walkie-talkie to his mouth. "Ted, where are you?"

"About forty feet from you, sir."

"Stop right where you are. It looks like an oiler named Cagayan may have killed Hensen. He's due to report at Main Control in about fifteen minutes. I want him alive! Is Jerry still at Main Control?"

"Far as I know."

"Join him there."

"What does he look like?"

Mike looked at Acosta and Patti Savage.

"He's remarkably small and thin," said Patti. "Filipino."

"Very small and thin," repeated Mike to Ted. "He's a Filipino."

"Roger."

"And I Roger that, Boss," said Jerry's voice. "I'm at Main Control."

"Art," Mike then said, turning to Covington, "please seal the ship the best you can from the main deck down and post men at any scuttles or hatches that must remain open. They're not to try to stop this guy. If they see him they're to get out of the way and report to us."

"Roger."

"Dave, secure the site. Are you equipped to lift fingerprints?"

"Yes."

"Then see if you can find any . . . Also see if you can find any blood that might not be Hensen's"

"Okay."

"Alex, we're going to pay a visit to Cagayan's quarters. Rodriguez is going to be our guide."

Alex nodded. Rodriguez looked far from happy.

"Captain," said Dr. Savage, "if you're done with me, I'd like to get back to my patients. I seem to have quite a number at the moment."

Covington looked at her.

"Sorry. I didn't mean that the way it sounded."

Covington then glanced at Mike.

"Of course," said Mike. "And we all hope like hell there won't be any more customers for you this voyage."

"What about Ray, Boss?"

"Let him sleep for now. I don't see how he's gotten around the past few days on that ankle."

"Pills," said Dr. Savage over her shoulder. "My pills, but they won't keep him going forever."

A few minutes later, for the second time in twenty-four hours, Covington passed the word that the fire and flood doors would be closing, and thirty seconds later bells started ringing and red lights flashing as the heavy steel barriers slid into position.

* * *

His mind and heart racing, Cagayan worked his way aft along the fourth deck, hanging on to the rail every step of the way. When he reached the aft end, he stepped carefully onto the ladder and climbed down even more carefully, his feet slipping on the treads and his hands on the rail as the ship did its best to throw him overboard. He repeated the process on the next ladder.

Once on the boat deck he paused to look around and catch his breath.

There wasn't a soul in sight and he was certain there wouldn't be. There was no way the boatswain was going to send anybody on deck in this weather without a very good reason, and even the stupidest passenger wasn't that stupid. Satisfied, he moved rapidly to a large metal chest. He opened the chest and withdrew a pair of bolt cutters. He then trotted forward to the aftmost boat.

Shit! There *was* somebody besides him on deck. Somebody—probably some half-assed passenger out for a thrill—was standing next to the boat looking out into the storm. He slipped into the shadows, his hands tightening on the cutter handle, uncertain whether to attack or to wait. Waiting, at least for a minute or two, seemed the least disruptive. Within a few seconds, the figure turned and, hastened by the howling wind, hurried through one of the doors, leaving Cagayan all alone again.

Confident he had no further company, Cagayan tripped the pelican hooks that secured the boat's two wire gripes. Now only the boat's weight was holding it in its cradle. He then used the bolt cutter to cut the forward falls, the wires by which the bow of the boat was raised or lowered. He finished his preparations by setting the controls on the winch he'd so carefully greased a few days before, to pay out when the strain of the boat's weight pulled on them. After preparing the three boats on the port side, he hurried around to the starboard side and repeated the process.

When he'd reached the aftmost boat on the starboard side, he paused a second to gently massage the cell phone. Then, with the closest thing possible to a song in his heart, he started forward again, tripping the gravity davits holding each boat.

* * *

Their sidearms drawn, Mike and Alex followed Rodriguez through a maze of narrow, almost dingy passageways leading to the crew's quarters. Except for asking the two or three people they encountered if they'd seen Cagayan recently—none had—they maintained silence.

Rodriguez stopped and turned toward them. He pointed ahead and to the right, toward a door. Mike nodded, then motioned for the young engineer to stand back. After nodding at Alex, he tiptoed past the door and stood a moment, his face pressed up against the bulkhead on the far side.

This was the bad part, he thought as he took a deep breath. What was waiting for him? A shotgun? A pistol?

He reached out with his right hand and tried the knob. It was locked. He stepped back from the bulkhead and, after another nod to Alex, charged into the door, using his left shoulder.

Fortunately, the lock was far from substantial.

With Alex two steps behind, Mike allowed his momentum to carry him into the room. It proved to be a small dormitory with six built-in racks and chests of drawers, a table and several chairs. The compartment smelled strongly of people crammed into a small, poorly ventilated space for long periods of time. It was empty.

"Jerry," he said into the walkie-talkie, "he's not in his quarters, so you be alert. We're on our way."

"Roger."

* * *

Once released, each lifeboat started to slide down two inclined ramps leading over the side of the ship, groaning and squealing slightly as it went. As each boat moved toward the edge of the deck, its davits—the upper arms of its cradle—pivoted out, morphing into the cranes from which the boat was supposed to hang.

With a thump, each of the davits stopped rotating out. Normally, the boat would then hang suspended fore and aft by its falls. But with one set of falls cut, the bow of each boat toppled down toward the pounding waves, while its stern falls paid out slowly. The ten-ton steel boats were now hanging—bows down—over the side. The sharp-tongued waves immediately attacked them, lunging and snapping. The boats began to pound with thunderous fury against the side of the ship, doing who-knew-what damage to the *Aurora* and shattering themselves.

Cagayan would have liked to stay and enjoy the spectacle close up, but he might be spotted. Anyway, he told himself, he had to warm up again before he continued. He threw the bolt cutters over the side and dashed up two outside ladders in the howling wind. All the way, until he slipped back into the funnel where the engine room's roars and groans out-shouted everything, he could hear the boats pounding themselves into scrap. This, he thought, should really scare the shit out of them.

* * *

"Ms. Smith," called out the helmsman, a look of shock mixed with suspicion on his face.

The mate of the watch turned and walked over to the console and looked where the helmsman was pointing. Six red lights in a row were blinking, indicating that all six of the ship's lifeboats were being launched. "There must be an electrical problem," she shouted over her shoulder as she headed out the pilothouse door onto the port wing.

Oh my God, she thought as she looked aft and down, cringing from the wind as she did. There was no electrical problem. There was a very big, very real problem. All three boats were grinding their way outboard; she could now feel it through the deck. Then, to her utter horror, one of the boats reached the end and toppled out, its bow plunging down toward the breaking waves. She turned and ran back into the pilothouse, where she immediately paged the boatswain.

"MacNeal," squawked the walkie-talkie. Fortunately, thought the mate, he's one of those guys who's wide awake the second he wakes up.

"Listen up, Boatswain, because this is hard to believe. Somebody has launched all six lifeboats and it looks as if the forward falls have been cut. Get up there with some men pronto."

"Shit!" replied the boatswain. "I'm on my way."

The mate then stepped into Captain Covington's sea cabin to notify him of the inexplicable disaster. "Do you want me to stop, Captain?"

"No. Not with these monsters chasing us." He paused, deep in thought. "Try reducing speed to six knots and see how the ship reacts. If she becomes hard to handle, we're going to have to put some more turns on again."

* * *

"It must be Cagayan," said Mike into the walkie-talkie when Covington advised him of the lifeboat disaster. "We're going to have to reverse our strategy—instead of trying to trap him belowdecks, we're going to trap him above. How's Ellison doing at closing the gaps?"

"He says he's got most of them filled."

"Good. Tell him the target is above him, not below. I also want you to get all the passengers in one place . . ."

"The Main Dining Room's the largest, but there'll be standing room only."

"That's unfortunate, but it won't kill them and this guy we're chasing very probably will, if he gets the chance. I'm going to wake Ray Fuentes and have him organize security there. You have any men who can be trusted with weapons?"

"A number. I'll have Mr. Winters work with Fuentes."

"Good. And have Ellison join them when he's finished

posting men below. The four of us are going to hunt this SOB before he comes up with something else."

"Jerry," he then snapped into the walkie-talkie, "our man is on deck—he's just launched all the lifeboats . . ."

"What? In this weather? Is he trying to trash them?"

"It looks that way. I want you and Ted to meet me and Alex at the suite. We'll arm ourselves properly and track this bastard down."

"Roger."

* * *

"What the fuck's that?" demanded Brad when he felt the rumbling of the lifeboats as they rolled over the side.

"No idea," replied Wendell Gardner. Gardner stood and looked out the window onto the storm. "Can't see anything. Something must have broken loose somewhere. If it's important, they'll tell us."

When Chrissie had thrown Brad out of her suite, he'd ended up in a cabin on the main deck, one level below the boat deck and two below Chrissie's suite. He'd started drinking tequila early and was still at it, in his cabin, explaining to Wendell what was wrong with everybody else in the world.

"Fuckin' ship's a disaster."

Wendell smiled. He enjoyed getting people cranked up.

"And this bullshit about having to go jam ourselves into the dining room with a million retards. Those navy guys are on a power trip. Whenever they don't know what to do, they dream something stupid up for us to do. If something bad's going to happen, it's going to happen where all the people are. We're much safer here, drinking in peace."

Wendell didn't bother to answer, although he did intensely dislike the military.

A few minutes later the tour guide noticed lights moving around on the deck outside the window. He returned to it and looked out. "Something's happening. I'm going to take a look."

Brad waved his consent.

Three minutes later Wendell was back, soaked and frozen. "Somebody's launched all the fucking lifeboats," he cried, a note of fear clear in his tone. "There's no way they can get them back aboard. If something happens to the ship, we're all dead."

Brad looked up at him. "Bullshit." He then passed out on the couch.

* * *

Boatswain MacNeal stepped out onto the port boat deck and immediately wished he hadn't. He'd failed to dress properly and it was now too late to do anything about it. He cursed himself for his stupidity, then again when he saw that all three boats were gone, each set of falls bouncing and twitching like a fishing line with a shark on it. He struggled into the wind and across the icy deck to the rail and looked down, flashing a hand spotlight as he did.

There they were, he thought with a mixture of surprise, anger and fear. The remains of the three boats were right below him, tangled up in one dark mass, pounding against the ship's side and against one another as they were dragged through the churning water. How in God's name was he going to recover them?

* * *

James Ives was scared, but more than that he was angry. He hated being stuck in the middle of a crowd. He hated it all the more when he was being shoved and stepped on by people who were even more panicky than he.

"It will be okay, dear," he reassured his wife—just to keep her quiet, if for no other reason—as they were carried down the passageway toward the Main Dining Room. They passed a media crew standing in a cabin, documenting the surrounding chaos. God! he thought. That's the end! To be shown round the world trapped and surrounded by a mob of terrified idiots. It was enough to make him almost forget his own fear.

"Please move along as rapidly as you can."

Ives looked to the side and saw one of the navy guys in his blue coveralls standing in a cabin. The guy who'd been limping ever since he arrived. He looked sick. Barely able to stand.

"They're gone!" somebody behind him shouted. "The lifeboats are gone. The crew must have taken them. They've left us here to die."

What shit, he thought as somebody rammed him from behind, almost knocking him to the deck.

"Keep moving there." It was that Ellison fellow. The security director, or something like that. "Don't stop, damn it! Keep moving! That's right, all the way back."

The room was already crowded, and Ives guessed that only about half the passengers had arrived. As the mob behind pushed him ahead, he forced his way to the left, toward the windows, dragging his wife with him.

When he finally reached a window, he jammed his face against it and placed both hands on either side, attempting to block out some of the light. He couldn't see much, but he could see enough. There were lights moving around on deck, and the dark blobs that should have been there—the lifeboats—were missing. Maybe they were there, but he didn't think so. Whoever had been shouting was right. The goddamned boats were gone. They were all dead.

The room was becoming uncomfortably hot and noisy, even though most of the passengers thought they were talking quietly. The air began to vibrate with terror as more and more realized they now had no escape.

* * *

"Shit!" said the first of MacNeal's men to arrive on the scene. "What the hell do we do now?" There was a note of despair in his voice.

"When I tell you, we're going to cut that mess loose,"

replied MacNeal in the most confident, authoritative voice he could muster. "For now, you find the bolt cutters in the boat tool chest while I check the other side."

"Okay, Boats."

"Remember, don't do a damn thing until I tell you."

"Okay, Boats."

Both men were shouting to be heard above the storm.

MacNeal ran through the superstructure and out onto the starboard boat deck, where he found two of his men hanging over the side, looking down. He joined them to discover that the situation wasn't quite as bad. All three boats were there, being dragged stern first, but none had swamped. They weren't as tangled, and they hadn't been beaten to shit by the waves' pounding them against the ship's hard side. At least not yet.

"Bridge, this is MacNeal," he shouted into his walkie-talkie.

"This is Covington, Boats."

"The boats on the port side are a total loss, Captain. When you're ready, I want to cut them away before they beat their way into the ship. I think we may be able to salvage one or two of the starboard ones."

"How soon before you're ready to cut?"

"Four or five minutes."

"Very well. I'm going to stop the port shaft now. Just before you cut the first boat, let me know so I can turn away. All we need now is a rat's nest of one-inch wire wrapped around the screws."

"Aye, Captain." He then turned to the two men, who had now been joined by three others. "While I'm cutting away the boats on the other side, I want you to use the spare blocks to re-rig the forward falls on davits three and five. And find the longest damn boat hooks you can."

There were a total of three deckhands waiting for him when MacNeal made it back to the port side.

"You have the cutters?" he demanded.

"Yes, Boats."

"Good. Now two of you stand by the number six aft davit. When I say 'now,' you're going to cut the fall and jump the hell back because the wire's going to whip around like an angry sidewinder."

The two men moved aft while MacNeal put the walkie-talkie to his mouth. "Bridge, this is MacNeal."

"Yes, Boats?"

"We're ready, Captain."

"Very well. I will start a slow turn to port in thirty seconds. As soon as the first boat is astern, I'll shift the rudder. Once we're back on our base course, I'll advise you so we can ditch the second one."

"I understand, Captain."

"I am starting to turn . . . Now!"

MacNeal waited until he could feel the ship's stern beginning to slew to starboard and then shouted "Now!" Straining, the two hands squeezed and twisted the bolt cutter's handles until the wire parted with a snap. And then fell, limp.

"Christ, Boats, it's not paying out!"

"God damn it," groaned MacNeal as he looked over the rail. The aft boat was hopelessly tangled with the others. "Bridge, this is MacNeal. We've cut the falls for boat six but it's so tangled with the others that it won't budge."

* * *

Within ten or fifteen minutes Marcello Cagayan's patience ran out. He loosened the strap on the rifle and put it over his shoulder. He then collected up the spare magazines and stuffed them into his jacket pockets. He'd heard the announcement directing all the passengers to the Main Dining Room. Except for the boatswain's people trying to save the boats, there'd be nobody on deck but him. He exited the funnel for the last time and made his way down to the second deck, all the way aft. From there he could see the empty davits and the men working on them. He would have liked to see what was left of the boats themselves, but they were hidden by the hull. He could see the men on both sides of the ship—they were now only about thirty yards away—but he realized that to get a decent shot he was going to have to lean out over the rail. Being right-handed, he decided to work on the starboard side. He checked to make sure a magazine was inserted in the rifle then leaned over and waited, the wind jamming him hard against the rail.

* * *

"Roger," replied Covington, who'd been watching the operation from above. "I'm going to get back on course and then we'll trying freeing four and see if the two of them will leave."

"Roger."

Once Covington had turned the *Aurora* back downwind, he turned to port again and told MacNeal to cut away the number four boat. The cutters clicked and the cut wire jumped a few feet, then collapsed. "Captain, the two of them are now riding on number two's falls."

Covington pounded the rail in frustration as the ship continued to turn slowly. He was very conscious of what he didn't know—just how many yards of one-inch wire were trailing back from the tangled mass of boats. If it was more than fifty, and he came right, to get back on the base course, he ran the very real risk of getting the wire tangled around one or both screws. If he kept turning much longer, he would soon find himself back across the trough, in the position that had almost killed them before. "Cut away number two right away, Boats. Then pray."

"Now! Cut!" grunted MacNeal.

The wire parted with the crack of a small cannon and flew through the sheaves and over the side. While MacNeal watched the tangled mass drift astern and off to one side, Covington watched as the bow swung to the left, soon to be pointing directly down the alley between the two monster waves on each side, the joystick gripped in his right hand.

"There," he finally mumbled to himself. The mess had passed astern. He flicked his wrist, moving the joystick and the rudder to the right. The ship was not a racing yacht, but she did respond in time to avoid Covington's worst nightmares. MacNeal and his three helpers raced back through the ship to the starboard boat deck.

* * *

"The target's a young Filipino engineer named Cagayan," repeated Mike as he slipped into a set of chest armor. "We don't know where he is at the moment but he's almost certainly not below. He's either on some weather deck or someplace in the superstructure. We also don't know if he's armed or not."

"Are we assuming he just killed Hensen or are we assuming he's a terrorist?"

"Very good point. There's nothing in that message guaranteeing that a terrorist is aboard. If there are any other explosive devices aboard, they may be controlled by timers or GPS position indicators. But we don't know, so we're going to have to assume that there are other devices and that Cagayan controls them. That means that we want him in condition to tell us what and where they are."

"How're we going to find him?" asked Ted.

"We're going to sweep the interior spaces, starting on deck four and working down. As we go, we're going to lock every lockable door. So get your armor on. Also bring night vision gear and rifles, in case we end up chasing him on one of the weather decks."

* * *

When Boatswain MacNeal reached the starboard side, he found that the men he'd left there had made considerable progress re-rigging two of the damaged falls. "Okay," he said, "this isn't going to be easy, but we have to get a hook through the forward ring on two of those boats. Then we'll be able to lift them level, maybe without beating everything to shit in the process. Any volunteers to dangle and get the hook in place?"

"I'll give it a try, Boats," offered one of the younger and more ambitious deckhands after a pause.

"Good . . ." Before MacNeal could finish the sentence, another young hand who was working partway up the davit, reeving the wires through the sheaves, arched his back and cried out. Without another word the kid dropped into the storm.

"What the hell!"

Then Gibson, the hand who had volunteered to dangle, collapsed on deck, clutching his chest.

"Everybody take cover," shouted MacNeal. "Get under the overhang of deck three and get into the shadows." He grabbed his walkie-talkie.

17

The Drake Passage

"Boss, this is Alex," whispered Mike's walkie-talkie, barely audible above the wind that was howling along the fourth deck. "At some point very recently the target was hiding in the funnel—on what Jerry tells me is called a blower flat—and it looks very much like he had a rifle hidden here."

"We're on our way." He then called Covington.

Mike and Ted continued forward, using their night vision gear to scan every corner and every shadow. When they reached the funnel, they found Jerry standing outside. "He's been here, Boss, and he left some wrappings that look as if they were secured around a rifle."

"So where the hell is he now?" Mike asked, thinking aloud.

"Bridge, this is MacNeal," whispered the walkie-talkie again. "There's a shooter someplace on this ship. He just shot two of my men. There's nothing we can do about these boats until we get some cover. And send Dr. Savage."

"Ted, you get down there and keep those men under cover. The rest of you spread along the starboard side. We're going to go down deck by deck. Maybe the bastard's still there, waiting to get another shot."

"Bridge, MacNeal, this is Chambers. Make sure Dr. Savage stays in the superstructure. Take your casualties to her. We only have one of her."

"Roger."

"Roger."

* * *

Wearing his enhanced vision goggles, Mike moved carefully down the port side ladder leading from the aft end of deck four to deck three. At the forward end of deck four Alex did the same thing, while Jerry remained on the starboard side of deck four, carefully scanning everything he could see below him.

Once Mike and Alex had reached deck three, they worked their way over to the starboard side and then, crouching, advanced slowly toward each other. When they reached each other, they repeated the process, working down to and along the boat deck, with Jerry watching from deck three. As they went, they could hear the three remaining boats beating themselves to death.

"Captain Chambers . . ."

"Is that you, MacNeal?"

"Yes, sir," said the boatswain as he stood up behind a steel locker. "You think he's moved on?"

"He's not above us."

"Can you cover us for another few minutes? We've got to cut those boats away."

"Will do. Alex, take the forward end of deck three. I'll take the aft end and Jerry the middle. We'll be in position in three minutes."

While Mike filled Jerry in, MacNeal called Covington. "The navy's arrived to cover us, Captain, so we'll be ready in five minutes to cut away the starboard boats—or what's left of them."

"Very well. I'm stopping the shaft now."

"Now, Captain," said MacNeal a few minutes later. After a brief pause he stood up in a crouch, bolt cutters in hand, and scurried over to the aft davit of boat five. He raised and positioned the cutters and with a grunt rammed the handles together. The wire parted with a crack and went whipping through the sheaves and over the side.

"First one went like a dream, Captain. Should I try the next or . . ."

"Go ahead, try the next one."

Snap. The second boat was gone.

"Get that last one, MacNeal, while you're hot. I've still got a minute or so before I have to turn back on course."

"Roger."

Snap.

"That's it, Captain. They all look clear from here."

"Good work, Boatswain. Now secure any trailing lines and then get your men under cover unless Captain Chambers has work for them."

"Roger," said MacNeal, exhaling a massive sigh of relief as he did.

"Okay," he said to his men, "police this area up quickly. Make sure there's nothing that's going to drag overboard."

"MacNeal?"

"Yes, Vido, what is it?"

"I hear everybody's looking for Cagayan. Do you think he's the one doing all this?"

"There's a lot people don't tell me. Get over there and help secure those wires."

"I've talked to him sometimes, and I think I noticed something that navy guy may want to know about."

The boatswain was about to blast Vido over the side, but he restrained himself. He wasn't a bad kid. Right off the farm, so he didn't know much, but he was a good worker and never gave anybody any trouble. "Okay, Vido, let's step out of the wind for a minute and you give it to me quickly."

"Okay, Boats. The thing is he's got a cell phone that he always carries around and plays with a lot. He never shows it to anybody, but I've seen him take it out of his pocket. Sometimes, when hc thinks nobody's looking, he puts his hand in his pocket and sort of pets it."

"A cell phone? Out here?" MacNeal looked at the boy a moment, on the verge of telling him he was a fool, but then he thought better of it. A cell phone was basically a radio, and a radio might be very useful to detonate bombs.

"Vido, you did the right thing. Stay here with me a moment." He called Mike Chambers—who was standing almost precisely where Cagayan had fired from a few minutes before—and reported what Vido had noted.

* * *

"A cell phone! That would certainly fit," said Mike after MacNeal had completed his report. He then passed the word to Covington, the chief engineer, Dave Ellison and the other four Trident Force members that when Cagayan was located, he was under no circumstances to be allowed to operate the cell phone.

"Does that mean kill him if necessary?" asked Ray.

"Affirmative. If necessary. We have to assume the phone is a detonator. There's simply too much at stake."

"Roger."

What the hell to do next? Mike wondered, momentarily at a loss. There was at least one more explosive device but, for some reason, Cagayan was in no hurry to detonate it.

It didn't make much sense, but then again maybe it did. To a terrorist. If he intended to sink the ship, he could presumably do it at any time, but it appeared he was more interested in terrorizing the passengers a little more before he killed them. Destroying the lifeboats was a good start, but what would he try next?

One widely quoted rule of sound military thinking is to always evaluate the enemy in terms of his capabilities—which are often knowable—not his intentions—which are generally not. Since Cagayan was able to move practically anywhere on the ship, and do practically anything, his capabilities were essentially limitless. Mike was going to have to make the best guess he could about the bastard's intentions.

The best way for him to further unsettle the passengers—and give the media something to spread around the world—was to get right up in their faces and hurt them, Mike decided.

"Trident Force," he said into his walkie-talkie, "I suspect the target's next move will be some sort of direct action against passengers. We're going to concentrate all our efforts on deck three in the vicinity of the Main Dining Room. Ray, leave Ellison at the dining room entrance and you patrol the approaches. Alex, you work with Ray. Jerry, you and I will establish an outside perimeter on deck three."

"Roger."

* * *

Shivering, his teeth chattering, Cagayan had ducked into a linen locker at the aft end of the third deck while the Trident Force was moving into position to cover MacNeal. He used a sheet to wipe the slush off his face, then took a deep breath and held it when he heard a group of passengers hurry by, headed for the dining room. One of them kept reminding the others, in a strident voice, that without the lifeboats they would all die.

It felt good to shoot those men, he thought, and now was the time to move on. He listened carefully, his ear pressed to the door, and heard nothing. He opened it and stepped out into the passageway. To his right he could hear the growing rumble from the dining room. That would be his final stop. He would walk down to its entrance and detonate the bomb in front of them. Tell them, if necessary, just what he had done. But before, he wanted one more jolt of power. He turned to the left, certain that more passengers would come along.

He heard talking up ahead. Up ahead and off to one side, in a cabin. He checked his rifle and then dashed down the passageway and through the open door of the cabin, swinging the AK-47—which was as big as he was—in front of him.

There was a media team there. The blond reporter along with video and sound guys. With them was that singer. With a shout he jumped through the door, swinging the rifle from side to side as he did.

The video guy immediately swung his camera in Cagayan's direction, while expressions of shock, then horror, crossed Chrissie's and Jessica's faces. Marcello Cagayan smiled into the camera then pulled the trigger, and the room was filled with a thunderous, pulsing roar.

* * *

"Oh my God!" cried a man, one of the many hundreds jammed into the dining room. "Somebody's shooting in the corridor."

Unease, uncertainty, flashed into even greater fear. Where could they go? What could they do? They were trapped here, barely able to move, unable to escape. They were sitting targets waiting to be shot down. The fear turned to panic, and hundreds—some sobbing and crying, a few screaming—struggled to get out. Through the doors to the galley. Through the one door leading out onto the weather deck. Anywhere but through the main entrance, where the firing was coming from. Ellison and the three armed deckhands under his control struggled to keep them in, but it was to no avail. Within seconds the passageway and the deck were filled with passengers fleeing in all directions. Most had no destination in mind. All they wanted to do was get out of that trap.

"Get in here!' shouted Tim as he struggled to drag Dana and Katie into a booth along one side of the room, out of the lethal flood of terrified passengers. "Hang on! Pull!"

Dana made it. Katie did not. Caught by the torrent, she was torn from Tim's grasp and carried downstream until she stumbled and fell, overrun by the raging current.

* * *

Cagayan looked down at the forms crumpled before him. It was nice to be able to look down on people. Especially the singer, who still seemed alive. He looked into her hazel eyes and saw pain and fear, and it gave him another jolt of pleasure. She'd been hot stuff an hour ago but not anymore. He raised his rifle and watched her eyes follow it. He slammed the butt into her face then jumped back, momentarily surprised at the amount of blood that erupted from her mouth. Elated, he turned and sprang out into the passageway, where he turned to face the mob of terrified passengers. So confused were they by now that some were trying to force their way toward him while most were trying to get away, all so desperate to be someplace they weren't that they were knocking one another down and running over the fallen. He opened fire and watched them crumple as he forced the living back toward the dining room.

Suddenly, all seemed to go silent as the crashing booms of the rifle blasts in the enclosed space stopped. It was now possible again to hear the terrified sobs and shouts of the victims.

"Shit," mumbled Cagayan as he withdrew the empty clip and fumbled in the pocket of his coat for a fresh one.

Ray Fuentes, his leg throbbing, his head spinning and his stomach churning, leaned against one of the bulkheads in the cabin. He knew Cagayan was at most twenty feet down the passageway to his left. By pressing his head against the bulkhead, he could peer out the door and see that all the passengers were some distance to his right, piled up at the door to the dining room. If only he could hold himself together for another minute, he would have a clear field of fire.

Gritting his teeth, Fuentes edged around the door frame into the passageway and jammed his left side up against the bulkhead as he pushed his Glock before him with both hands.

So intent was Cagayan on reloading that he never noticed the figure dressed in blue coveralls who oozed out of the cabin, steadied himself and discharged five heavy .45-caliber rounds at almost point-blank range, tearing the scrawny monster's chest to pieces and blasting the mangled remains back several feet.

* * *

The passageway was still thick with smoke when Alex reached it, Mike and Jerry not far behind. With her eyes focused intently on the pile of rags and blood and her trigger finger tense, she approached Cagayan. One close look assured her he was absolutely dead. She then walked over to Ray and crouched beside him. "You okay?"

"No worse than I was an hour ago."

"I'll get Dr. Savage."

"Just get me into the bed in that cabin. Dr. Savage doesn't have time right now for me."

After getting Ray onto the bed, the three Tridents returned to the body and looked down at it. "Tiny mother," remarked Jerry. He then knelt down and reached with two fingers into a blood-soaked pants pocket. "Here it is," he remarked as he pulled the phone out.

The three looked at one another then nodded, in unspoken agreement. Jerry slowly opened the phone. "Four,

four, four, four has been punched in," he remarked. "I bet my pension that if I push call we'll all be blown to hell."

"Please don't," said Mike as Jerry carefully closed the phone and handed it to his boss.

There was the sound of a door opening at the far end of the corridor.

"Oh Christ!" There was a pause, then, "These three are gone. Get pressure on this girl's wounds. Stop the blood. Then we'll figure out what to do next."

"Ellison, this is Savage," squawked their walkie-talkies immediately thereafter. "You have any casualties in the dining room?"

"You'd better believe it!"

"How many?"

"Maybe twenty. Maybe more."

"Get everybody out of there except the wounded . . . and any doctors or nurses we have aboard. I'm going to need a lot of help."

"Ellison, this is Chambers," cut in Mike. "Use the armed men from the ship's company to escort the passengers back to their cabins."

"Roger."

"God damn it!"

Mike turned and looked down the corridor to see Captain Covington standing in the passageway, looking in at Chrissie Clark. The captain's face, initially red from the weather, had turned white. "I don't know what to say," he mumbled as he walked up to Mike. "It's good you were here. What, exactly, happened?"

Mike explained.

"It might be prudent to pass the word that nobody, under any circumstances, should touch their cell phones."

"An excellent idea."

"You think this is the end of it?" asked Covington after directing the mate of the watch to pass the word about cell phones.

"We've still got at least one explosive device to find."

"Do you think Cagayan was alone?"

"I get that impression."

* * *

When Mike returned to his suite several hours later, he found his team all there. Ted and Alex were doing stretching exercises, hoping they would help them unwind. Jerry was dozing, and Ray was established in one of the beds, totally out of it.

"Ray okay?" asked Mike.

"Dr. Savage says he'll be fine, someday," explained Alex. "After they do a little work on his ankle. So what's the score, Boss?"

"The score," said Mike, anger now flashing in his blue eyes, "is one maniac, one drug dealer and one deckhand dead and one wounded; eleven passengers and three media persons dead and thirty passengers wounded; one dead congressman and a ship that might very well self-destruct at any time."

"Ship's still afloat, sir," offered Ted, trying to be positive.

"What about the singer?" asked Alex.

"Alive. Dr. Savage says she'll probably make it, but she'll need a tremendous amount of reconstructive surgery."

"And the little girl who got trampled?"

"A broken arm and a few bruises. Captain Covington's hoping to medevac the worst cases out this afternoon, assuming the weather doesn't get much worse. And another tour ship, the *Polar Duchess* is headed south from Ushuaia. We'll probably rendezvous tonight."

"We going to be able to transfer the passengers under these conditions?" asked Jerry with a skeptical tone.

"Probably not unless we have no choice, but at least she has boats and she'll be with us."

"Captain," said Ted, "a day or so ago I remember Mr.

Acosta mentioning something about that fuel tank near the void Cagayan stuffed Hensen into."

"What?"

"He was explaining about how stubborn Mr. Montalba can be at times, and he mentioned that during the overhaul the chief wanted the yard to inspect the outlet and siphon in that tank but somehow it didn't get on the original work order list. At first the yard didn't want to do it, but Montalba made such a scene they finally went ahead and drained thc tank and inspected the siphon. Since it was in good shape and no work had to be done they didn't bother to gas-free it, they just closed it up again. He's not even sure it made it to the final list, since it was really a very minor item and it was still a sore point with a couple of the yard's supervisors."

"And I'm the one who keeps saying whatever we're looking for was probably placed during the overhaul . . ."

"Yes, sir."

"Not only are you a credit to the SEALs, you're also a credit to all the shipfitters in the navy."

"Kind of you, sir."

"Jerry!"

"Sir?"

"Ready for a swim?"

"Always, Captain."

"I'll tend," offered Alex.

"I've got another job for you. I want you to go through the chief engineer's records of who signed off on what during the past few days. I want a complete list of all the spaces Cagayan supposedly searched."

"I can see how we're going to spend the rest of the trip," remarked Alex. "Where's the cell phone?"

"In Captain Covington's safe."

* * *

Jerry Andrews, dressed in a black dry suit, stood and watched as Mike and Ted finished unbolting the inspection port into fuel tank number two. Once the cover was removed, Kim Ackerman shined a flashlight down into the hole, revealing the ugly brown surface of the diesel about ten feet down. It certainly wasn't Jerry's first dive into a fuel tank, but he hoped it would be his last. The stuff didn't move right, didn't feel right, and if it got to your skin you ended up with a nasty rash.

"The bottom of the tank's about twelve or thirteen feet below the surface," said Mr. Acosta as he lowered a Jacob's ladder into the hole. "And the baffles are ten feet high and ten apart," he added, referring to the low walls built into the tank to prevent all the oil from moving at once when the ship rolled, thereby endangering the ship's stability.

Jerry gave him the thumbs-up sign then turned to Kim. "Okay. My helmet, please."

Kim checked to ensure that air was flowing from the two big, steel bottles they had rolled into position, then fitted the fiberglass helmet over Jerry's head and locked it closed.

"You read me, Jerry?" asked Mike into the communicator.

"Roger," said Jerry, "going down."

After picking up the wand for the sonar search system—its cable was bundled into the umbilical with the air hose and communication wire—the master diver started down the ladder with Kim carefully tending his umbilical. The ship rolled, causing the ladder to sway and the oil to shift slowly. Seeming to pay little attention, Andrews continued down into the pitch-black pool then stepped off the ladder and started to sink, only to come to a shuddering halt with his helmet and shoulders still above the surface. "Damn it, my butt landed on one of the baffles," he said as his helmet tilted forward and he disappeared.

"I've reached the forward end of the tank," he reported

a minute or so later. "I'm proceeding to the starboard side and starting there."

"Roger."

"I'm between the starboard side of the tank and the first baffle. I'll start waving the wand. You be sure to tell me the second you spot an irregularity, so I can check it out. The visibility's zero or less."

While Ted and Acosta kept their eyes focused on the sonar display, Mike hung upside down through the port and, using a brilliant, halogen light, studied every square inch of the tank that was visible.

"Be sure to give me plenty of slack," said Jerry. Kim complied, making sure the buoyant umbilical was floating out and over the baffles before plunging down to the diver.

"Nothing?"

"Nothing."

"I'm all the way aft. I'm going to start down between the first and second baffles now."

"Roger."

"Damn!" grumbled Jerry three passes later. "I think I just tripped over the siphon."

"Okay," said Mike. "Mr. Acosta, please pay special attention now and see if you can spot any irregularities when he scans the siphon."

The second engineer, who had been staring intently at the display, looked even harder as the ghostly image of the two-foot-high pipe rotated on the screen. "That looks clean to me, Captain."

"Very well."

"Jerry, I want you to follow it over to the end of the tank—to the discharge."

"Roger."

"That's it!" shouted Acosta a few minutes later. "The siphon goes through a simple flange when it leaves the tank. There's something next to the flange that I've never seen before. It looks round . . . or maybe a hemisphere!" As he spoke, he pointed at the ghost image.

"Tell Jerry to find it and check it out by hand."

"Roger."

"It's like a hemisphere, all right," reported Jerry a few minutes later as, surrounded by what could have been the blackest of pitch, he saw with his hands. "More like half an egg. About two feet long and maybe one high and one deep."

"Your evaluation?"

"A large-shaped charge designed to blow a hole in the end of the tank."

"How's it attached?"

"I would guess either magnetic or suction. You want me to try to pull it off?"

"Hell no!"

"Good."

"You think it's booby-trapped?"

"I wouldn't be surprised. That's why I'm still alive at my advanced age. Whoever planned this attack is pretty damn sophisticated."

"Leave it and stand by for a few minutes."

"Roger."

Mike then pulled out his walkie-talkie and asked Covington to come below and join them.

"You don't want to remove it now?" said Covington after Chambers had explained the situation to him.

"No, not now. We have the detonator, but we have no idea whether or not it's booby-trapped. The odds look better to me to leave it. Once we get to Ushuaia, we can do it right."

"Ummm," remarked Covington skeptically.

"How much of the oil can you transfer to other tanks?"

"Maybe half."

"I suggest we transfer what we can while flooding the tank with nitrogen from the firefighting system. After the transfer is complete, cover the surface of what's remaining with foam and then pump it over the side. That way, even if it does blow, the damage will be limited. If we manage to meet *Polar Duchess* in twelve or so hours, we can probably hold out—especially if we keep the ship buttoned up."

"Understood. Now, who's going to explain all the oil we're dumping to Rod Johnson?"

"Remind him that diesel is much less destructive than bunker fuel. Especially out in open waters."

"I'm sure that will make him feel better."

* * *

The farther north *Aurora* got, and the more the day advanced, the better the weather became. By 1300 hours, when the first helicopter reported its imminent arrival, the winds were down to a breeze-like forty knots and the seas a modest ten to fifteen feet.

On learning of the helo's approach, Covington turned *Aurora* into the seas and slowed in order to reduce her motion and make it more predictable. As the first aircraft approached—an Argentine naval one—the first five evacuees were brought on deck.

MacNeal watched as the craft edged in, then hovered directly overhead, lowering a stretcher as it did. Once the stretcher had touched the deck, the boatswain and two men rushed for it. They disconnected the wire from the stretcher. MacNeal and one of them connected the wire to one of the occupied stretchers—one of six the ship carried—while the third man carried the just-delivered empty off. MacNeal waved his arm in big circles and the helo whisked the first patient up and away, then returned for the second.

The first five transfers went faultlessly, and the first helo sped off over the horizon as the second sped in to repeat the process.

The first four transfers went like clockwork, but during the fifth—the patient was Chrissie Clark—near disaster developed. Just as Chrissie, her broken jaw wired in place and her bullet holes all patched, was being lifted off the deck, the helo was knocked to one side by a gust of wind and the stretcher was dragged across the deck toward the bulwark, screeching as it went.

The boatswain and several hands jumped forward, grabbed the stretcher and raised it as they were all dragged toward the side. Thanks primarily to luck, they got Chrissie up and over the bulwark just in time. The injured singer then swung in a great arc away from the ship. On the return swing she barely avoided a bath in the shimmering, oil-fouled waters as the pilot finally managed to regain control and haul her up. Later, much later, when the incident was described to her, Chrissie said she was sorry she'd been so doped up at the time. She'd missed it all.

The last four of the fourteen persons whom Dr. Savage considered seriously enough injured to risk the transfer were called for by the same contract supply helo that had delivered the Trident Force. All went smoothly.

The operation had a large number of spectators. While most had, by now, expressed the strongest possible desire to be "off this damn ship," none expressed any wish to leave as the wounded were. Except Katie, now wearing a new cast on her left arm. She thought it looked like great fun—as long as you didn't have to be shot already in order to be allowed to do it.

Most of the other passengers smiled and admired her cast, especially when she pointed out Arthur Covington's signature on it. A few averted their eyes and edged away, embarrassed, it would seem, and hoping not to be recognized as having been one of those who contributed to her injury.

* * *

At 2215 hours, to the immense relief of everybody aboard *Aurora*, the brightly lit cruise ship *Polar Duchess* appeared on the horizon. An hour later she had approached and circled in order to steam back to Usuaia alongside the *Aurora*. Her boats were all swung out, just in case they were needed in a hurry.

18

Rio de Janeiro

At first, Mamoud al Hussein paid only limited attention to the live broadcasts from *Aurora.* They were, after all, mere puffery—focusing almost exclusively on just the sort of petty minds in which he had no interest. But as the situation became more confusing to him, when things that he had no hand in started happening, he began to pay attention. By the time Marcello Cagayan launched his campaign of destruction and death, Mamoud's eyes were fixed with horror on the TV. But it wasn't the pain and suffering that horrified him, it was the seeming failure of his plan, which Omar's little monkey had clearly hijacked. Al Hussein loathed disorder and illogic. He considered both to be the most odious forms of insanity. Now it was just this form of insanity that was driving what had been *his* plan.

Yes, the little whoreson had terrified half the world and made the Brotherhood of Faith a feared name, but what of the last two charges? For Mamoud, there was more to the affair than terror. His ego was involved. His ability to conceive, to manage, to organize, to execute. And now, to his shame and fury, it was not his plan being displayed on every TV in the world. It was the mad caperings of a little Filipino nonentity.

It took Mamoud several minutes to get his anger under control. To move on to the next question: If it was not his plan being executed, then were his defenses still intact? Or had the vicious little lunatic exposed him to new danger?

He had, all along, assumed that once his plan had been executed the world's eyes would turn to Tecmar. He was certain that, in the end, while there might be whispers, the world would agree that whatever had happened had happened despite management's best efforts. And, as for himself, he was clearly above it all. He was a friend, a confidant—in some cases almost a savior—of countless men of great importance. His engineering textbooks were used at the most prestigious universities around the world. He wasn't some ignorant tribesman from who knows where. He was more scientifically and technologically advanced than 95 percent of the American population.

While some might whisper vague suspicions, he was, in the end, as safe as was the king of Saudi Arabia.

On the other hand, he thought, as he finally got his breathing under control, the little creature's performance had been so mad that no sane person would ever associate it with any but the most obviously insane. Some minor desert Mahdi with delusions of grandeur. He would stick with his initial plan, even if Cagayan had not. He picked up his phone and called Roberto Palmeira, Tecmar's COO.

"Have you been watching the TV, Mamoud?" asked Palmeira.

"Yes. It's stomach-turning."

"I will never understand the terrorist mind. I know about poverty, religious fanaticism, drugs, but it still escapes me. I hope to God it's not connected in some way with the overhaul."

"Unfortunately, I'm beginning to suspect that some

connection does exist, and even if it doesn't, I'm afraid many may believe it does. Or may wish to believe it does."

"Do you want me to call the federal police and have them redirect their investigations?"

"Yes, and I would also like you to call the United States Embassy and see if it would be possible for the Rio FBI office to send a team. If something happened here, I want to know about it. If nothing happened here, I want the world to know that nothing happened here."

"As you've pointed out on several occasions, Mamoud, it's logically impossible to prove a negative statement."

"Indeed it is, but we must do our best."

19

Ushuaia

There was a stiff breeze blowing as *Aurora* approached Ushuaia harbor. There was also a light rain, a high-powered drizzle that obscured much of the town and the mountains beyond. The temperature, however, was well over sixty degrees, mild for the world's southernmost city, even at the height of its summer.

Mike Chambers was standing alongside Covington as the pilot boat surged up to the ship's starboard side, delivering not only the pilot but also Commander Artemio O'Brien, the captain of the port.

"Good morning, gentlemen," said Covington to the two Argentine mariners, both of whom he knew, having sailed out of Ushuaia for some time. He then went on to introduce Mike.

"You two have had a very difficult voyage," remarked O'Brien as the pilot walked out on the wing of the bridge to conn the ship.

"Yes," replied Covington with little enthusiasm.

"I'm sorry I have to put you on a buoy for the time being. We can move you alongside a pier once we're certain the ship is safe. We'll get all the passengers off just as soon as we are moored."

"I wouldn't want it any other way, sir."

"And you, Captain Chambers? Are you satisfied with my desire that our people should remove the charge and take custody of the detonator—which will be immediately flown some distance away so our technicians can examine them without the risk of doing further damage?"

"It's your harbor, Commander, and my people are very beat-up and tired. When you're tired, you make mistakes. I'm also very much aware that you've had more experience with terrorists than we have."

O'Brien turned and looked astern, out toward the Beagle Channel. "At one point in our not so distant history we had the misfortune of having terrorists on both sides. It was very uncomfortable for those of us in the middle, especially those of us who may have known a little more than the others and found what we knew hateful, yet failed to act decisively. But that, I hope, is over forever in Argentina."

Chambers looked down at the Argentine's left hand, which was missing the pinkie and ring finger.

O'Brien followed his glance, then smiled slightly. "That is not the result of the 'Dirty War.' That is the result of frostbite. And youthful stupidity. When I was younger, I served in a supply ship down here, and one winter I was a little careless. Far too careless."

"About the press. It appears that those who are aboard have no desire to stay. However, I'm sure there are more ashore."

"Our people have no more desire than yours to have them looking over their shoulders when they're trying to disassemble bombs. There are plenty of passengers to talk to, and if any press get by me, throw them off and blame it on us."

The conversation petered out as a large harbor tug came alongside. The pilot stopped *Aurora*'s engines and used the tug to edge the ship toward the rusty mooring buoy, which had once been painted white. Lacking an anchor windlass, Boatswain MacNeal had to make use of the smaller tug to pass one of the ship's anchor chains to the buoy and secure it. The job was completed with surprising speed, and a few minutes later the first passenger ferry appeared—this one assigned to bring ashore those of the wounded—excluding Ray—whose injuries had not been considered serious enough to justify the many risks of being medevaced.

"Arthur," said O'Brien quietly as he and the pilot were leaving the bridge, "we both will be very busy the next few days, but after that I hope you will find time to dine with Gloria and me. She insists."

"Yes, thank you. I doubt I'll have a choice, right?" Covington smiled for the first time that morning.

A few minutes after O'Brien, and then Mike, had left the bridge, Arthur Covington, his back just as straight as ever, walked slowly down to the landing stage. He felt it was his duty, undoubtedly one of his final duties, to say good-bye to all the passengers, the vast majority of whom had chosen to fly north in the morning, directly back to the United States, where many would immediately grab their phones to call their attorneys. Or so Covington assumed.

It hurt to think that his future and his reputation would, in the end, be decided by one or more civil juries composed of men and women who had never been to sea at all, much less to the Southern Ocean. And he had little confidence in the owners. They wouldn't hesitate to damn him with the faintest of praise then throw him to the lions.

Well, if worse came to worst, O'Brien could probably get him a job skippering one of the tourist boats that bounced up and down the Beagle Channel.

The departures were much as he'd expected. James Ives told him he was calling his lawyer the instant he got ashore. Brad, Chrissie's ex, tried to take a swing at him but stumbled and would have fallen into the boat had Dave Ellison not caught him.

And *there* was one surprise, thought Covington. I still

don't really like the man, but he's done a good job. As good as any of us.

The good-byes, however, were not all painful or embarrassing. Senator Bergstrom and Babs each shook his hand, smiled and left, making no more wake on their departure than they had throughout the voyage. Linda Williams was so busy talking to Rod Johnson that she hadn't even noticed Covington. Penny Evans, sad but dry-eyed, thanked him for his efforts and told him she would always admire him. That elderly woman whose name he could never seem to remember—the one with a husband named Fred who always smiled and never said anything—told him she and Fred had sailed with at least forty captains "over the past century or so" and he was the greatest of them.

And then there was Katie: "We've had a tough time, Captain Covington, but you've saved us all. Thanks."

"I understand you three are among the few who've decided to take a few days to visit Tierra del Fuego."

"Yes. We're all very excited. We're going to see llamas."

"Not penguins?"

"Are there penguins here too?"

"Yes."

"Penguins and llamas, then. Have you seen where that navy guy wrote his name on my cast?"

Covington looked and saw, "To Katie with Love, Ramon Fuentes."

"He's a good guy, Katie."

"Yeah, the greatest."

* * *

"These are marvelous machines your people come up with," said Commander O'Brien as he and Mike watched three Argentine technicians struggle to get an advanced imaging device—similar to a CAT scan—down into the now-empty number two fuel tank.

"Unfortunately, they're too damn heavy and bulky for teams like mine to tote all around the world."

"I can understand that."

While the two officers watched part of the Argentine explosive ordnance team rig the scanner, other members were filling the voids outside the tank with sandbags in the hope they would absorb some of the blast—just in case things didn't go as planned.

Two paper cups of coffee later, the device was rigged and in operation. The display was spectacular. Every wire, every resistor, every diode was visible. It took the two electronic technicians less than ten minutes to make their pronouncement: There were two different charges in the same device, with their detonators both wired to a very basic radio receiver powered by a small lithium battery. No evidence of a booby trap. In sum, an only slightly complex, magnetically attached limpet mine—although one of no recognizable origin.

"A piece of cake," the young lieutenant in charge said with a grin, as he supervised the placement of a preprogrammed robot next to the device and the removal of the scanner. Half an hour later the device was being towed ashore, on its own little makeshift barge, for further study. Very careful further study by more robots.

"I'm sorry you can't stay another day or two, Captain," said O'Brien as they climbed a ladder into the superstructure. "This is a harsh land but it has its beauties. At any rate, a helicopter will pick you up at dusk and take you to the naval air base to meet your jet. With luck, the media will know nothing until it is too late for them to try to chase you."

"Thank you, Commander."

"Tell me, do you think you found all the devices? It's something that has always bothered me. If you find one, how do you know there're not others?"

"I always worry about the same thing."

"Yes? I plan to have this ordnance team spend another three or four days taking another look. A new set of eyes."

"Let me get you the job list from that last overhaul. I still think it's the best guide we have."

"I'm sure it will be more than just useful. Will you join me for a quick drink at the ship's bar? We'll probably have it all to ourselves."

"Are you buying?"

"Arthur is. I'll tell him later."

When Mike got back to his suite, he found the team all packed and ready to go, Jerry having stuffed Ray's duffel for him. Ready but also dejected.

"What's your evaluation, Boss?" asked Alex. "Did we win or lose this one?"

"It's a hard call, but I think we did win. If we'd lost, we'd damn well know it."

He looked around the room and decided to take a note from O'Brien's book. "We've got at least an hour before the helo arrives, and none of us is going to be driving anything for the next day or two, so let's have a drink. What can I get for you, Alex? Ted? Jerry? What about Ray?"

"He's dead to the world, Captain," said Ted. "We're going to have to carry him to the helo."

20

South of Alexandria, Egypt

A man of many names, one of which was once Omar, sat back from the window of the all-but-abandoned five-story apartment building. His silenced sniper rifle was held in place by small sandbags on the table in front of him. The room, he speculated, had last been occupied by a woman, or a girl. What other possible explanation was there for the peeling plaster's having been painted pink?

Smiling, the man returned his attention to the recently cleared field about a quarter of a mile away. Not only had they cleared the land, but they'd already started pouring the foundations for the huge new solar panel factory that was scheduled to rise there soon. It was undoubtedly a giant step forward for the local economy. Fortunately for him, despite its obvious value, a group of local dissidents had taken offense and were protesting its construction loudly.

The man saw motion at the door to the construction office trailer and bent forward to look through the sniper scope. There, filling most of the scope's field, was Mamoud al Hussein, flanked by two engineers, stepping out of the trailer. Although al Hussein had so far escaped being firmly connected with the cruise ship attack, he still represented a threat to the man. He was the only living person who knew of the man's connection to the affair.

The man saw no reason to wait—he squeezed off two shots, the second aimed slightly lower than the first. Al Hussein slumped backward, and the two engineers, driven by instinct, recoiled while his bodyguards crouched down and scanned the area around them. The man fired two more shots into his still-exposed target. He then stood and walked rapidly out of the room, along the hall and down the stairs to the alley behind the building. Waiting there for him was an ancient motorbike. He kick-started the engine and then sputtered almost sedately through the maze of alleys that meandered among the block of tired old buildings onto a main street, merging unnoticed with the passing mass of humanity.

His problem was solved, and the local dissidents, even though they had played absolutely no role, would garner all the credit.